THE ENGINE

written and illustrated by
Richard Crist

A Truth Engine Book

Published by Truth Engine Books.

ISBN: 978-0-692-26831-5

Disclaimer: Every effort has been made to make the instructive parts of this book as accurate as possible, but no warranty or fitness is implied. The information provided is on an "as is" basis. The author and publisher shall have neither liability nor responsibility to any person or entity with respect to any loss or damages arising from the information contained in this book.

CONTENTS

CHAPTER 1
THE MYSTERIOUS CAVES IN THE CATSKILLS

Talking to a dark-haired girl who stood next to him, twelve-year-old Robert sat in his wooden chair in the tiny rustic classroom. The last class of the night had just ended for the five or six students. Robert looked toward the doorway that led to the back room. At that moment he realized that the teacher, who somehow had conducted the class while hidden, was about to show himself by bursting past the hanging cloth that covered the opening—and a moment later, it happened. The teacher rushed into the classroom and toward the children. The charge terrified Robert. *I can't look at his face*, he thought.

The next instant Robert was wide-awake. The clock by his bed read 3:35 a.m. A warm summer-night breeze blew in through the nearby open window, but he was shivering. This dream always frightened him. Not the learning part of course, but the last part, when the teacher entered the room.

The katydids were calling in the tall elm trees that bordered the field behind the house. *The same nightmare—again*, he thought. Yet something about the dream always had seemed to him to be distinctly undreamlike: although he never could remember what the lessons were about, he knew with certainty that a number of classes always took place during the night, each one covering a different subject, and that the sequence of the classes was always the same. *Such detail in dreams*, he thought, *wasn't usually that regular or predictable.* He closed his eyes and fell back to sleep.

The next morning Robert bounded down the stairs and joined his mother and father at the table for breakfast.

The dining area was in one corner of the large living room, part of the original colonial-era house that made up the core of a series of later additions. Robert's father, Steve Bennett, had bought the place five years before, as a second home. He ran a well-known, lucrative graphic-arts studio in New York City, and every year, at the end of June, he moved the entire firm upstate to the Catskills for the summer—his three artists always could find places to stay there and were happy to spend two months in the country with their families.

"So what's up for today?" Robert's dad asked, sipping his coffee.

"I'm gonna look for the old tanner's cabin. I figure it must be farther up the creek, near the rock wall." The wall was on their property, toward the northwest.

"Don't go climbing that wall," said Elizabeth, his mother, as she spooned scrambled eggs onto his plate. "I've seen that wall. It's very high, and it could easily collapse. Promise me you won't climb it."

"I promise, Mom."

"You know, it could all just be a folktale," Steve said. "There may not be remains of any cabin up there at all."

"I know. But if it's there, I'll find it," Robert said. He was determined. In fact he felt compelled to take on this search. This was his mission.

Right after breakfast, with a compass and penknife in his pocket, he took off across the turnpike and up to the end of the dirt road that cut through the field across from the house. Then he hiked up into the forest.

It took him about five minutes to get to the creek. He followed it upstream for a couple of hundred yards until he reached the old wall. His plan was to look on the far side of the creek for the cabin's foundation. He crossed the creek on stepping-stones and went uphill, a little farther into the woods.

After exploring the far side of the creek for a while, he approached a low, natural, rocky ledge. At one end of the outcrop, he saw the result of a recent mini mudslide. Some large mud-covered rocks at the base of the ledge looked like they had slid down from the top not long ago. Robert remembered the terrific thunderstorm they'd had a couple days before and figured it had caused this. A vertical crack had sliced through that part of the ledge.

As he approached the crack, he saw that, since it was long, and fairly wide in places, and because the sun was in just the right position, enough light fell through the crack and onto interior portions of the rock to allow him to see pretty far in. Normally he wouldn't bother investigating a crack in a rock, but something about this one fascinated him. He even wondered for a moment why this particular crack might seem special but wasn't able to identify the reason.

He got close to the opening and peered in. He had the distinct impression that the narrow gap opened into a larger opening at the back. Near the bottom of the crack, the shadow of Robert's head obscured the sunlight, but as his eyes grew accustomed to the dark, he spotted a small, flat, light-colored rectangular object on the floor of the opening.

What is that? he wondered. He picked up a stick and used it to try to maneuver the object out of the crack but was unsuccessful.

Now his mission had changed, and he hurried back to the house. After picking up a flashlight, he looked around for something he could use to grab the object and pull it out. In the backyard, on the bench by the grill, he found his dad's charcoal tongs and decided they would do the job. Carrying his two archaeological tools with him, he hurried back up to the site.

After Robert checked the cavity with his flashlight and found nothing else in there (he couldn't see into the larger cavern behind the space in front), he inserted the tongs into the crack. The job was much harder than he thought it would be. He found he could lift the object, but trying to get the tongs and the object out together kept resulting in failure. And the sound of distant thunder added a bit of urgency to the operation.

Finally—very, very, carefully—he was able to dig out the artifact. He laid it in his palm and examined it. It was shaped roughly like a stick of gum with rounded corners but was a little bigger. The main part consisted of a long, gray, piece of what looked like silver. On one side of this silver piece were three identical lines of small, delicately formed letter-like shapes.

Over the past several years, Robert had put together a small but varied collection of foreign coins, so he knew that if the figures were letters, the writing wasn't Chinese or Arabic or Greek. He had no idea what the language was.

Attached at each end of the object were two half-round decorative finials made of what looked like real gold. He tried to pull the finials off, but they seemed firmly attached and appeared to be only decorative.

The sky grew darker as storm clouds moved in. Robert made it back to the house just as it began to rain.

"Hey, Mom. Look what I found. What is this?"

Elizabeth was sitting at the dining-room table, reading the paper. She looked closely at the object in Robert's hand. "What is that, Robert? I don't know what it is," she said. "Where did you find it?"

"In a crack in a rock ledge," he said as he sat on the sofa. He turned on the table lamp and held the piece close to the light to study it. It was raining hard now, and the roar could be heard through the screen door. Robert looked out at the summer storm and thought how the delicious smell of the strawberry bush near the house seemed to be strongest when it rained. Then it occurred to him that this storm could cause another mudslide and that he might have to move some rocks and mud to uncover the crevice.

Later that evening, he showed the object to his dad. Steve was intrigued by the piece but also baffled as to what it could be. "Part of a child's toy or something?" was his best guess.

The little object that Robert found

But to Robert this was an artifact from a long-lost civilization, and later events would prove him right. Proof was not to come this summer, though, or the next, or for many years. When he went back to the rock ledge the next day, he did have to uncover the crack again. Using a flat rock, he pushed the mud away from the cleft. A close look at the rock and soil around the cavity, however, didn't suggest that further investigations could easily be carried out, so he put the project on hold for some future time when he could double his efforts.

When Robert was thirteen, his dreams about the classroom ended. In the last one, he finally looked at the teacher's face and saw only an ordinary-looking man. He woke up without feeling fear.

Twenty years later

Robert sat in the office of Steve Bennett's lawyer, Glenn Pearson, as the attorney studied some documents. He put the papers down and looked at Robert. "Well, Dr. Bennett, since your mother died three years ago, and since you have no siblings, everything goes to you."

Robert nodded. "My dad and I talked about it several weeks ago."

"This is a rich estate." Pearson picked up the papers again. "Your father sold his business…um…"

"Two years ago," Robert said.

"Yes. It was very successful—it grew tremendously over the last decade or so." He looked at one of the pages. "There are several large bank accounts. And he left you an apartment here in Manhattan, a house and land in Europe—near Lake Geneva—and three hundred acres and a house in the Catskill Mountains. The entire estate is valued at more than seven million dollars."

"I hadn't realized it was quite so much."

Pearson looked over his glasses at Robert. "Steven told me that you have a PhD in…is it archaeology?"

Robert nodded.

"That's interesting. He also told me you were teaching at a university in Pennsylvania, is it?"

"Some teaching, some fieldwork. I'm on a sabbatical right now, though, trying to regain focus on my academic work, reformulate future plans."

"Single. No kids…"

Robert sensed that Pearson wanted to make conversation. "Almost married a couple times. But it didn't work out," he said with a little laugh, embarrassed that he was being so open with someone he hardly knew.

"Are you going to keep the properties?"

"For now, yes. I was thinking of renting out the house upstate. I'm going up there this week to go through Dad's things."

"That's quite a lot of property up there."

"Dad called it his 'lucky find.' He acquired it as a result of chance meetings and having the finances just when he needed them."

Two days later Robert drove up to the house in the Catskill Mountains. After arriving, he went to work boxing up the things he wanted to take back to Pennsylvania with him. The rest would be sold at an open-house sale.

At about eight o'clock that night, he went up to his childhood bedroom to decide what to take and what to leave behind. He looked at the books in the bookcase. Donnelly's *Atlantis: The Antediluvian World* and Churchward's *The Lost Continent of Mu* were on the shelf. These books had helped shape his childhood decision to become an archaeologist, even though he no longer found their evidence for lost civilizations convincing.

Also on the shelf, and equally formative in Robert's life, were editions of Plato's *Timaeus* and *Critias*. These books contained Plato's account of Atlantis, an island that, Plato claimed, had sunk beneath the sea nine thousand years before his time; Robert still found these texts interesting. Plato implied that the story had come to him through the oligarch Critias, the uncle of Plato's mother, and Robert found it a little improbable that Plato would falsely attribute a story to such a close relative and contemporary.

Although Robert had decided that reasons to disbelieve in Atlantis outweighed reasons to believe, he disagreed with those of his colleagues who summarily dismissed the notion that highly advanced civilizations, lost to history, might have existed on earth.

Going through the top drawer of his desk, he picked up a sealed and folded envelope; he felt something inside it. After tearing the envelope open, he pulled out the silver-and-gold artifact that had so intrigued him all those years before. He looked closely at it. *Real silver*, he thought. *And this looks like real gold.* "You're the reason I'm an archaeologist," he said to the little object.

The next day was bright, cold, and windy. The leaves of the maple trees next to the house and along the turnpike shimmered pure yellow in the early autumn light. Robert put on a jacket, grabbed a flashlight (so he could look into the crevice again), and walked up toward the ridge, a place he hadn't seen since he was twelve. It was a beautiful day for a walk, he thought, and the place where he'd found the mysterious object all those years ago seemed as good a destination as any.

He found the wall, crossed the creek, and after a search, located the stony ridge. He looked for the crack where he'd pulled out the artifact, but that part of the ridge was completely covered up by soil and vegetation. Recalling how he'd seen what had appeared to be a larger space beyond the little rock shelf where the object was lying, he inspected—now with the eyes of an accomplished archaeologist—the top of the ledge, looking for a deep crevice. There was no crevice, but he noticed the forest floor above the ledge seemed unusually flat. He picked up a stick, poked it into the flat area, and struck rock.

How big is this rock? Robert wondered, and kept poking with the stick at different spots until it sank into soft earth. Using this method, he was able to draw a complete outline of the stone in the dirt. He realized he'd drawn a perfect square that was about five feet on each side.

"That's curious," he said. "A flat, square rock with a space under it…"

He stood back and looked at the outline and considered how he might investigate further.

Choosing a spot at random, he used a stone to scrape the dirt away from the rock's edge. "Even more curious," he said, when he saw a line of tiny, barely visible notches inscribed along the edge. *This is definitely interesting*, he thought. *I'll need a shovel.*

Robert went back to the house, got a shovel from the garage, went back to the site, and started to clear away the dirt from the square stone. Near the middle of the square, he uncovered a manhole-cover-size, flat, stone disk. Inscribed into its center was a line of letters that closely resembled those on the little artifact—in fact Robert recognized the words as ones that appeared on the artifact. *Really interesting.*

After going to the house again and returning with a crowbar, he went to work to lift the disk. He found he could slip the crowbar under the edge of the disk and lift the stone slightly. He went around the disk several times doing this, until he was able to lift it up and push it aside, exposing a round hole that went through the big square and led to a cavity beneath.

He took the flashlight out of his pocket and shined it into the hole. The floor of the cavity was about seven feet below the opening; a metal ladder led from the floor up to the hole. *Did someone, in the last hundred years maybe, build some kind of cellar here, or a bomb shelter?* But how would the perplexing inscriptions fit in?

He cautiously lowered himself through the hole and, standing on a rung of the ladder, shined the light around the cave. He saw that he was in a small room of the cave. He looked at the wall in the direction of the rocky ledge and spotted the little stone shelf, with a crack behind it, upon which the artifact he'd retrieved years before had lain. Shining his light to the right, he saw a wide passageway that led deeper into the earth. Opposite to that opening was a metal gate, with a second gate beyond it, and a short tunnel beyond that. Since the short tunnel went toward a hillside on the outside, Robert assumed it served as a second exit.

Just to make sure he wouldn't get trapped in the cave somehow without anyone knowing, he went back to the house and taped a dated note on the front door that read, "Went for a walk in the woods near the stream." The owner of the local bookstore, who had been a friend of Robert's when they were kids, was going to stop by the next day to buy some books. If anything happened, at least someone would know where he was. He put on his boots and a thicker coat, tucked a pen, a notebook and some aluminum foil for samples into his pants pocket, and went back up to the cave. It was now well past noon, but he figured he could have lunch later.

Again Robert turned on his flashlight and went down into the cave; this time he climbed off the ladder at the bottom. Making sure he had solid purchase with each step, he slowly made his way down the incline into the passageway to the right. Within a few yards, he came to portions of a wall that apparently had once sealed the tunnel. It seemed that an old cave-in had destroyed the seal, and he was able to squeeze through the opening and continue his descent. After a few more yards, the passageway opened into a rock-walled room.

What Robert saw as he shined the light around the room took him aback. This was a small chamber, in the center of which stood a strange-looking vehicle, rusted and in pieces, but apparently complete. It was clearly a vehicle; he saw two big spoked wheels, two little ones, a pair of large headlights, and a body with a compartment that had a seat in it.

He studied the car carefully. Close examination revealed fine, well-crafted detail. In several areas, for instance, where there were hinges, he saw complex structures. He could see under the hoodlike panel and made out a simple-looking engine of some sort. He also saw the wheels' axles but couldn't spot how they might be connected to the engine.

Was the device a concoction of recent times—perhaps a hoax or the work of an eccentric inventor? Was it a remnant of an ancient lost civilization? If so, where were the remains of their cities, their factories?

Robert couldn't shake the feeling—and his was an educated feeling—that the little gold-and-silver object, the writing on the rock, and now this incredible vehicle were genuinely strange and belonged to a much earlier time. His enthusiasm began to soar. Had this privilege been given to him—the privilege of uncovering a true lost civilization? Was this—what was happening right here and right now, with only himself as a witness—a historical event, on a par with Calvert and Schliemann's discovery of Troy?

Get a grip, he thought. *What are the chances that an advanced civilization existed in North America then all but disappeared, leaving only a vehicle in a cave in the Catskills? Vanishingly small for sure.*

The vehicle as Robert discovered it

He realized he needed to date the site before he would allow his imagination to run away. Since there was absolutely nothing in this chamber that was familiar to Robert—at least as far as he could see—that connected the site to any known culture or period, he would have to find other means of dating the site. He looked around for organic materials that might be submitted to radiocarbon dating, and located the remains of three tiny plant stems near a small, plain, rectangular ceramic box that may have been a planter. He also saw remains of a wooden wall that apparently had once enclosed the space. Rows of metal pins lined the cave walls, and a small piece of wood was still attached to one of the pins. *Plants and wood,* he thought. *This site can't be very old.*

He picked up a piece of wood and a sample of the plant debris for testing and wrapped them in foil.

Shining his flashlight up to the ceiling, he saw a small, shiny, black dome that may have been a lighting fixture, but he couldn't find a switch anywhere in the room. He then left the chamber and continued down the narrow tunnel.

Robert counted his steps to the next chamber: twenty-seven. This room was somewhat larger than the first and was surrounded, inside the rough stone walls of the cave, by a smooth, segmented, curved granite wall, rounded at the top, which didn't reach the ceiling. In the center of the room stood a large bronze statue of a weird-looking bird whose body was shaped like a high-sided bowl. The body/bowl was about five feet in diameter from rim to rim. On the bowl's right side was a small staircase—the bird and stairs being of one piece—which facilitated entry into the bowl.

The floor of this chamber was uneven though covered with flat rocks. Here and there several pools of water had collected. Short metal posts were set into the floor in a straight line that extended from the bird to the room's inner wall.

The cave bird as Robert discovered it

He left this chamber and walked 121 steps through a steeply down-sloping, high-roofed passageway to a third—and apparently the last—room. This room, like the others, seemed to Robert to have been roughly hewn out of the natural rock, though it was difficult for him to be sure. The ceiling and floor, as well as the back wall and the walls to left and right, all were totally unrefined in appearance. But the far wall, the wall Robert had faced when he had entered the room, was completely flat. In the center of this smooth, gray, highly polished wall was a door—or at least a set of inscribed lines delineating the shape of a door and its plain casing.

Above this door shape, also inscribed in the flat surface, was a symbol that featured two-overlapping rings. Like everything else in these chambers, the symbol seemed utterly unfamiliar to Robert. Although he was confident he would remember its appearance, he took out his pen and his little notebook and, holding the flashlight under his chin, drew a sketch of the figure.

Robert studied the door and considered what it might take to get through it. He felt that if he could open the door he might find out who had created these

The two-rings symbol

caves—if indeed someone had created them—who had made these strange objects, and why the objects had been interred here.

After reexamining the strange objects he'd found, he decided it would be dark outside soon, and he wasn't sure how much longer his flashlight would hold out. Elated, he quickly climbed out of the hole, covered it with pine branches, and went back to the house.

The next morning Robert sent the plant and wood samples to a radiocarbon dating laboratory in New England for testing. Wanting to spend the whole day at the site, he called his friends to break a dinner date for that evening and phoned the bookstore owner to cancel the visit. Then he hiked back to the caves with a tape measure, a camera, a battery-powered lantern, and a bigger notebook. No matter how old the site turned out to be, he thought it would be worthwhile to document it.

The strange motor

After descending into the cave, he took a few minutes to reexamine the car. The engine didn't seem to have any moving parts and was very simple. He

A power source?

Reconstruction: graphical reconstruction (GR) #NY1521: the full-size car in the first cave, as it would have originally appeared

could find no fuel tank, so he guessed the car had been powered by electricity—but the only battery-like object he saw was a two-and-a-half-inch-diameter, smooth, white, Saturn-shaped object, with two wires attached to it, a thin one on top and a thick one underneath. Could such a small object have powered the car?

He spent the day taking pictures, making measurements, and drawing a map of the site. Then he went back to the house, found a tarp in the garage, and took it up to the site to cover the opening. As he walked back to the house, he thought about his find. *Maybe a reclusive sculptor lived in this area once,* he mused. *Maybe—say, sixty or seventy years ago—the sculptor created these strange objects for his own private gratification.* Robert contemplated this explanation for a moment. *No,* he thought. *The car was not handmade. It was surely the product of a sophisticated manufacturing process. And how realistic is it to suppose that the massive bronze bird came into being as the product of one person's secret art project?*

This was a genuine mystery.

CHAPTER 2
THE BURIED BUILDING

The next morning Robert hauled a small gas generator and a few power tools up to the caves. Among his dad's art-studio equipment he found some lamps and tripods, and he set up a lamp on a tripod in each of the three chambers.

He went back to the house for lunch, where he got a call from Mr. Pearson in Manhattan, who asked him to stop by to sign some papers. Robert made an appointment for the next day. Then he returned to the site to continue to map and photograph the cave complex.

The next day, Wednesday, he drove down to the city, arrived at the lawyer's office a little after noon, and signed the papers. He spent the night in his apartment on West 72nd Street.

On Thursday, Robert went to a hardware store on West 3rd Street and bought a second generator, some lamps, and a couple of SureFire flashlights. He left the city in the late afternoon and arrived at the house in the Catskills that evening. Intending to break through the inscribed doorway in the third room the next day, he went to bed.

In the morning he received an e-mail from the lab with the results of the radiocarbon tests. He was stunned. The lab dated the plant remains to 13,730 ± 300 years Before Present (BP) and the wood to 13,890 ± 300 years BP. Because the plant parts had been associated with a planter, and the wood clearly had been attached to the wall, Robert felt sure the results truly reflected the age of the nonorganic objects, which meant the car and bird had been sitting in their sealed chambers for an incredible fourteen thousand years.

How could these plant and wood remains have survived for fourteen thousand years? he wondered. *The lab techs must have been surprised too.* Older plant remains had been found at Ohalo in Israel, but those had been carbonized, and Robert knew that some researchers believed that uncharred, dry, botanical remains could not be ancient. The cave-in might have unsealed the chambers as recently as, say, a few hundred or a thousand years ago, but that would only partially explain the survival of the plant stems and wood. Nevertheless Robert could not easily discount the results.

Everything pointed to the fact that there existed a sophisticated culture, unknown to archaeology, in this part of the world at that time.

He sat at his computer, thinking about how and when he might inform others of his momentous find. He faced a dilemma: The public needed to know about this ancient site—this was the bottom line for Robert—yet the finely detailed, obviously purposeful mechanisms on the car had by now convinced him that the vehicle may well have been the product of a technology more advanced than our own. Disclosing such a find in the wrong way could cause problems. Not only would the history books have to be rewritten, but also this single find, as incredible as it seemed, could actually have a significant and unpredictable impact on industry and the economy. The civilization whose artifacts he was uncovering was in no way primitive, and Robert knew that these ancient people may have discovered technologies and methods that surpassed those of the modern world. He thought about how, in recent times, the mass-produced automobile had destroyed the horse-drawn vehicle market and he imagined that such disruptions, as wonderful as their results would be in the long run, could follow from the revelation of his discovery. He felt uneasy being alone at the center of something that could change the world. What weighed most heavily on Robert, however, was his realization that the government, foreseeing military applications, might not only cover up these newly discovered technologies, which, he thought, *might* be a legitimate thing for them to do, but also cover up the find in its entirety. To do so, he felt, would be criminal.

He decided the best way to continue would be to keep investigating on his own, to keep good records of his work, and to put into safekeeping some pieces as evidence until he could figure out a way to ensure that an attempted disclosure wouldn't result in a complete cover-up.

Now it was time to break through the doorway.

He went up to the site and walked through the caves to the third chamber. Studying the smooth wall, he noticed an irregularly shaped area of the doorway with a slightly different color than the rest of the wall. Perhaps at some point this door had been breached and repaired. A few quick tests of the wall appeared to show that it was made out of some kind of plastic-like substance, slightly translucent and soft enough to cut through fairly easily; obviously it was a material that hadn't broken down with age. Robert first drilled a small hole all the way through the wall at a point within the doorway markings. Not detecting any noxious fumes, he decided to keep at it. He found that if he cut well within the doorway outlines, his jigsaw blade was long enough to saw through the material to the other side. He slowly cut out a large block of plastic at about eye level. When he shined a light through the opening, he saw a big, decorated, wooden door about twelve feet away. The space was enclosed by walls and a ceiling that were made of the same plastic material as that of the cave wall. Cutting out sections of the plastic doorway, he created an opening large enough to walk through. Then he set up a lamp inside the newly opened space, close to the wooden door. Examining the door, he identified it as being made of ebony. There was a blue, metallic U-shaped latch on the right side of the door attached to a metal plate with a narrow slot in it that might have been a keyhole. He looked for hinges, but none were visible. He pulled on the latch, but the door was closed tight. The next challenge would be to get through this door without damaging it. It was past 9:00 p.m., and since he had shopping to do and hadn't eaten since breakfast, he left the site for the night.

After dinner, Robert went to bed but couldn't sleep. How would he get to whatever was on the other side of that ebony door? He imagined there might exist another wall that the door was set into and thought he might uncover that wall by cutting into the plastic enclosure—but he wasn't at all sure this idea would work. Maybe he could dig under the door to see what was there. Or perhaps, if that slot was a keyhole, he could pick the lock.

Suddenly he sat upright in bed. "Could it be a key?" he said out loud. He jumped out of bed, turned on the light, went to the desk, and picked up the little silver-and-gold artifact. He looked at it carefully; it seemed to be too smooth to function as any sort of key. Sitting at the desk, he retrieved a tiny screwdriver from the top drawer. He had tried to pull off the gold finials several times before but had given up each time, assuming they couldn't be removed. But now he would try again, harder. He put the screwdriver blade into the crack between the silver part and one of the finials and very gently tried to pry the crack open. The blade slipped out. He tried again and again until he managed to fit the blade into the crack in just the right way so that when he pried, the crack opened a tiny bit. When he applied more pressure, the crack opened wider. With a tug he pulled off the finial and placed it on the desk. When he tipped the artifact over, a tiny black key fell onto the desk.

It was clearly a key; it looked to be made of iron, with a square bow, a three-part shank, and teeth of different lengths.

"OK!" he said. He jumped up, got dressed, and slipped the key into his pocket. *Could a lock mechanism still work after fourteen millennia?* He put on his coat and grabbed a flashlight. *It could. It could, if it were made to last. Anyway,* he thought, *even if it doesn't work, the key will give me a clue about how to pick the lock.*

He left the house with the flashlight and walked up toward the site. It was well past midnight when he arrived. He started the generator, turned on the lights, and went down into the now well-lit cave. When he got to the ebony door, he held his breath and inserted the key into the slot. He felt the key's teeth engage something inside the door—a little more pressure, and suddenly he heard a loud click. Grabbing the handle, he pulled on the door and felt it move. With more effort he pulled it open farther. Grasping the door with both hands,

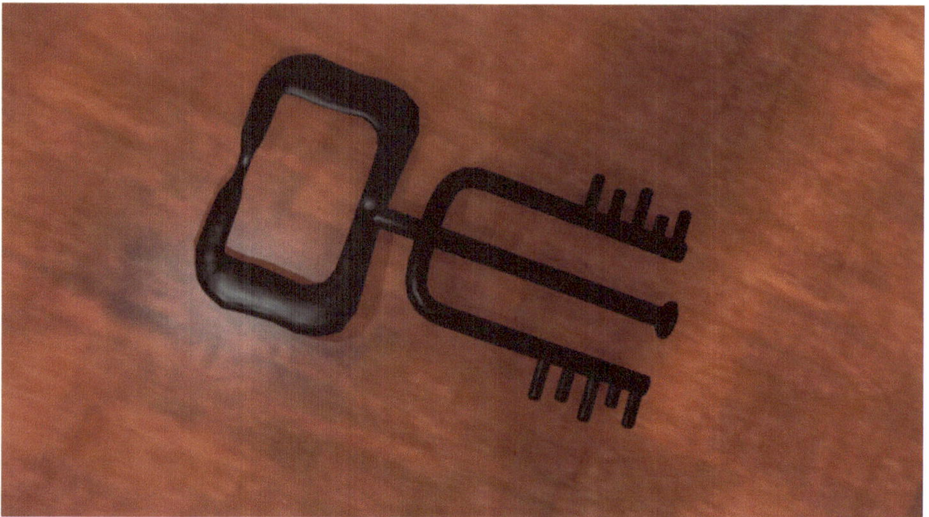

The iron key

he opened it more and more until there was just enough space for him to fit through. He slid through the opening far enough to be able to stand on the other side of the door. The air inside was musty but breathable. He took out his flashlight, turned it on, and shined it into the space.

What Robert saw astonished him: he was in a room filled with a marvelous jumble of objects. There were parts of what was once a wooden throne-like chair; big metal bowls of various sizes and shapes; a large, decorated, spoked wheel that appeared to be made of bronze; and several wooden boxes. The objects were strewn around in something of a clutter; the thought occurred to Robert that whoever had broken through the sealed door the first time may have tossed things around, looking for something. That was exactly what had happened to King Tutankhamun's tomb; in fact, he thought, *This is how Howard Carter must have felt when he peered into that tomb and saw "wonderful things."*

Robert trained his flashlight on a model bird, its wings outstretched, which sat atop a vertical pole. Having had a lifelong interest in prehistoric life, he recognized the bird as an archaeopteryx.

The first room Robert entered

He assumed it was a model, because archaeopteryx had become extinct many millions of years before the end of the Pleistocene epoch. As he walked farther into the room and looked back in the direction he had come, he saw on the wall a map covered by a thin layer of dust. It was a map of a land he couldn't identify. To the right, in an alcove, on a boxlike pedestal, sat a large sculpture or model of a strange animal that Robert thought looked prehistoric. In the middle of the room, half buried in the rubble, lay a statue of a human figure that he judged to be made of

Reconstruction: the room Robert entered, as it looked fourteen thousand years ago

polychromed metal. The figure wore a robe and a strange mask. On the floor, Robert noticed what appeared to be the pieces of a game set.

Shining the flashlight onto the wall opposite the entrance from the cave, he saw black wooden shelves divided into large square compartments, each containing a rolled-up bale of fluffy, cloth-like material. Between two sets of shelves was an open door. He carefully made his way to the door and went through it into a spacious mostly empty room that reminded him of the interior of an old barn. The floor was stone, mostly

Reconstruction: the game in the room

covered by old boards—clearly the floor was originally wood. He shined his flashlight around the room, focusing on a group of objects near the far wall. He walked carefully toward these objects, glancing back to make sure he could see light through the door he'd just come through; he wanted to be able to get back there if his flashlight failed.

At first he thought he was looking at a group of large jars, but when he got closer, he had the distinct impression that the elongated spheres and the cylinders, interconnected by wires, were parts of a machine of some sort. *It represents our solar system*, he thought. *This big object is Jupiter. This one has a ring around it; it's Saturn. And that greenish one on its side is Uranus, and the other green one is Neptune—and there's Pluto.*

He noticed some paper or parchment pages hanging off a little assemblage that might have represented the asteroid belt. Looking at them closely, he saw that these ancient papers had diagrams on them that exactly resembled modern astrological charts—though the symbols on them were different from those with which he was familiar.

Reconstruction: the astrology machine, as it looked fourteen thousand years ago

On the wall was a metal box that looked just like a modern electrical panel. He saw what appeared to be indicator lamps, as well as buttons and what

The astrology-machine control panel, with electricity applied

looked like incoming and outgoing wires. The panel had the same symbols on it that were on the parchment astrology charts, so Robert surmised it might control the solar system machine. Since the symbols seemed to label the lamps, he guessed the panel simply turned the planet units on and off.

He noted that if the operation of this machine somehow was supposed to simulate the workings of the solar system, then these ancients had conceived of the planets as functioning astrologically in pairs: There was a control lamp on the panel for each pair. Robert thought he could identify the pairs from their relative positions on the panel: sun and moon,

Venus and Mars, Jupiter and Saturn, and Uranus and Neptune. Neither Mercury nor Pluto was a member of a pair.

But what in the world did this machine actually do?

Robert noticed a staircase in the middle of the room that led up to another level. As he shined his flashlight up to that level and saw wooden structures there, it dawned on him that he was in a building that had been buried under the earth.

How could a building be buried? It could, if it were enclosed in a mound.

The only other fixture in the room was an enigmatic round table surrounded by a circular arrangement of bars.

Shining his light in the direction from which he had entered the room, he noticed two other doors along the same wall. Each had a different word inscribed above it. He walked closer to the door he had come through to get a better look at the word, but the letters, like those on the key case, were totally unfamiliar to him. He decided to call the cluttered room through which he had entered this building from the caves the "Entrance Room."

The writing above the other two doors was equally enigmatic.

The enclosed table

Reconstruction. The door through which Robert entered the big room

Reconstruction. The writing above the door through which Robert entered the big room

There also was an open door on each side of the room. Robert walked through these doorways into alcoves, and found an ascending staircase in each one.

He didn't want to stray too far from the door through which he had entered until he had set up lighting; besides, he was feeling a bit overwhelmed and figured he'd better get some rest, so he went home and to bed.

The next morning he returned to the site and installed lamps inside the big room. Then he carefully studied the wood of the central staircase. It seemed solid; there was no detectable degradation. *Perhaps the wood was treated*, he thought, *to prevent fungal and bacterial damage*. If there was any degradation due to physical or chemical mechanisms, it was undetectable. So, flashlight in hand, he walked up the stairs. On the next floor, he found himself in a very long hallway that led to a door at the far end.

Reconstruction: the upstairs central hallway, as it looked in antiquity

At the top of the stairs, he found three large cubical stands; on top of each was a large closed book. *This is amazing*, Robert thought. *But can they be read?* Noting that the people who had occupied this building used books in codex form rather than scrolls, he went to the book farthest from the stairs. He shined his light onto the book and, with extreme care, opened it just enough so he could see one page. Small pieces of brittle paper or parchment fell out as he held the book open. The page was filled with simple color drawings of people doing various things: Two reddish-skinned men with blond hair and beards, and dressed in robes, stood in a street beside a building and talked to a man wearing a squarish red hat who peered out of an upstairs window. In another picture on the same page, the two men on the street stood talking to a woman in a beige dress patterned with small red flowers at the building's open door.

On the page he also saw writing that resembled the writing on the key case, as well as on the stone that covered the entrance to the caves and above the doorway through which he'd entered the big room.

He knew these marvelous books would be a major focus of his work in the coming weeks. He would allocate time to study them while continuing to explore and document the rest of the building.

He discovered that the door at the far end of the hallway couldn't be opened. The only way he could get out of the hallway was to go back down the way he had come.

Over the next two days, Robert explored the rest of the building, setting up lamps in each newly entered area. He found that this very large wooden building seemed to be divided into three parts; in his notes, he simply called them "left," "right," and "middle." The big room with the astrology machine in it, as well as the central upstairs hallway, constituted the entire middle part of the building.

Most of the left, or western, side of the building was composed of rooms that contained what seemed to be hundreds of bookcases, the shelves of which were bare, except for a few wooden bookends here and there. *If the shelves were filled in the past,* Robert thought, *someone had removed all the books.* Also in this wing he found a group of rooms on different levels, connected by staircases. In one of the rooms, he found a table, on top of which was a stack of three slide mounts, not much different than modern mounts, each of which contained a film frame that appeared to be solid black. On the uppermost level, he saw a telescope aimed at a screen some distance away in the building's right side—on this level, just below the roof, there were no intervening walls.

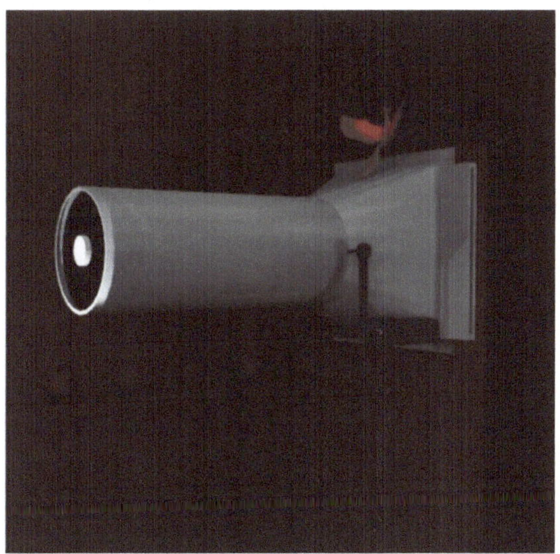

Reconstruction. The telescope

On the right side of the building, a curved hallway filled with abstract sculptures led to a room with a large pedestal inside. On top of the pedestal was a large projector. Also in this room was the screen at which both the telescope and the projector were aimed. In the center of the room, next to a bronze sculpture of a tree, stood a small templelike building that contained a desk, a chair, an ivory box on a table, and an open book. Robert inspected a few of the book's pages. They weren't paper but were made of a flexible, plastic-like material. At first all the pages seemed to have nothing on them, but as Robert looked more closely at the two on top, he made out very faint images of the interior of a room. He could make out walls, some furniture and a round window. The pages underneath the top ones were blank.

He walked over to the ivory box and lifted its lid. The box contained a smaller, similar box, which contained an even smaller box, which seemed to be empty.

Reconstruction. The sculpture-filled hallway

Reconstruction: Another view of the sculpture-filled hallway

Reconstruction: a chair and desk on the first landing below the telescope room

Reconstruction: the templelike building

Reconstruction: The projector

Reconstruction: the projector in operation fourteen
thousand years ago

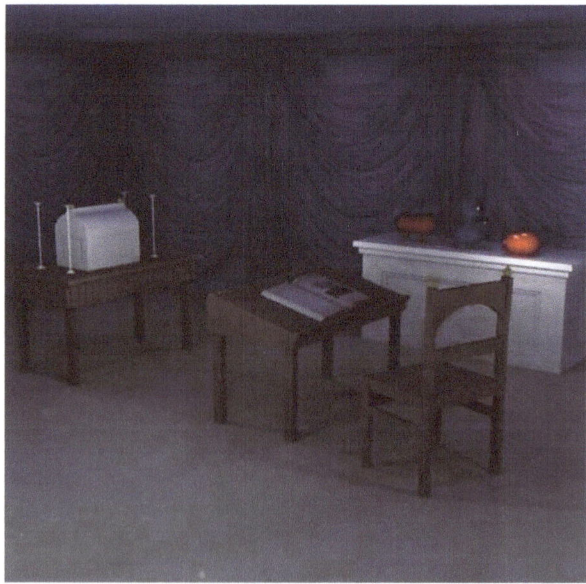

Reconstruction: the interior of the templelike building,
as it appeared in the distant past

In the building's left side, near the foot of the stairs that led up to the rooms that ascended to the telescope, Robert found a closed door that he was able to push open easily. He entered the space and looked around. Aiming his flashlight at a group of boxes on the floor, he saw that each box sat at the foot of a stand topped by a small shield. The room showed no sign of having been rummaged through, as the Entrance Room had. Perhaps whoever had broken into the building had been quickly removed and the entryway resealed. Robert's attention was drawn to the box/shield assemblage in the center. Although a thin layer of dust covered the shield, he could make out the painted image on it: a wheel surrounded by clouds and red flames. What had attracted his attention was a piece of parchment that hung from the stand. Looking closely at it, he saw it was a handwritten page. He made a mental note to photograph this page as soon as possible.

Reconstruction: the room of shields, as it appeared in the distant past

Robert spent the next three and a half months cataloging and documenting everything. Of course this wasn't what he'd agreed to be doing on his sabbatical. In his application to the dean, he'd promised to travel to Greece then Turkey for the purpose of expanding his expertise in classical archaeology. Normally a change like this would require a professor to submit a statement of revision of plans for approval, but doing so was out of the question. Furthermore Robert had no idea what kind of report to submit upon his return to the university, if he returned at all. He had made up his mind to refund his salary for this period and felt sure no one would blame him for what he was doing.

Robert turned his attention to the two unopened doors just to the west of the Entrance Room door. When he opened the door in the center, he found that it led to a room about the same size as the Entrance Room. Although the Entrance Room was in shambles, the objects in this room were intact and clearly all in their original positions. Poles supporting short horizontal beams leaned against all four walls, and from these beams hung clumps of silvery threads that reminded Robert of hair or moss. Scattered here and there among the hanging strands were small gemlike ornaments. Centered in the room was a large, decorated mahogany desk that would have been imposing when new. On the wide front panel of this well-crafted piece of furniture was carved a six-letter word in the same unknown language Robert had seen before. Seated in a chair behind the desk was a sculpture that, like the one in the Entrance Room, seemed to represent a masked person. Here, though, the mask had the form of a round, yellow head without ears, nose, or mouth, but with small black dots for eyes. The life-size body of this doll-like sculpture was dressed in a heavy, quilted cloth robe whose original colors—rose, purple, green, and orange—could still be made out.

Robert eventually was able to open the third door along the same wall and enter the third room. This room was filled with hundreds of pieces that fit together as parts of a machine. After looking closely at the pieces, he realized they hadn't formed a functioning whole; rather, the objects formed a sculpture that represented a machine.

He found a structure below the left wing of the building that seemed to be some kind of furnace. He also found an electrical generator and located electrical outlets throughout the building. He discovered a kitchen and bathrooms, and made plans to map the building's plumbing.

Robert now turned his full attention to the three large books, which he called the "Hallway Books." He had already spent weeks photographing all the pages of these books and had set up a space in his house to study the photographs.

Eventually Robert realized that the Hallway Books constituted keys to three different languages. The first book, the one farthest from the stairs, was a universal key to what he assumed was the natural language of the people who had built this edifice. It was universal because it taught the language, defining its words and illustrating its grammar, by means of pictures. Although the pictures fairly quickly gave way to pure text further into the book, there nevertheless were many interesting images that illustrated activities, costumes, animals, and vehicles of land, sea, and air. The book also contained a guide to pronunciation, using illustrations that depicted, in cross-section, the lips, palate, and tongue. Robert discovered that the language itself was called "Atl" by its speakers, who called themselves "Atlanians"; their land was called "Atlan." It may have taken twenty years for the Rosetta stone to be deciphered, but because the pictures in this book so clearly conveyed the meanings of the words, because Robert had some linguistic training—he'd studied ancient Greek in graduate school, and taught himself to read Sumerian cuneiform in college—and because the author, or authors, of the book had laid out the order of lessons so well, it was only a matter of three months (of very hard work) before he had created a fairly complete—although basic—Atl-English dictionary.

The similarity of "Atlan" to "Atlantis" wasn't lost on Robert. Before his discovery of this place, it seemed to him unlikely that a great civilization could have existed at the end of the Pleistocene epoch only to disappear with barely a trace—and that's why he found it difficult to fully accept Plato's story of Atlantis as a true account. But now it was clear to him that an advanced culture had in fact existed at the end of the last ice age and had in fact left barely a trace. So now he had no problem accepting, as a working hypothesis at least, that Atlan and Atlantis were one and the same place. Although Plato had claimed that Atlantis was an island in the Atlantic Ocean, not a region in the Catskills of New York State, Robert suspected that the land of Atlantis could well have been large enough to encompass many regions.

It occurred to him that this first book, which he had come to call *The Universal Dictionary of Atl* (*UDA*), because of its clever pictorial definitions, which built complex notions out of extremely simple ones, could be of interest to philosophers.

The second book translated Atl into a universal artificial language that the Atlanians had invented and that they called "Wahte." Robert called this book *The Atl-Wahte Text* (*AWT*).

The third book was, according to its introduction, "essentially a textual and diagrammatic representation of a philosophical analysis of the world." Robert called this volume *The Philosophical Language Text* (*PLT*). He tried to follow the exposition but couldn't make sense of it and decided to put it aside for a while.

Now, in late April, he was able to translate the writing on the silver-and-gold key box. The thrice-repeated line on the left read, "Heroes speak." The three lines on the right each read, "We flourish." Robert wondered what the purpose of the repetition might have been.

The single line on the stone that covered the cave entrance said only, "Heroes speak."

And now Robert could read the word above the door to the Entrance Room. *Tasatl* meant "truth." The word above the center door was *shanshal*, meaning "goodness," and above the third door was *lyytoy*, "beauty." He discovered that the word carved into the desk in the center room, *talaso*, meant "examiner." He decided he would now call the Entrance Room the

The beginning of *The UDA*

"Room of the Truth Examiner." The next room would be the "Room of the Goodness Examiner," and the last would be the "Room of the Beauty Examiner."

Robert also was able finally to translate the handwritten note in the Room of Shields. This note, in a hurried hand, read as follows.

Today, as I directed that the last volume of soil be placed upon this venerable building, they told me they will immediately plant grass on the new hill. I was buoyed by my premonition that this wonderful place will not be forever hidden beneath the earth. But the destruction of our institutions has been so complete that it will not soon be rediscovered either. The chaos that has taken over our country has destroyed much but also permits much to be put aside for you—you who discover these products of our labors of more than five thousand years. You may have entered through the caves. I know this is not the end of our Truth Engine but is merely an interregnum. I implore you who find this to carry on our work—please let the work of our ancestors not have been in vain. It may even represent your own salvation. But do not make the mistakes we made. Beware of the Anti-Engine. Be clear about the nature of the cycles. If you do not yet know of it, seek out and find the Great Place for Humankind, which contains the deepest secret of the Engine. Look in the room of the double glass.

I am now ready to leave this place for the last time. WheelCloudFire will carry me through the air to my home, which I also will bury. We will encase the house; we will build the plastic (?) shell above and below, treat everything with *kalmat* and mix *shuutek* into the air, and seal the shell. Then earth movers will be brought in from the sea to finish the hill, and in years to come, travelers will see only a natural hill there. In the box below, you will find the coordinates of my house—they are extended (?) from the center of the earth, from the Map of the First Time that was carved from the living rock and that became the face of the lion, near the wide northern river. I will now live a simple life with my wife. We will live by my secret place that I have called the "Great Stream."

The note was signed "Kholoruuf, chief logician of our beloved Truth Engine."

Robert had no idea what *kalmat* and *shuutek* were, but at least the note supplied a small clue as to how people in Kholoruuf's day would have preserved a building and its contents and as to why the organic material he'd found in the cave might have been preserved for such a long time. These people had developed a science dedicated to this kind of preservation.

The note left Robert with many questions: What was this "Truth Engine" of which this Kholoruuf spoke? What was this engine that was so valued by these people? Since the *UDA* covered only a somewhat basic Atl vocabulary, he could find no answer there. And what was the "Anti-Engine"? What did Kholoruuf mean by "cycles"? What was the "Great Place for Humankind"? Could Kholoruuf's buried house be found? If so, could the answers to Robert's questions be found there?

Indeed, in the box below the shield, Robert discovered a map showing the East Coast of what we know today as America and, across the Atlantic, the entire continent of Africa. There was a dot apparently at the location of the very building Robert was presently exploring and where the map had been left. Next to the dot was the two-rings symbol and a rectangle that was given a length of "1." From the dot a roughly horizontal, straight line was drawn, which ran through a point in what is today Egypt. Down from that point, two straight lines extended; one was offset ninety degrees from the first line, and the other, offset at a specified smaller angle, precise down to four decimal places, intersected with a dot near the South African coast. This line was associated with a number, again extremely precise, which presumably specified its length.

Robert assumed that the rectangle represented the building that he was at this moment exhuming, and took its length as the unit. He had a hunch that "the First Time" in Kholoruuf's note referred to something at Gizah. He knew that the Sphinx, since it had been carved from the local bedrock, had been "carved from the living rock" near a "wide northern river," and that maybe "the First Time" somehow related to the Sphinx, a statue of an animal that, presumably, once had a lion's face. It was an extremely tenuous connection, he knew, but it was all he had, and he accepted it provisionally. He'd discovered in the *UDA* that the Atlanians had divided their circle into 384 degrees, so he could determine the exact angular offset of the second line. Based on this data and these assumptions, by making use of the Internet and the public library in New York City, he came up with a very precise location for the third dot on the west coast of South Africa, not far north of Cape Town, very near a coastal town called Melkbosstrand.

Also in the box under the shield, Robert found a second key, much like the one he'd used to unlock the ebony door.

Robert knew what he had to do now. He had no teaching duties to fulfill—he would deal with the issues concerning the sabbatical requirements later—and because of his inheritance, his financial resources were, practically speaking, limitless. He would put off renting out the house in the Catskills. There was absolutely nothing preventing him from fully investigating the South African connection.

CHAPTER 3
A CHANGE OF LOCALE

Before focusing on South Africa, Robert wanted to get a better sense of how the ancient building in the Catskills fit into the surrounding topology. He threw a pair of binoculars into the passenger seat of his car and drove to an outcrop that was locally well known for affording a view of the area. Looking down from the mountain with the binoculars, he located his father's house and the road that led up to the archaeological site. Scanning the area, he made out a straight ridge that ran east to west. *That's the buried building,* he thought. *They must have held it in great esteem to go to such lengths to preserve it.* He could see the little hill, next to the large mound, at the top of which he'd discovered the entrance to the caves—and he could discern the stream following the contours of both hills.

Returning to the site, he picked a spot on top of the large ridge that covered the building and dug into the earth until he uncovered a hard surface. He examined this surface and determined that it was composed of the same plastic material that had enclosed the entrance to the building in the cave. He concluded that a huge shell surrounded the entire building.

He built and installed a secure camouflaged cover for the cave entrance and covered the square stone with soil and leaves. It was time to make plans for a solo expedition to South Africa.

Although Kholoruuf's map provided exact measurements, Robert assumed that once in the new site's vicinity, he would still need to make a search. The first step would be to see whether he could find references to any mysterious archaeological discoveries that might have been made in or around Melkbosstrand.

An entire month of research at the New York Public Library turned up only one significant item—but that item supplied a major clue: an obscure South African science journal had printed a paragraph from a letter attributed to an astronomer, Sir John Herschel, son of the more famous astronomer Sir William Herschel. The letter was written in the 1830s to John Herschel's friend Charles Babbage. John Herschel had traveled to South Africa and set up an observatory at Wynberg. In addition to astronomy, Herschel was interested in botany and geology. He wrote:

> Thomas [Maclear] tells about a farmer who described to him Nell's Rock, near Cape Town, as being composed of an unusual waxlike or hornlike stone, one small face of which had, at some point in the past, been polished and inscribed with an enigmatic sign composed of two intersecting circles, side by side, surmounted by a circle and with a diamond underneath, which the farmer had drawn for him.

Robert suspected at once that the site referred to in the letter was the site he was looking for. "Near Cape Town" was vague, but he had learned from the map that the location of the rock, or the small hill, must be near Melkbosstrand.

A library and Internet search for "Nell's Rock" uncovered only a recreational area in Connecticut. It was time to go to South Africa.

Did he know anyone with a Cape Town connection? Yes. Kevin Sorrell, a sociologist he'd met in London at a conference, owned a place in an upscale Cape Town suburb called Fresnaye—Kevin had pronounced it "Fray-nay"—and had offered to rent part of the house to Robert, if Robert should ever want to vacation there.

Robert had kept in contact with Kevin over the years and had written to him about his dad's passing. Kevin was now living with his wife and son in London but still had the house in Fresnaye.

"Hi, Kevin. It's Robert Bennett in America," Robert said when he called Kevin. "How are you doing?"

"Oh. Hi, Robert. Good to hear from you. I'm doing very well. And you?" Kevin spoke with a Capetonian accent.

"I'm good. I'm at Dad's house…the one in upstate New York. Just clearing things out."

"That can be tough."

"Yeah. But you know, when I was going through my own things, in my childhood bedroom, I came across something that put me on a very interesting archaeological path. I really want to tell you about it, but…ah…I have to…Well, I have to be completely secretive about it at this stage. I'm sorry," he said.

"Well, Robert, that's very, very, mysterious. So something perhaps forgotten from your childhood now influences your future."

"I promise, as soon as I can tell *anyone* about it, I'll tell you first."

"Hmm. Now you've made me very curious. Secret archaeology."

"I'm calling because this project, as it turns out, is taking me to South Africa of all places, and I was wondering if you still have that place available there and if I might be able to rent for a while. It might be as long as a year."

"You're going to South Africa? Really? Well, no…I have a couple of tenants in the Fresnaye house now, but…uh…" he said, pondering the question. "Actually you can use the guesthouse. No one's living there now. In fact you can stay there for free."

"I don't mind paying rent, Kevin. Really. Not at all. You know, Dad left me a pretty big inheritance."

"Nah. You can stay there for free. It'll be good to have someone else there to kind of watch the place. You can be a welcome guest in the guesthouse."

"That's great, Kevin. Thanks so much. I'm thinking I may be going there very soon."

"You can move in tomorrow, as far as I'm concerned," Kevin said. "I'll call the tenants on the ground floor and tell them to expect you—and you can get the key from them."

"Thanks for your help. I appreciate it."

"Now you'll have me wondering what this archaeological project of yours actually could be. Hmm. Very interesting. Listen, you'll love the place. It's choice real estate. It's way up there on Lion's Head, and there's a pretty nice view from the guesthouse. If you have a pen handy, I'll give you the address."

After the call, Robert transferred the image files of his discoveries to a flash drive and put his hard drive into a safe-deposit box at a local bank.

The guesthouse really was choice. It was the first time Robert had been to Cape Town, and the city enthralled him. From the front windows of the guesthouse, looking down across Avenue Saint Bartholomew, he saw, between rooftops and tropical plantings, the blue water of the ocean, and from the front patio, the whole stretch of the sea was visible. He had rented a car at the airport, driven to the house, and gotten the key from Mr. Besch, one of the first-floor tenants. Now he was unpacking his things.

It was about three fifteen in the afternoon. Kevin had warned Robert to be careful walking about in Cape Town, or even driving in certain areas, at night, so he decided this would be a good time of day to take a drive to a grocery store and stock up. He rang the Besches' bell and asked Mr. Besch where he might do some shopping. The man suggested a place on Regent Road in nearby Sea Point. Robert locked his front security door, drove to the store, and brought back enough food to fill the refrigerator. He spent three hours setting up his computer, ate dinner, listened online to Beethoven's "Kreutzer Sonata," and got ready for bed. As he emptied his pockets, he pulled out the envelope that contained the silver-and-gold key case. He'd hurriedly put it into his pocket on his way out of the house in New York. Now, he wrapped it carefully in a towel and placed it on the closet shelf behind some folded shirts.

The next day Robert got up at 7:00 a.m., feeling well-rested. He threw open the big front windows to let in the warm, fragrant morning air. *What a beautiful city*, he thought.

The town of Melkbosstrand, whose name means "Milkwood Beach," was about thirty miles up the coast from Fresnaye. With as much precision as he could, he would first drive up to the spot he'd identified as the place where Kholoruuf's house lay buried, just to see what was there. If he didn't see Nell's Rock sitting there—and he fully expected not to—he'd chalk up the misstep to bad calculations and return to Cape Town to do some more investigating.

After breakfast he drove to Melkbosstrand. He had researched the route and had no trouble getting there. Just to get a sense of the place, he drove along Beach Road. The town impressed him as being a pretty, lively, seaside village.

But he knew exactly where he wanted to go. He turned onto one of the avenues and drove southeast then just a little way out of town. He pulled over at the place he'd calculated would be nearest to the site, near enough to the exact spot to be able to see whether a hill was there. He got out, placed a pair of binoculars to his eyes, and scanned the more or less open landscape.

As he'd expected, nothing jumped out as unusual. There were low hills, fairly far from the road, but nothing that stood out as an example of the mound builder's art, and he couldn't see how any of the hills might be called a "rock." He got back into the car and drove around the area. He saw more small and medium-size hills but nothing especially interesting.

Next step: more research, Robert thought. He'd compiled a list of archaeological and geological groups in the area, and he would now inquire at each about Nell's Rock.

He went first to the department of archaeology at the University of Cape Town, where he spoke with several faculty members. None of them, however, ever had heard of Nell's Rock. They took Robert's number and said they'd ask around. He didn't mention the symbol that supposedly was carved into it, but it was because of the carving that he felt archaeologists might be familiar with it. Then he checked with the geology department and got identical results.

Next, from the university, he phoned the Cape Town office of the Archaeological Society. He spoke to a council member of some standing in the archaeological community—Robert recognized the name—who also was unaware of the existence of any such rock and who also took Robert's number.

The next day Robert bought a used white '87 Toyota 4Runner and returned his rental car.

He decided that, no matter how his search went, he would not be returning to his university in August. He would repay his salary along with the health care and retirement contribution that the institution had paid on his behalf during the sabbatical. He called the Office of Faculty Affairs to inform them of his decision.

He spent the next three months following up on other leads but had no luck. He also went back up to the field in Melkbosstrand several times. He talked to the neighbors and received permission to enter the land to investigate—but nothing came of it.

Near the end of September, he decided to move his focus to another piece of terrain, a field a little to the south of the first that contained a number of hills that looked promising. He drove up to the field and parked. Standing on the road, Robert scanned the field. The landscape in this area was more rugged than at the previous site. The hills rose more abruptly from the surrounding terrain, looking much more like Robert's mental image of what Nell's Rock might look like. But nothing seemed particularly anomalous.

It was still early, so he decided to investigate an archaeological data center and reading room in Cape Town whose address he recently had discovered on the Internet. He drove down to Kloof Street and parked near the address. From there he walked half a block to the tiny storefront on whose window was neatly painted, ARCHAEOLOGY READING ROOM. He opened the glass door and went in. Inside were two tables with computers on them and several wooden chairs. Bookshelves filled with books lined three walls.

A pleasant-looking middle-aged woman seated at a desk at the far end of the room looked up.

"Hello," Robert said.

"Hello," the woman replied. "May I help you?" Her accent was American.

"I hope so." Robert walked over to the desk. "I'm trying to get information about something but haven't had much luck."

"What is it? I'll try to help."

"I'm looking for information on a geological feature in this area called 'Nell's Rock.' Have you ever heard of it, or can you suggest how I might be able to track it down?"

The woman raised an eyebrow when he mentioned the name of the rock. Robert thought for a moment that the name might be familiar to her.

"No," she said. "No, that's not something I've heard of at all. Do you know any more about it?"

"Not really, just that it's quite large."

"Do you have any idea—even a rough idea—where it's located?"

"I think it's in Melkbosstrand," Robert said, and immediately wished he hadn't. He wanted the details of his investigation to be as covert as possible.

The woman raised an eyebrow again and wrote "Melkbos" on a piece of paper. "I've never heard of such a thing," she said. "Please give me your name and number, and I'll ask around. I know some people who might know."

Robert gave her his name and number and she wrote it down.

"I'm sorry I couldn't give you any information," she said. "I hope you get your answer."

It was now past two o'clock, and Robert stopped in at a pizza place on Kloof Street for lunch. He finished eating at about ten minutes of three and decided it wasn't too late in the day to go up to Melkbosstrand again to check out the field that had become his new focus.

Traffic wasn't good, and it was early evening when he got back to the field he had surveyed earlier that day. He parked, got out, and scanned the field with his binoculars. *I'll have to find a way to check out each of those little hills*, he thought. *Am I going to have to investigate every big rock and hill along this whole coast one by one? And it may not even be here.*

"Wat sien jy?"

Robert took the binoculars from his eyes and turned to see a brown-haired boy, about nine or ten, in blue jeans and a red-and-white striped T-shirt. "What? I'm…I'm sorry. I don't understand."

"What do you see?" the boy asked, switching from Afrikaans to heavily accented English.

"I'm looking for big rocks or odd-looking hills. Do you know of any around here? Have you ever heard of Nell's Rock?"

"No. I never heard of that," the boy said.

Great. Another dead end, Robert thought. He'd planned to talk to the people here, but only if other means failed. *If the neighborhood kids don't know about it, I've got a problem.*

The boy looked at a beetle crawling on his own shoulder and swiped it off. "Nell's *Koppie*," he said, almost under his breath.

Robert felt a chill. "What?"

"Nell's Koppie," the boy said again. He pointed into the field. "It's over there. It's got a picture on it."

A surge of excitement coursed through Robert. He knew, from his archaeological studies, that the word *koppie* was Afrikaans for "hill"—and this *koppie* had a *picture* on it. He couldn't believe his good luck. The calculations had been right on and had brought him to within a half mile of the site. He'd begun to think his search would be a protracted one—perhaps lasting many years— yet it looked as if he'd achieved his goal in only three months. "Could you show it to me?" he asked.

"Sure. I can take you there."

"I'm Robert," he said, holding out his hand.

The boy shook his hand. "I'm Willem."

Willem took Robert down to the corner and walked with him up the road toward a house and driveway.

"Are you an American?" the boy asked.

"Yes. Is this your house?"

"No. This is Mr. de Bruin's house. That's him there." He gestured toward a rather disheveled-looking man dressed in tan trousers and an undershirt who was pushing a wheelbarrow filled with dirt across his backyard. The boy shouted to Mr. de Bruin, "He wants to see Nell's Koppie."

Mr. de Bruin frowned, paused, waved his hand as in disgust, and went back to work.

"It's on his land," Willem said, "but he doesn't mind us taking a look at it."

"He seemed a little upset."

"Ah, he's all right. He's just like that."

Robert followed Willem into the scrub. "Any snakes in here?" he asked the boy.

"You might see a *koperkapel* in the grass or a *boomslang* in a tree. Just stay on the path and watch where you step."

They arrived at a grass-and-bush-covered hill, the northeastern part of which appeared to be a large multifaceted rock or complex of rocks. Robert looked up at the *koppie*. It was big enough to have a large house inside it. Willem led Robert over to a flat, vertical surface on the rock and knelt, pointing to a place near the ground. "There's the picture," he said.

Robert bent down and looked. There he could make out a group of inscribed lines that delineated precisely the same symbol he'd discovered in the cave in the Catskills. He carefully examined the surface itself. Unlike the gray plastic in the New York cave, this material had the variegated color of a natural rock, but there was a translucency to it. He took out his penknife and sliced into a rough part of it, cutting off a sliver. "Strange, huh?" he said.

On their way off the property, Robert stopped and introduced himself to Mr. de Bruin, who was now sitting on his back porch.

"Hi," he said. "My name is Robert Bennett. I'm an archaeologist."

The man seemed not to want to be bothered but was polite enough. "Pieter de Bruin," he said.

"So this is all your property here?" Robert asked.

"*Ja*, out to the next road way over there."

"That's a very interesting *koppie* over there, Pieter."

"I don't call it interesting. I call it weird."

"Have any idea who drew that diagram in the rock?"

"No, I don't. It's been there as long as my family's owned it, and that's a long time."

Robert nodded and looked toward the hill. "Has there been any archaeological work done on it that you know about, since your family owned it?"

"No. And if there had been, I'd know about it."

"What would you think about some kind of an archaeological excavation being done there now?"

"I wouldn't be for that, Robert."

"I'd be willing to pay for permission."

Pieter sat back in his chair and smiled. "Well, that's another story," he said.

Robert ended up with a signed agreement with Pieter that gave him permission to excavate at the *koppie* for six months, starting from the first excavation, in exchange for thirty thousand rand, which converted to a little more than three thousand dollars.

As he drove back to Fresnaye, he thought about Nell's Koppie. How could it have remained intact for fourteen thousand years? It made sense to him actually. For thousands of years, the inner shell had been buried in an earthen structure of perhaps the same height as Monk's Mound in Illinois (but conceivably much smaller in length and width) that looked like a natural hill among many similar natural hills. In recent times perhaps, part of the shell had been uncovered, but since then, Nell's Koppie remained the property of a single family and was simply ignored.

How easily everything had come together for him! Incredibly, in just *three months* he had found what he had been looking for.

Thanks to the precision of Kholoruuf's map, Robert found the right field on the second try. But he was amazed he'd been correct in the first place about the Sphinx as being the origin of Kholoruuf's coordinates. He was also amazed he could identify the exact hill so easily.

I must be getting assistance from the cosmic powers, he mused.

Now Robert faced a dilemma: Section thirty-five of the South African National Heritage Resources Act required a permit to excavate the site, but getting a permit would make the site known to the South African government. If the government were to learn what was interred within Nell's Koppie, it might decide to take the property over (with compensation, of course, to Pieter). And if they realized the advantages to appropriating Atlanian high technology, officials might initiate a wholesale cover-up.

Robert's mission was to make sure that never would happen.

He could start to excavate without a permit, and if the government got wind of it, the consequences might not be severe. But Robert wanted to obey the country's laws. An application for permission might not need to be specific; after all, he wasn't sure there was a house inside the hill. How could he describe his "full motivation" on the application form? He needed to mull it over.

The next day he pulled his 4Runner out onto Avenue Saint Bartholomew and headed north to take another look at the site. He didn't notice the black Mazda pull out from the curb and begin to follow him.

Robert drove up to the Melkbosstrand field again, parked, and wearing high boots this time, hiked over to the *koppie.*

The Mazda pulled up to the side of the road some distance away.

Robert looked closely at the engraved diagram and took some photos of it and of the rest of the hill. *If it's OK with Pieter, I'll put a security fence around the hill,* he thought.

Using a laser distance measurer, he took key measurements and jotted them down in his notebook. After examining other accessible parts of the *koppie*, he drove back to Fresnaye.

Robert spent the next day at the guesthouse working on an application for permission to excavate. He also created a rough map of the site using the measurements he had taken as well as his photographs.

In the evening a storm moved over the Western Cape. Robert was in the kitchen when his doorbell rang. He went to the door, turned on the porch light, and looked out the door's window. No one was there. When he opened the door and looked out, he found a note taped to the door. Over the sound of the rain, he heard a car door slam. Then he heard a car pull away and drive north on the avenue. He brought in the note and read it. It had been typed on a word processor.

Dr. Bennett,

This evening the site you discovered, Nell's Koppie, and the land around it, has been expropriated. Pieter de Bruin will be compensated. You have led these people to something they have been seeking for years. They intend to contact you soon to find out how much you know. It is imperative that you go to them first, without delay—but it could be dangerous for you to approach them while they are at the koppie *before you've been invited.*

They are the Grayling Conservancy. Tell them that someone at SAHRA has told you this.

Regardless of what they tell you, they are set on seeing to it that the public will never learn about any part of this discovery. That is how zealously they will guard any technology they find. And they will sell whatever they find to the highest bidder.

I know you, and I know you believe this site's cultural treasures must be made known to the world. If you can convince these people that you know what is within the koppie, *they will want you to work with them, and you can influence what happens only if you work with them. If you have knowledge about what is inside the* koppie, *tell them some of what you know but not everything. Be warned: If it becomes clear to them that you know more than what you've told them, your home and possessions will not be safe.*

These people are not to be trusted—they can be dangerous. Be careful.

Robert knew that SAHRA was the South African Heritage Resources Agency. But "I know you"? *Who could have written this note?* Robert wondered. *Who do I know who could have written this?*

Although it was already eleven thirty at night, Robert put on a raincoat, got in his 4Runner, and drove in the rain up to Melkbosstrand. He went to a spot where he could watch the hill without being seen. Sure enough, the area around Nell's Koppie was lit up. Several white SUVs and a black van were parked in the field next to the *koppie*, and people in rainwear were installing a security fence.

How could I have led them here? he wondered. *How did they catch on to what I was up to?* He thought about his visit to the archaeology reading room, where he'd communicated a little more information than he'd intended. *They've been seeking this for a long time. What better way to track archaeological activities in the area than to operate a data center within a reading room?*

The writer of the note was right. The site had been taken over. He turned around and went back to Fresnaye.

That night Robert did an Internet search and found the location of the Grayling Conservancy. It was on Rheede Street in Cape Town. He thought about what an intruder might find in any of his houses. He had brought all his notes relating to the site in the Catskills with him to South Africa. He opened his desk drawer and took out the stack of notes. Looking through them he realized none of them could lead anyone to the site. To throw any intruder off, he took a sheet out and wrote in pencil a set of numbers on it, simulating the notes someone might make if he were adding up costs. He wrote "*lira*" after a couple of the numbers, and "*kurus*" after another. He smiled. *Maybe they'll think that I found the site in Turkey,* he mused.

To get rid of references to the car, with its high technology, he copied, by hand, the two pages of notes where the car was mentioned, leaving out any mention of it. He folded the original two pages and put them in his pocket to throw away somewhere. Next he copied the map of the first cave but left out the car and stuck the original in his pocket. He also removed all references to the note and map that Kholoruuf had left in the Hall of Shields. Then he put the stack of notes back into the drawer. He got a slice of bread, scattered a few tiny bread crumbs on the top sheet, and very carefully closed the drawer.

He would keep his flash drive, with the image files on it, in his pocket.

Satisfied that there was now nothing in any of his residences to reveal the location of the site in the Catskills, and no mention of the car technology, not even in his computers, he went to bed.

Early the next morning, Robert drove to the offices of the Grayling Conservancy. As it turned out, they were about a block from the archaeological reading room on Kloof Street. He parked and walked into the building. He found himself in a foyer, facing a door, with a door to the left and one to the right. The door to the right was marked, GRAYLING, so he opened it and walked in.

It was like walking into someone's living room, except a receptionist's desk stood along part of the far wall, to the right of a wide, closed door. Robert noticed the large paintings, landscapes mostly, hanging on the royal-yellow walls. There was an expensive-looking sofa against the wall to his left, and several rather elegant wooden chairs here and there around the room. The ambiance was clearly meant to be comfortable and welcoming, yet he felt he would not be welcome here.

An attractive, slender, black woman in a deep-blue dress sat behind the desk.

"Hello," Robert said.

The woman turned from her computer screen and looked at him.

When he realized there would be no response, he spoke again. "I believe people here might want to talk to me." he said. "My name is Robert Bennett."

"Professor Orten is just on his way out of the building, but perhaps he can see you." The woman had an American accent. She threw the switch on her intercom and spoke into it. "Robert Bennett is here."

"I'll be right out," said a male voice on the other end.

Professor Orten. The name rang a bell for Robert. George Orten was a well-known archaeologist in the United States. In fact Robert had spoken to him briefly at a conference. *Could this be the same man?* he wondered.

After a few moments, the wide door opened.

Robert recognized George Orten immediately. He was a tall, balding man with a round face. At the conference, Orten had been wearing a suit, but now he was dressed in gray trousers and a wrinkled blue-denim shirt open at the collar.

"Hello, Dr. Bennett!" Orten said with a smile that seemed overly expansive and probably insincere. "We've met, haven't we?"

"Dr. Orten. Yes, in Vancouver."

"Yes, I remember that. Please come in."

They went into Orten's office. It had the same expensive ambiance as the reception area, but there were two sofas in the room and more chairs than in the reception area. Orten closed the door and sat behind his desk. "Please take a seat, doctor," he said.

Robert sat in the armchair that faced the desk.

"How are you doing?" Orten asked, still coming across as being a little too friendly.

"Fine, Professor. I heard you might want to talk to me about a certain discovery I made."

"Where did you hear *that*?" Orten asked, still smiling and seemingly surprised.

"I've got friends at SAHRA."

Orten's smile broadened. "And who at SAHRA told you *that*?" he asked.

"I'd rather not say."

Orten stopped smiling, looked down, and shuffled some papers on his desk. "Oh. All right. I see." He looked up at Robert. "Ah, well it's true," he said. His tone was still friendly. "I wanted to ask you some questions—things I'm curious about…if you don't mind answering them."

"I don't mind," Robert said, "and I was hoping you could answer some questions too. For instance why you took over my site."

Orten smiled again. "What I'm most curious about…What is your interest in Nell's Koppie?"

Robert sat back in the chair. "I read a letter written by John Herschel to his friend Charles Babbage that described it. He called it 'Nell's Rock.'"

"I've seen that entry in that journal. But how did you know it was at Melkbosstrand?"

"Someone I spoke to said they thought they knew the rock and it might be there," said Robert. "Actually I'm not sure who it was. Do you have anything to do with the archaeology reading room around the corner?"

Orten rested his elbows on the desk and leaned forward. "Tell me, Dr. Bennett, why are you so *interested* in that hill? Or…let me put it this way: Do you have any idea what is to be found at Nell's Koppie that would interest us archaeologists?"

Remembering what the mysterious note had advised, Robert told him, "I believe there's a house buried there, a whole house—from a culture that was flourishing at the end of the Pleistocene epoch."

Orten looked at Robert and nodded slowly several times. "And what makes you think *that*?"

"I have my secrets, Professor."

"Ah! OK." Orten stood up. "I guess we all have secrets. Look. You must be angry at us for taking over like we did. I'm sorry, but it's just the way it had to be done—so we did it." His eyebrows raised, he looked at Robert. "It's legal.

The conservancy even *owns* the land now. Why don't you come up there tomorrow, and I'll let you see what we've discovered so far. I run the show up there, so you won't have any problem getting in. Come up tomorrow night, after dark, because we'll be putting up security fences tomorrow during the day. But remember it's important that we don't *blab* about this to people—you know, you've been guarded about it yourself. But since you know about the site already, you might as well take a look."

"I'd like to see it," Robert said, getting up.

Orten guided Robert to the door and opened it. Then they shook hands. "Good," Orten said. "See you then."

Robert left the building thinking about how he hadn't been able to ask the professor many questions, but he figured there would be time for that later. He had expected to be angry at Orten and his group for what they had done, but he wasn't. What he felt instead was a sense of acceptance at what seemed a fait accompli, a little fear, and an eager anticipation that hadn't dissipated.

CHAPTER 4
YOU'RE ONE OF US

The next day Robert waited until dusk then drove to the site. When he arrived he drove around until he found a spot where he could access the field from the road. As he pulled into the field, a man with a rifle slung over his shoulder stepped in front of his vehicle and signaled for him to stop.

The man walked up to Robert's window. "This is private property," he said.

"Professor Orten invited me. My name is Dr. Robert Bennett."

"OK. Hold on." The man walked a short distance away from the 4Runner, spoke into a two-way radio for a few seconds, then waved Robert in.

As Robert drove up to the *koppie*, he found a temporary chain link fence had been put up around it. Noticing that the rock area of the hill was lit up, he parked near the *koppie* alongside some other vehicles. Orten's crew had dug a trench below the two-ring symbol and had broken through the doorway, the entrance to the hill's interior. Two portable generators were running, their cables stretching into the hill. A man carrying a sidearm in a holster stood beside the entrance, talking on his radio and watching Robert.

Orten came out of the hill and stood by the doorway. "Hi, Dr. Bennett," he called out, smiling. He gestured toward the opening. "Come on in and take a look."

Robert was excited to see what was inside the hill but didn't feel safe. He got out of the 4Runner and walked through the open gate and up to Orten. They shook hands then walked together into Nell's Koppie.

And there it was. The house of the man who had written the note Robert had found in the Room of Shields, the note that had spurred his trip to South Africa, the house of the man who had signed his name as "Kholoruuf, chief logician of our beloved Truth Engine." Unlike the building in the Catskills, which had been solidly embedded, like a fossil, within its plastic matrix, Kholoruuf's house was situated inside a hollow plastic shell. The doorway in the side of Nell's Koppie led directly into the expansive interior of the shell. Robert could make out the imposing facade of the house about forty-five feet away.

The House of Kholoruuf inside the underground shell after Orten had set up lighting

As Robert walked toward the house with Orten, he wondered how much Orten and his group knew. Did they know Kholoruuf's name? Had they come across the term Robert had translated as "Truth Engine," and if they had, were they as much in the dark about what the term referred to as Robert was?

Orten's crew had set up lighting between the hill's entrance and the house. The house was larger than Robert had expected it to be. Its exterior walls were made of gray wooden boards attached vertically to the house's frame. A porch with a railing ran across the entire front, and there was a closed front door that appeared to be made of metal. Two rows of windows were situated below a large windowless expanse. At the peak of the roof, barely visible in the dim light, about a foot below the plastic shell's ceiling, was the sculpture of a bird sitting on a sphere. Supporting structures connected the roof to the plastic enclosure, and metal rods supported the corners of the house.

About ten people were on the porch by the door. The inside of the house, or at least what Robert could see through the windows, appeared dark. He guessed the crew hadn't yet been able to open the house's door.

To the left and right of the building, near the enclosure walls, he saw the straight trunks of several ancient palm trees. "There's a sign of transatlantic commerce," Robert said to Orten as they approached the stairs that led up to the porch.

"What's that?" asked Orten.

"Royal palms. A Caribbean species."

"Interesting. I hadn't noticed that."

Robert had commented on the palms in order to set a friendly tone with Orten, but now he wished he'd said nothing. He wanted to be welcomed into this group, but he already may have made its leader feel foolish.

As they reached the porch stairs, Robert looked up at the people near the house's door. They were all looking at him as well. The men in the group were mostly in their twenties, though two seemed older. They were dressed in slacks and button-down shirts and polo shirts. Two women were with them. Robert recognized one of them as the receptionist at the archaeology reading room. The other was a raven-haired, blue-eyed woman in her early thirties whom Robert instantly thought might be the most beautiful woman he'd ever seen. One of the men carried a gun on his belt, but all the others, except Orten, carried only a flashlight in a holster.

"Robert, I'd like to introduce you to our team," Orton said. "Dr. Robert Bennett, this is Scott, John, Eddy, Will…ah, Jimmy, Harry, Jonathan, and Ben." He looked at the reading-room receptionist. "You've met Karen."

Robert nodded to each member of the crew as they were introduced. He tried remembering the names—using a mnemonic technique he'd learned—and thought he'd succeeded.

"And this is Jennifer, my right-hand gal," Orten said, gesturing toward the stunning blue-eyed woman.

Robert nodded and said, "Hi."

Jennifer gave him a rather icy stare and nodded slowly.

"We're trying to figure out the best way to get into this place," Orten said, as he and Robert climbed the porch stairs. He noticed Robert looking down at the steps. "The wood's been treated somehow to prevent degradation. Believe me, it's stronger than it was when the building was occupied."

Orten and Robert joined the group on the porch.

"Let me try it," Robert said, walking up to the door. He saw that the latch was a near duplicate of the one on the ebony door he'd entered from the cave in New York. He remembered the words of the mysterious note—"Tell them some of what you know"—and took from his pocket the key from the box under the shield at the Catskills site. *This probably won't work*, he thought, *but if it does, I'll wow this bunch.* He inserted the key in the lock and turned it. He felt it engage and heard a click. Then he pulled the latch, and the door opened easily.

He looked at the group and saw astonishment on the faces of the team members.

Orten laughed. "This man has secrets!" he said. "How much do you know, Dr. Bennett?"

"A few things," said Robert.

Orten smiled and looked at Robert as if sizing him up anew. "Will you tell us where you got that key, Dr. Bennett?"

"Not quite yet, Professor."

Reconstruction: The House of the Chief Logician of the Truth Engine, as it would have appeared when Kholoruuf lived there fourteen thousand years ago

Orten turned to his crew. "Let's go in," he said. "Bring one of those lamps up here."

One of the men handed Orten a flashlight while another went down the steps to retrieve one of the spotlights. Orten looked at Robert, then to the man he'd introduced as Jimmy. "Give Dr. Bennett a flashlight," he said.

As Orten entered the house, Jimmy handed Robert the flashlight.

Because he was nearest the door, Robert stepped into the house behind Orten. The others filed in behind him. Robert stopped and shined his light around. He and Orten were in a short hallway with a railing at the end and a space beyond. To the right he saw a shallow alcove that contained a dusty but clearly polychromed life-size statue of a man sitting straight-backed on a decorated cushion, his legs folded beneath him. The man had long, straight, yellow hair and a ruddy face. His patterned robes were of an overall greenish hue. *Could this be a statue of Kholoruuf himself?* Robert wondered.

In front of the seated man, reminding Robert of the tableau in the room at the Catskills site that he had entered from the cave, were two small tables. On one was a game set, and on the other was a thick square tablet inscribed with a circle divided into twelve sections. Robert took it to be an astrological chart, like the one in the New York site.

To Robert's left was another alcove. This one contained an exact duplicate of the statue in the alcove opposite to it—that is, of the polychrome Kholoruuf—except that it was colored a uniform gray.

He walked a little way down the hallway and saw a second pair of alcoves. The one on the right contained a group of colorful flags. In the other alcove, he saw a round jar on top of a tripod, behind which were six gray statues of robed men and women seated behind a large curved desk.

Walking to the end of this short hallway, he saw that Orten had stepped out onto a balcony-like landing. Robert stepped onto it beside him.

"Hold up." Orten told his crew.

Robert looked around and saw that Jennifer was just behind him. He directed his flashlight to his right and saw a closed gate, behind which was a staircase that led to a lower floor. In front of him, his flashlight dimly illuminated a large room below the balcony.

Reconstruction. The view of the stairs leading to the second-floor hallway, from the entrance landing

Reconstruction. The stairs that led to the second floor

Prominently, in the center of this lower space, was a room-size wooden structure in the form of a vertical cylinder.

Reconstruction: the Core Room, as it looked in the distant past

To Robert's left, as he stood on the balcony, he noticed a stairway that led to a higher floor. He took two steps up and shined his light up the stairs, illuminating a pair of strange-looking, nearly identical animal figures on wooden platforms on either side at the top of the stairs. The sheep-size creatures' bodies and oddly splayed front legs were covered with brown hair. Each animal had a thick neck and a gray, pear-shaped head topped by a crown of fluffy yellow hair. The beasts looked nothing like any species with which Robert was familiar.

Orten was quietly surveying the scene. "A historical moment," he said to Robert.

"Yes, it is," Robert answered. *But,* he thought, *will it only be recorded in a* hidden *history?*

"Let's get some lighting in here," Orten said to his crew as he inspected the wood of the ascending stairs.

The crew brought lamps into the house and placed one in the hallway and another on the balcony. Almost the entire lower floor below the balcony could now be seen clearly. The members of the group who weren't setting up the lighting were strolling from one part of the hallway to the other, looking into the alcoves and taking photos with their cell phones. Robert remained on the balcony. As he peered down at the lower floor, he now saw a big, empty bookshelf to the left. The fact that it was empty disappointed him greatly. To the right of the bookshelf stood a large, round table. To the far right, at the back of the building, he saw what looked like a kitchen area. Spherical pots hung on a rack above what appeared to be a stove with a number of burners on top. To the right of the stove was a long sink.

Two men hauled another lamp and cables up the stairs to the upper story. Robert followed Orten, Jennifer, and a couple of the others up the staircase. At the top of the stairs, he found himself looking down a hallway. Then he looked closely at one of the two otherworldly animal models that stood to left and right at the top of the stairs. The direction of the animal's hairs, the variation in the hairs' length and color, and the

Reconstruction. The upstairs hallway

wrinkles on the areas of bare skin all looked incredibly realistic.

Partway down the hall on the right was a door with an odd little cluster of three sculpted shapes above it; each shape consisted of an organic-looking cone topped by a small sphere. Beyond this door was a gated opening. At the end of the hall, on the left, was an open door.

One of the men tried to open the first door on the right but was unsuccessful. Robert followed some of the others through the open door at the end of the hallway into a room that he immediately felt must have been Kholoruuf's study. Shining his flashlight around, he saw a desk, two wooden chairs, a piano-like instrument, and cabinets. The room was in some disarray, as were the other parts of the house. Robert knew this part of the world wasn't seismically active, but he had to assume the house had suffered some earthquake damage over the many millennia.

Reconstruction. The glass doors in Kholoruuf's study

Reconstruction. The logician's desk

Reconstruction. The archaeopteryx display and atlas in the study

Reconstruction. The piano-like instrument and the door to the bedroom

Reconstruction. The bookcase, color generator, and game set

Reconstruction. The elaphrosaurus painting and the sculpture

Books and paintings filled the room. Robert was excited to see two bookcases that, unlike the empty ones on the lower floor, contained scores of books. There was a cabinet surmounted by a dusty display featuring a life-size model archaeopteryx surrounded by ginkgo leaves. The wings of the prehistoric bird were spread, like the one in the Room of the Truth Examiner in the Catskills. Beside this display was an open book on a cabinet. Robert gently brushed the dust off the book and saw it was an atlas, but at first glance he couldn't identify what area the map on the open page depicted. On the wall, above the atlas, was a framed map showing what he thought might be the same area.

Then he noticed a dusty painting on the wall to his right. He looked more closely and was able to discern the painting's subject matter. Robert was startled. It was nothing he could have expected: the painting showed a very birdlike, feathered dinosaur walking past two small beings huddled behind a tree.

What he found most strange was that the two beings looked like aliens from space as they had been pictured in modern representations. As he walked around the room, he found hanging to either side of a closed door two more paintings picturing other dinosaurs with these alien-like beings.

In the middle of the back wall, on a half-round table, sat a game set very similar to the one he'd found in the Catskills.

Elaphrosaurus

Allosaurus

Stegosaurus

A crew member brought in a lamp and set it on a stand in the middle of the room. The light revealed an incredible array of archaeological treasures.

Orten walked over to Robert. "You're like me, aren't you, Doctor? You can't *wait* to explore this house, can you? To discover the utterly *amazing* things it most certainly contains? If you join us, I'll let you investigate what you want to investigate, and when you want to investigate it. What do you say?"

Robert didn't have to think about it. "I accept your invitation, Professor Orten. Absolutely."

This place definitely had captured Robert's sense of wonder, and he wanted to see more. But more important, he recalled the words from the note: "You can influence what happens only if you work with them."

"Good. Good." Orten said. "But you know, we might be dealing with technologies here that in some ways surpass our own. You must appreciate these are delicate matters that may require us to keep this under wraps for a while. Do you agree to that?"

"Yes, I agree," Robert said. He was perfectly fine with participating in the cover-up—*for a while.*

"And do you agree to report to us at our meetings any discoveries you might make while you're a member of the team?"

Robert nodded.

"Welcome to our group then," Orten said, patting Robert on the shoulder. "I'll get you a key to the gate. Now, as far as compensation goes, shall we say you're a volunteer?"

"Of course."

Orten shifted his gaze and looked past Robert. Robert looked over his own left shoulder and saw Jennifer, who clearly had been listening in on the conversation. She looked at Robert then turned and walked away. Her cold stare, and the abrupt manner in which she turned away, gave him the impression that she wasn't happy about his joining the group.

One of the men was examining the spine of a book in a large bookcase. "It's the same writing," he told Orten.

"With all those books," Orten said, "maybe we can begin to translate it." He turned and said to the group, "Let's stick together as we look around."

Robert walked over and looked at the same book. The Atlanian characters on the spine read, *Keesat Merat Atlanosh*. "*Keesat Merat Atlanosh*," he said under his breath. *History of Atlantean Kings*, he thought.

For the rest of the evening, the team explored the remaining parts of the house as a group. Robert was eager to get a sense of the place, so he stayed with the others—though he was looking forward to taking a closer look at the books in Kholoruuf's study.

A couple of the doors were found to be unlocked and easy to open. The team, with flashlights lit, went through the door that was flanked by the dinosaur/alien paintings and discovered a bedroom. Next to the bed, on a desk, was a machine with a flat screen and an odd-looking keyboard. "That's got to be a computer," Orten said to no one in particular.

Beyond the bedroom was a room filled with astrological wheels and what seemed to be other astrological implements made of wood, metal, and ceramics. So *Kholoruuf was a collector of astrology equipment*, Robert thought.

In the next room was a discovery that amazed everyone. At the far end of this high-ceilinged space sat a large vehicle. Its shape reminded Robert of an old-style bathtub, not streamlined. It was supported underneath by wheelless appendages—similar to the landing gear of an airship—that seemed to have been designed for vertical takeoffs and landings, although the craft had neither wings nor rotor blades.

"Let's make this a priority," Orten told the crew. "I want to know all about its engine."

The flight mechanism seemed to be in a boxy structure mounted above the front part of the machine. Behind this structure was a kind of fin or rudder that looked as if it could be swiveled for control purposes. The entrance portal, on the side of the vehicle toward the back, was open, and the team members took turns exploring the interior. An empty compartment in the rear seemed to be a cargo hold. In the front, at a higher level, were seats and a control panel.

On his way out of this room, Robert shined his flashlight around. He noticed a narrow ascending staircase tucked into a space that was the back part of the gated opening in the entrance hallway.

Robert pointed to the staircase. "I wonder what's up there?" he asked the crew.

They went up the stairs in small groups. Robert went up with Orten and Karen. At the top of the staircase, they came

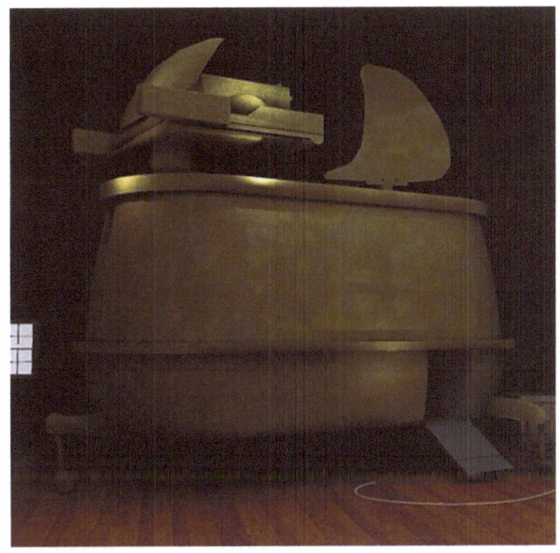

Reconstruction. The airship

to a round opening in the roof. Above the opening was a gazebo-like structure with cushions on a curved bench that encircled the opening.

After descending the stairs, everyone returned to the study. Orten tried to open the east door but couldn't. He turned to Robert. "Do you think your key might work on this door?" he asked.

Robert looked closely at the door's keyhole and saw it was simply a round hole. There was no way that the key's three-part shank and teeth would fit into it. "No," he said. "I'm sure it wouldn't."

In the hallway, Orten tried but failed to open the door with the odd sculpture above it.

At the landing downstairs, the crew stopped to look at the open lock on the gate at the top of the descending stairway. It was an odd sort of combination lock with a number of adjustable wire pins. Orten swung the gate open, and the group went down to the lower floor.

At the foot of the stairs stood a large rectangular table. The main room consisted primarily of open space and took up the entire eastern half of the floor. Near the southeast corner of the room was a mountain gorilla, apparently the product of a taxidermist's art, sitting on a thick, gnarled, moss-draped branch. Just east of this mounted animal, against the wall, was a many-legged table. On the table was a glass case filled with small metal objects that perhaps had served as coins in the distant past.

Toward the back, occupying the northwest part of this floor, was the kitchen, with its ceramic and metal cooking utensils along with a stove and refrigerator. To the south of the kitchen the crew saw a room containing a large circular table with a complex sculptural centerpiece. Behind the table, a painting on the wall depicted a group of people in a room, all apparently participating in some sort of event. And here, against the south wall, were the empty bookshelves Robert had seen from the balcony.

The room-size vertical wooden cylinder, another structure that Robert had seen from the balcony, dominated the space. This floor-to-ceiling

Reconstruction: the CEANA Gate, as it once looked

cylinder apparently constituted the curved external wall of a central room. A door led into this cylinder, but it was locked.

Next to the north side of this central room was a three-foot-wide circular opening in the floor with stairs that led to a lower level. At the bottom of the stairs was another door that could not be opened.

Robert wanted to explore all of this on his own, but he was most eager to translate some of the texts in the study.

As the group emerged into the night air, Robert decided this was as good a time as any to try to get more information from Orten. "Can you tell me how it is that you were so curious—or knowledgeable—about Nell's Koppie? Or is that one of *your* secrets?"

Orten raised his eyebrows. "About five years ago, some surveyors, on a hillside in Finland, discovered a tiny house that had been encased like this one. In the house were ancient versions of modern appliances—there were electric lamps, a stove, a refrigerator, and a furnace. The house apparently got its power from an external electrical source, long since gone. The site was dated to an astounding fourteen thousand years BP. In a garage attached to the house, they found an automobile with an incredibly simple-looking engine. It was clear that this car had been powered by a tiny but extremely powerful battery—or some kind of tiny source of electrical power, maybe even something nuclear—but only the socket for this power source was intact; the source itself was missing. Imagine. A little round thing, the size of a walnut could power a car. This power source, if it can be found and reverse engineered, could revolutionize our world's power-source technology."

So Orten is *focused on the technology*, Robert thought. He remembered how the note on his door had warned that the group planned to cover everything up because "that is how zealously they will guard any technology they find." Robert was as resolved as ever to find a way to prevent such a cover-up. He reflected on Orten's words—*A little round thing the size of a walnut.* That was exactly how he himself might have described the little Saturn-shaped object he'd found in the car in the Catskills. He'd suspected it was a power source, and what Orten said seemed to confirm that suspicion. Now Robert was fairly sure that he had knowledge of something these people desperately wanted. He was a little surprised that Orten was so forthcoming about the battery but figured Orten wanted him to know why there was such a need for secrecy. And after all, Orten may have entertained the thought that Robert might be corruptible.

"Whoever buried this house here," Orten continued, "must have done the planning for it in Finland. We found diagrams there showing this house as being encased and subsequently buried in a mound, along with a lot of apparently descriptive text we still can't read. There was also a map of the southwest coast of Africa, showing lines that we supposed represented paths along which equipment and materials were to be brought for the construction of this mound. These lines converged, but not in any precise way, on the southwest coast of South Africa. On the map at that point was a symbol consisting of two rings with a circle above and a diamond below."

"And then," Orten continued, "the Grayling Project, now the Grayling Conservancy, was born. This group, our group, in league with the US government—and the South African government of course—has been looking for this site for the past five years. Now we've found it…thanks to you. And I mean that. I consider you to have discovered this site."

Robert sensed that Orten would eradicate any record of his role in this discovery if it suited his purpose. But for now he would play along.

Robert nodded. "You certainly moved in quickly. How did you get permission from Heritage Western Cape so fast?"

"Well," Orten said, "going to HWC isn't the only way to get permission. By the way, now that I've told you some of what we know, how about telling us more about what you know, Doctor? You seem to know a great deal."

"As it turns out," Robert said, "I may have a lot to add to your work here. You said you can't read the writing these people used. Well, I can." Robert knew Orten and his people eventually would be able to translate the writing on their own, so he figured they might as well view him as being helpful. As a major concession, he would give them his Atl-English dictionary.

"Really!" Orton said.

"Do you believe in Atlantis?" Robert asked.

"No, I never have, Doctor."

"Well, these people called their land 'Atlan,' and the language is called 'Atl.' This is the house of a man named Kholoruuf, who was the director of a culturally important institution called the Truth Engine."

"Amazing," Orten said. "Anything else?"

"Not for now."

"Look," said Orten, "I've scheduled a meeting at my office for nine tomorrow morning. Will you come and fill us in…you know, about the language and the Atlantis connection, et cetera? Could you bring us your lexicon?"

"Sure. I'll be there."

"So, obviously, you've discovered a cache of artifacts somewhere. New Mexico? I know you've done work there. Turkey?"

"I can't give you that information yet," said Robert.

"But why would you not be more forthcoming on this, Robert?" It was the first time Orten had used his first name.

"I just feel it's necessary to keep things under wraps for a while, Professor."

Orten smiled. "For the same reasons *we* want to keep things under wraps perhaps?"

Robert shrugged. He wasn't at all comfortable talking with Orten or being in this place with Orten's crew, and even sensed some danger. But he knew it was important that he take part in all this, and Orten couldn't know for sure that Robert wouldn't go along with a permanent cover-up. And Robert knew he himself had a mysterious friend somewhere nearby who was knowledgeable about Orten's operation.

The next morning Robert showed up at Orten's office at the Grayling Conservancy at nine o'clock, carrying a folder that contained three hard copies, as well as a flash drive, of the Atl-English lexicon he had compiled before he had come to South Africa.

Most of the people who had been at the site the night before were there, and Robert was directed to the single empty chair. He sat down, placing the folder on his lap. Orten was seated behind the desk. Jennifer, dressed in a black T-shirt and blue jeans, sat in a corner where she could face the group.

Orten spoke. "It seems Dr. Bennett—he's joined our team now—has considerable knowledge about the civilization we're dealing with at the site." He smiled. "He won't tell us how he knows any of this. But he doesn't have to, does he?" Orten turned to Robert. "But anyway, what *can* you tell us, Doctor?"

Robert recognized that Orten's introduction reinforced his identity as an outsider. "The house buried inside Nell's Koppie," he began, speaking to the group, "was the home of a venerated man from the land of Atlan whose name was Kholoruuf. When he realized his civilization was doomed, he had his house enclosed in a casing, and then had an earthen mound built up around it to resemble a natural hill. This all happened approximately fourteen thousand years ago. Burying buildings in this way—a variation of mound building—probably wasn't something that originated with Kholoruuf; the procedure was called 'perochakh,' which means 'hilling.' Kholoruuf, it seems, was the director of a very important cultural institution called the Truth Engine. It's not clear to me yet exactly how this institution functioned, but I hope our site here will contain the answer to this important question. In addition I can supply a lexicon for the language of Atlan—the language was called 'Atl.'"

As Robert had expected, no one seemed surprised by what he'd said. Orten must have filled everyone in before he got there. He took two large manuscripts out of his folder—the two copies of the lexicon—and gave them to Orten. Then he handed him the flash drive.

"Thanks," Orten said, thumbing through one of the manuscripts. "Very interesting. We'll make copies of these."

The man Orten had introduced the night before as Eddy said, "So you're saying these discoveries belong to the Atlantean culture? You're saying Plato's story was true?"

"It looks that way," Robert told him.

"Anything else you want to tell us?" Orten asked.

"No. I'll stop there for now."

Jennifer glared at Robert. "So, Robert, we're supposed to sit here while you parcel out what you know bit by bit? We don't even know *how* you know these things."

Robert had expected not to be liked but nevertheless was taken aback by Jennifer's brusque tone.

Before he could respond, Orten stepped in. "Frankly I understand Jennifer's impatience, but I wouldn't express it the way she has. You're a volunteer here, Dr. Bennett. You don't have to tell us anything you don't want to. We want to know, but we're not going to waterboard anyone here. I thank you for what you *are* deigning to tell us."

One of the men laughed. Robert sensed Jennifer's comment mirrored the sentiments of many of the others in the group. As he looked around the room, he sensed hostility. *These are dangerous people*, he thought. *But they're just archaeologists, right?*

The rest of the meeting consisted of a brainstorming session regarding how to proceed at the site.

After the meeting the group, now in possession of the Atl dictionaries, decided to meet at the site. "Bring a lunch," Orten told the team.

As Robert left the building, he found himself walking next to Eddy.

"A beautiful witch, isn't she?" Eddy said. "She's like that to everyone. We call her the 'dragon lady.' Beguiling but as cold as ice. You'll find out. Just try to stay out of her way." He held out his hand, "Dr. Ed Peltier—Eddy to everyone here."

Robert shook his hand. "Thanks for the warning." Although he thought Eddy seemed nice enough, he still didn't trust him. At least he felt he knew where he stood with Jennifer.

CHAPTER 5
AN ADVENTURE FOR THE MIND

Robert drove up the coast to Melkbosstrand, stopping off at a big box store in Milnerton to buy a lunch bag cooler and an ice pack that he'd use the next day. It was almost eleven, so he bought a sandwich to eat on the way to the site.

As Robert drove into the field, he noticed a white camper parked near the hill with the other vehicles. Three workers were on top of the hill; Robert guessed they were installing vents. He parked, got out, grabbed his folding table, and walked up to the group beyond the fence. Orten had been speaking to the team members, and the meeting was just breaking up. Robert heard him say, "Our day ends at eight. Let's get to work."

Orten glanced at Robert but didn't greet him. Robert, carrying his table, followed the others into the hill and got his first good look at the exterior of the house; the team had cleared soil off of the top of the *koppie*, allowing the sun to shine, in a diffused way, through the plastic shell into the enclosure. He went up to Kholoruuf's study, where John and Will were setting up a table and two chairs in the center of the room. Robert set up his table near the large book cabinet, went back out, got a folding chair and his laptop out of the 4Runner, and carried them up to the study. He placed the laptop on the table and set up the chair while John and Will took pictures of the cabinet and its books in their original positions.

While John and Will documented the other artifacts in the room, Robert inspected the books. He selected one at random, gently took it out of the cabinet, and placed it on the table. He sat down and opened the book to its first page. This book was in better condition than those he'd examined in New York. He closed the book and carefully returned it to the cabinet.

The next step was to translate the titles of the books in the cabinet. He could do this without disturbing the books because the titles were printed on their spines. In New York he had worked hard to compile his Atl-English lexicon with its several thousand words—enough of a vocabulary, he felt, to be able to get an idea of the kinds of books Kholoruuf kept in his study.

Before the end of the day, sometimes using informed guesses, he managed to translate most of the titles. He found that the cabinet held books on logic, mathematics, history, philosophy, and the sciences. The books had titles such as *Physics Handbook, Beginning Physics, A Student's History of the Earth, Geography of the*

Central Islands, and *An Introductory History of the People of the Woods*. Other titles included *Truth-Engine Logic, Logic Basics, Mathematics for Dialecticians*, and *Introduction to the Early History of Atlan*. As he translated the titles, it became clearer to him that, for the most part, the volumes were basic treatises on their subject matter. Here was a collection of books quite capable of delivering a paideian education—an education designed to produce an enlightened citizen, a citizen with a broad grasp of cultural knowledge. But he did notice there were gaps in the range of subject matter; for instance, aside from a couple history books, there was nothing here about social or political matters, and, except for a book that taught musical performance skills, he found nothing pertaining to the arts.

Working into the evening, Robert compiled a catalog of the books by title, size, position, and cover color. He gave numbers to the titles he was unable to translate.

Around eight o'clock several crew members walked into the study from the bedroom and went into the hall. John looked at his watch. "Time to go," he said, and he and Will started to wrap up their work.

Robert picked up his notebook and laptop and left the study. As he entered the hallway, he saw that someone had found a way to open the door with the sculpture above it. He went up to the door, peered in, and saw Orten and several crew members inside. The most prominent pieces of furniture in the room were three large cube-shaped cabinets with legs. There was a chair in front of each. Robert walked in and examined one of the cabinets. It was a well-made, decorative piece of wooden furniture, probably quite attractive when new. An open pair of cabinet doors flanked a pair of large lenses installed about halfway up the front of the cabinet.

"A stereopticon?" one of the men asked, not speaking to anyone in particular. He placed his face up to the lenses and looked through them. "Nothing," he said.

On the way out of the *koppie*, Robert ran into Professor Orten.

"A productive day?" Orten asked.

"I felt good about it."

"We'll meet tomorrow morning at eight, in the white camper," said Orten.

Later that evening, at the guesthouse in Fresnaye, Robert formulated a plan.

Beginning with the most interesting translated titles, and those that might best promote understanding of Atlanian culture, he decided to take photographs of the first several pages and one internal page of about twenty books.

He took out his Canon SLR digital camera. With the depth of field afforded by an aperture of eight, he could focus in on the book's gutter and page simultaneously. For any pages that weren't numbered, he'd have to include in the shot a little piece of paper showing the actual page number. He decided to place a color card, to ensure accurate color, and a ruler into each photo. He would mount the camera on a tripod and use the camera's self-timer and flash to take the pictures. After taking the photographs, he would come home and translate the texts using the photos. Then he would write a report on each book, and prepare a presentation on each, for Orten and the team. When that was finished, he'd photograph twenty more, and put together reports and presentations, until all the books were documented. On days when he was at home translating, he would skip the meetings.

The next morning, as Robert drove into the field, he noticed two additional campers parked near the hill. Feeling the usual sense of danger that he felt around these people, Robert went into the white camper and joined the meeting. Several team members were already there. Some were seated, while others stood. An older, white-haired man with a white mustache, whom Robert hadn't seen before, sat near Orten and Jennifer. Robert expected Orten to introduce him to the man, but Orten just shuffled his papers. Robert looked at the man then at Jennifer and saw she was looking back at him. It was an odd moment, and Robert didn't know what to make of it; perhaps he didn't want her to think he was curious about the man's identity. Robert had begun to see Jennifer as the team member to be most wary of.

After several more team members arrived, Orten started the meeting, giving the floor to Robert. Robert told the group he'd translated the titles of the books in the cabinet, then he handed out copies of his list. He ran his translation plan past Orten and received the OK to proceed with it.

Other team members reported what they'd accomplished the day before. John and Will had been in the study with Robert and had taken a lot of photos and diagrammed the room and now would study the artifacts more closely.

Jonathan said he'd managed to pick the lock on the door with the sculpture above it, the door to the room he now called the "Room of Stereopticons," and gone in.

Eddy described his documentation of the bedroom and the Astrology Room.

The five other team members had been with Orten, investigating the flying machine. Scott, who seemed to be the team's mechanics and electronics expert, reported he'd investigated the craft's engine and found that it, like the car's engine in Finland, was missing its power source. The engines in both vehicles, Orten said, looked very similar.

The white-haired man broke in several times during Scott's presentation to ask questions. In his responses, Scott addressed the man as "General."

It was the general who ended the discussion about the flying machine, and he did it in a way that gave Robert the impression that the general, not Orten, was in charge of this meeting. "We'll not talk further about this airship today," the general said quietly.

"OK," Orten said. "Meeting's over. Jonathan, document everything in the Room of Stereopticons. Everyone else keep doing what you were doing yesterday."

Orten turned to Robert. "You do whatever you want to do," he said.

On his way out of the camper, Robert thought about how being ordered to be autonomous isn't real autonomy.

Robert spent the day carefully photographing the first several pages—and a random internal page—of each of twenty books. Since one of the books he documented was a text on music, he also photographed the sheet music that was on the piano-like instrument.

When he got home to the guesthouse shortly before 9:00 p.m., he turned off his security alarm, unlocked the door, and went in. Someone had been smoking a cigarette. Robert was sure he smelled it the instant he walked in, but it was now less distinct. He stood at the door, leaving it ajar. He knew he'd locked the door on his way out in the morning, and the alarm had been on, but someone had been in there. Was that person still there?

He carefully checked every room but found no one. As far as he could see, nothing had been taken or disturbed. The mysterious note had warned him his home would not be secure. It made sense that people at the Grayling Conservancy, if they were as corrupt as the note writer implied, would try to get a look at his personal records. He slowly opened the drawer that contained his stack of notes. Sure enough, there were no breadcrumbs on the top sheet.

So now they have a better idea of the site I found, he thought, *but they don't know where it is—maybe now they think it's in Turkey.* He smiled. *And they have no idea I discovered a car with a power source in it.*

There was nothing to do about the break-in, so Robert started his computer and loaded his photos into it.

After dinner he got busy translating the pages.

Geometry

The first photos he opened on his laptop were of the first pages of a book titled *Elementary Geometry*.

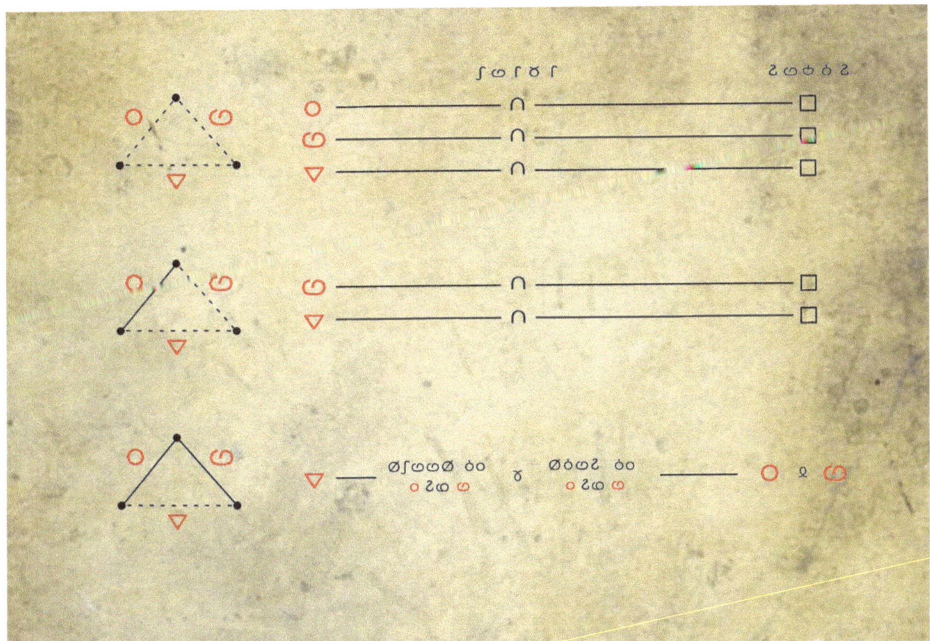

A page near the beginning of the book on geometry. The third figure shows a "bunch" consisting of three points with only two of the three distances between them known. The minimum value for the third distance (labeled "▽") is described as being equal to the "shorter of O or ☺ taken from the longer of O or ☺," and its maximum is "O plus ☺."

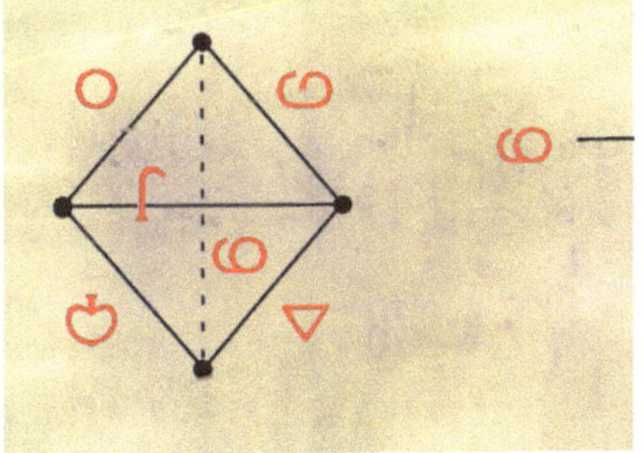

Another figure from the geometry book

There was nothing about angles between lines on these pages. Instead the focus was on maximum and minimum distances. Fixed distances among a number of given points can place limits on how short and how long other distances among them can be.

The author referred several times in the text to the combination of groups of points and the relations existing among them as *bunches*, the same word used in the *Universal Dictionary of Atl* for bunches of bananas, grapes, or flowers.

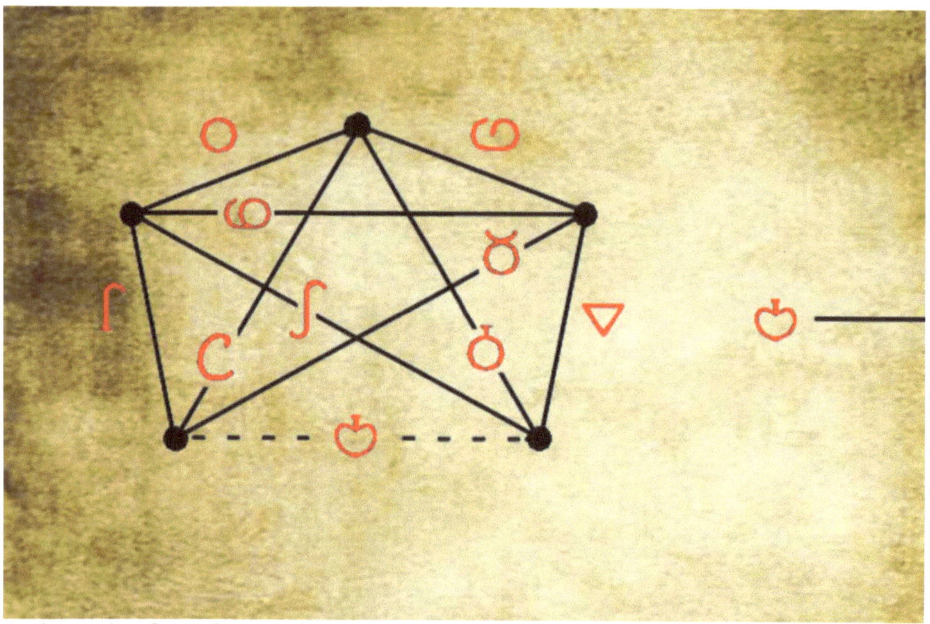

An interesting figure from the book on geometry. Robert translated the author's comments on this figure: "If you have a fixed structure (O, ⊙, ♉, ʃ, C, ⊙), then three distances (▽, ♂, ʃ) must be fixed in order to fix the distance ♺. This is why we say our space is 'three-dimensional.'"

Arithmetic

The next pages Robert translated were from a book titled *Mathematics for Dialecticians*. He was no expert in mathematics, but he felt he had a good handle on the Atl language, so he should be able to translate the introductory part of the text, the part on arithmetic.

As he translated the examples in this text, Robert discovered that Atlanian arithmetic had something in common with modern arithmetic. There were many different kinds of expressions, each composed of three numbers connected by special signs. For instance he decided that the Atlanian "2 – 3 – 5" must mean something like modern "2 + 3 = 5." But he was confused by their system. If "2 – 3 – 5" meant "2 + 3 = 5," then what did the Atlanian "2 – 3 – • ' 5" mean?

The author of the Atlanian text called expressions such as "2 – 3 – 5" *sum bunches*. Here was the word *bunch* again. But expressions such as "2 – 3 – • ' 5" were never referred to in the ancient text with the word *bunch*.

He reasoned that Atlanian "2 – 3 – • ' 5" had to be a *statement* meaning "2 + 3 = 5. But "2 – 3 – 5" was a *term* that named an "addition bunch," a group of numbers along with the relations among them, composed of 2 being added to 3 to equal 5. He knew of no modern term for such a group.

He now saw clearly that the Atlanian expression "•' – 3 – 5" was also a term. It meant "the first of 3 numbers that are in the addition bunch composed of "*some number*, 3, and 5." In other words "• – 3 – 5" meant "5 minus 3."

Similarly "2 – 3 – •" meant "2 plus 3." So the " ' " sign meant "equals."

As he worked on his translation, he was impressed by the neat consistency of the Atlanian system compared to our modern system. For instance in Atlanian our "12/6" was "• = 6 = 12," and our "2 x 6" was expressed as "2 = 3 = •."

Logic

Robert had taken a course in symbolic logic in college but decided he'd better brush up on the subject before translating the pages of the Atlanian book called *Truth-Engine Logic*. The next morning, he went to a bookshop at the V&A Waterfront and bought a book on logic.

After returning home and spending several hours giving himself a quick refresher course, Robert started his translation of the introduction to *Truth-Engine Logic*:

Throughout Atlan these rooms differ. The room of instruction at the Truth Engine in the capital city is ten strides long by ten strides wide. A very thick pillar stands at each corner. As the initiate enters this room, he or she faces a round desk and a chair near the far wall. At the far right, in the corner, is a large wooden panel-cabinet [*mish-panahk*]. In the middle of the room, between the door and the chair, the floor has been built around an old stone well that, it is said, is the well that was built by Atallas, the founder of the capital city of Atlan, who arrived as a keeper of livestock and later reigned as king. They say Atallas's farm stood on this spot.

The well is still a source of water.

The initiate steps into the room with a dialectician [*skeopashu*—referring to a particularly revered logician or debater] who will be his or her guide. To the initiate's left and right, two giant, gray metal statues of armored soldiers stand between the columns. Each soldier holds a light-flash weapon.

The guide shows the initiate to the chair. The teacher enters wearing a green robe, green sandals, and a tiny, bright-orange *namat* pin. Adopting a casual tone, the teacher speaks.

"Welcome to our school," says the teacher. "Look at these four figures." He pulls a panel from the cabinet. On the panel the following figures have been drawn.

⊗ ∇ ⊙ ◇

"I have chosen one of these four figures to serve as my example."

Being prompted by the guide, the initiate asks, "Which one is your chosen one?"

"I will not tell you, but I will give some clues as to how knowledge of one or two facts can lead to knowledge of another. Here I will show you the Three Laws." He slides a panel from the cabinet. On the panel is written in red letters:

The Deny-Other Law
Suppose I say that the chosen one is one of these: ⊗ ⊙.
Then you can know that the chosen one is not one of these: ∇ ◇.

The Add-Anything Law
Or suppose I say that the chosen one is one of these: ⊗ ⊙.
Then you can know the chosen one is one of these: ∇ ⊗ ⊙.

The In-Common Law
Or I may say that the chosen one is one of these: ⊗ ▽ ⊙.

<u>And I may add that the chosen one is one of these: ▽ ⊙ ◇.</u>

Then you can know that the chosen one is one of these: ▽ ⊙.

Robert studied the lesson. He thought about how the teacher hadn't really stated the laws but had produced concrete examples through which the initiate could infer the general rules.

The teacher asks the initiate, "Do you see how these are valid conclusions, how these are valid laws?"

"Yes. Clearly."

The teacher frowns. "But if you knew them already, why in the world would you care to make them plain to your conscience mind?"

The guide prompts the initiate not to respond.

The teacher continues, "Do you know why you receive these lessons here beside the well of Atallas, where these two soldiers are portrayed as guarding what we do here?"

"No," says the initiate.

The teacher says, "It was claimed that at the well of Atallas water was drawn from the center of the earth, from the eternal and unchanging realm. The Three Laws are of that eternal realm, so the well of Atallas is the symbolic source of the laws. To the uninitiated, the laws seem obvious, trivial, and without value, but we know they underlie the Argument Forms, which, together with the machinery of the Truth Engine, are such a powerful force against ignorance and evil that the men of iron here to our left and right must guard them. The dialectician is a lover of humanity, and the knowledge of these three simple laws allows him to fully manifest his love."

82 | Richard Crist

"That is the first of the two Foundational Lessons," the teacher says. "Are you ready for the second?"

"Yes."

Robert found it interesting that this book taught logic by describing a learning ritual. But he didn't clearly see why the Atlanians felt these laws were such powerful instruments of love.

He now had translated all the pages of *Truth-Engine Logic* that he'd photographed, but so far he hadn't come across anything relating to the sort of logic he was familiar with. Robert was curious about the second of the two Foundational Lessons, so, although it was past eight in the evening, he drove up to the *koppie* to photograph the next couple of sections of the book.

When he arrived at the site, the parking area was almost empty. Only the RVs and one car, which Robert assumed belonged to the guard, were there. He spent two hours photographing more pages of the logic book then went back to Fresnaye. The next day he translated the newly acquired text.

In this new section, the author presented what he called the "four statement models," which he described in the following manner:

The teacher gestures toward the four massive columns. "These columns," he says, "represent the Four Models. These models are the four statement models that serve as the Four Pillars supporting the Truth Engine. Each model is written near the top of the column that represents it. See up there?"

The guide tells the initiate to say, "I cannot see them. They are far above me."

The teacher points to the four columns and says, "These Four Pillars of the Truth Engine, these Four Models that allow us to manifest our love as we speak to one another, look like this…" Leaving the laws panel displayed, he pulls another panel out of the cabinet. On this panel is written, in bright gold letters:

ტ—ၑ ტ\ၑ ტ/ၑ ტ_ၑ

"These are the four wonderful pillars of peace and happiness that all dialecticians must know and revere," says the teacher. "Knowledge of these Four Models guides the logicians of the engine in their heroic battle for truth." He pushes the panel back into the cabinet and withdraws another one. On this one is written in black letters:

In these pillars ⏻ stands for any statement; ◌ stands for any other statement. The straight line means "and." When the line ends low next to ⏻ or ◌, a "not" is put into the ⏻ or ◌.

"At this point," the author wrote, "the teacher shows the initiate, step-by-step, how an argument should be constructed."

Robert read through the teacher's lesson on symbolic logic. It was clearer than the modern system. He learned the meaning of the connecting lines in the Four Pillars. The lessons directed the initiate how to translate ordinary language into the language of Truth-Engine logic:

Where "p" and "q" each stands for a statement:
For "p and q," write "p ▔ q."
For "p and not-q," write "p ╲ q."
For "Not-p and q," write "p ╱ q."
For "Not-p and not-q," write "p ▁ q."
For "If p then q," write "p Ƶ q" (literally "The true one is one of these: 'p ▔ q,' 'p ╱ q,' 'p ▁ q'").

So, for instance, for "I study and I do not learn," write "I study ╲ I learn."

Use of this terminology made it easy to apply the *Three Laws* in logical deduction. For instance:

The In-Common Law (IC) as applied to logic allows you to construct a conclusion by creating a third expression that has all and only the connector line(s) that the two premises have in common. For instance:

p ⊻ q

p ⊼ q
____

p ⊤ q

(You can see how this law works, if you write out the full meaning of "p ⊻ q" then the full meaning of "p ⊼ q": "The true one is one of these: 'p ⊤ q,' 'p ⁄ q,' 'p ＿ q.'" And "The true one is one of these: 'p ⊤ q,' 'p ⟍ q.'" Therefore the true one is the expression they have in common, namely, "p ⊤ q.")

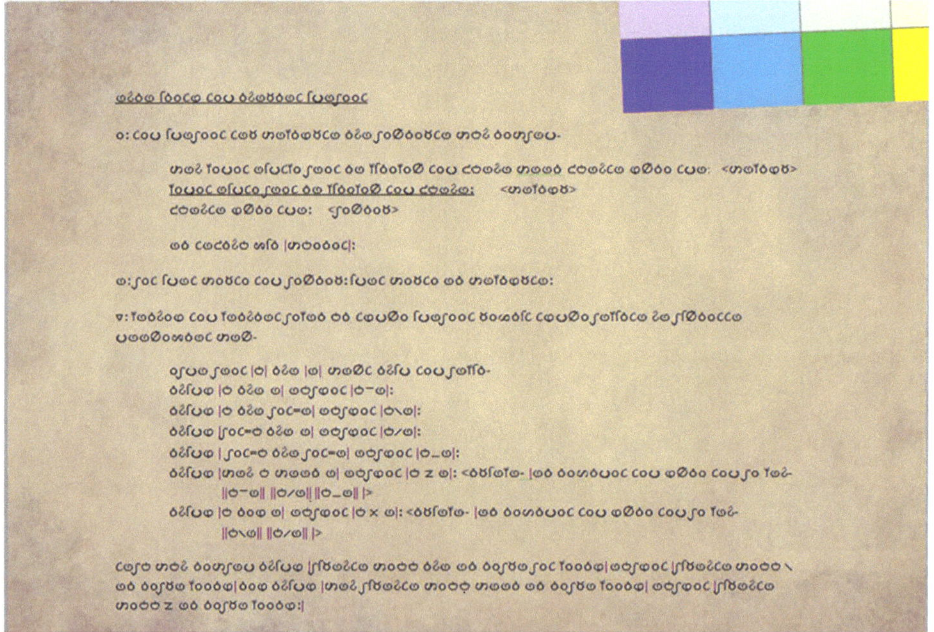

Truth-Engine Logic. Robert's photo of the page where the teacher's step-by-step lesson begins. (Robert included a color separation guide in the photo.) For Robert's translation of these pages, go to Appendix 1 on page 227.

But there were parallels to our system. For instance, Robert recognized *Ash-Katl* as being the same as the modern argument form called Modus Ponens: If p then q, p, therefore q.

According to the text, the full deduction for Ash-Katl was:

p **Z** q

<u>p **⌐** q</u>

<u>p **⎺** q</u>   by the In-Common Law

p **➚** q   by the Add-Anything Law

which was shortened to:

p **Z** q

<u>p **⌐** q</u>

p **➚** q

Robert looked at the Ash-Katl form. *Where have I seen this before?* He wondered. *I know I've seen something like this before.* He went to the closet, reached behind his shirts, and pulled out the towel in which he'd wrapped the key case. Unwrapping the envelope and opening it, he took the key case out and sat down on the bed to examine it.

Three lines of repeated text, he thought. *And each line is divided in the middle.* He looked carefully at what he'd thought was a decorative band separating the words on the left from those on the right and laughed out loud. He plainly saw what he'd never noticed before. He saw the vestiges of paint on parts of the design. By taking only the painted parts as included in the text, he could now finally discern the complete meaning. It read:

Heroes speak **Z** We flourish.

Heroes speak **⌐** We flourish.

Heroes speak **➚** We flourish.

which Robert now knew meant, "If heroes speak, then we flourish. Heroes speak. [Therefore] we flourish."

The heroes could only have been the logicians, Robert thought. *Somehow their speaking, and their use of logic, brought happiness to the people.*

Reconstruction: the key case, as it looked fourteen thousand years ago

Robert sat on the bed holding the little key case in his hands. Tears came to his eyes. In a way he couldn't quite understand, the revelation of the meaning of the inscription—the fact that the meaning finally was completely clear to him—was for him a milestone, as if a childhood dream had been fulfilled, something important accomplished. Now he would get on with things.

He decided not to cover much of the logical material in detail at the meeting (and of course he would say nothing about the key case), since he sensed the group would not be open to learning a logical system, even though this one was essential to the workings of the Truth Engine, a central institution for the Atlanians. But he did want to make the point to the team that the Atlanian systems he'd studied were more advanced than ours.

The next day, Robert made a chart to include as an appendix to his translation, which showed how sentences containing *and* (or *but*), *or*, and *if* are treated in Truth-Engine logic and in modern logic. In modern logic the dot (•) means "and"; the tilde (~) means "not"; (⊃) means "if…then"; (∨) means "or"; and (≡) means "if and only if." Here is Robert's chart.

Truth-Engine Logic	Modern Logic	Ordinary Language
I study ° I learn	no modern equivalent	
I study ▬ I learn	I study • I learn	I study and I learn.
I study ╲ I learn	I study • ~(I learn)	I study, but I don't learn.
I study ╱ I learn	~(I study) • (I learn)	I don't study, but I learn.
I study ▬ I learn	~(I study) • ~(I learn)	I don't study, and I don't learn.
I study ◤ I learn	I study	I study.
I study ◥ I learn	I learn	I learn.
I study ═ I learn	I study ≡ I learn	I study if and only if I learn.
I study ✕ I learn	(I study ∨ I learn) & ~(I study • I learn)	I study or I learn, not both
I study ◢ I learn	~(I learn)	I don't learn.
I study ◣ I learn	~(I study)	I don't study.
I study ✗ I learn	I study ∨ I learn	I study or I learn, or both.
I study ◿ I learn	~(I study) ⊃ ~(I learn)	I study if I learn.
I study ◺ I learn	I study ⊃ I learn	If I study, then I learn.
I study ✖ I learn	~(I study) ∨ ~(I learn)	Either I don't study, or I don't learn.
I study ✖ I learn	no modern equivalent	

The Atlanian method impressed Robert. Compared to our modern system, the Atlanian one had a polished, perfected look, as if it were the product of a longer—perhaps centuries longer—process of evolution. He knew that some very formal modern systems were more orderly than the popular version, but he realized that none of our systems had Truth-Engine logic's transparency.

He was also struck by the way Atlanian logic used only three axioms, whereas modern logic uses many.

He thought about how logic today is considered an esoteric study, of little practical value for anyone not involved in, say, computer programming, and wondered how it was that the Atlanians saw logic as an essential weapon in the dialectician's heroic battle for truth. How was this cold, abstract discipline transformed into a powerful instrument of love "as we speak to one another"? He wanted to understand the Truth Engine better.

[To see Robert's translation of part of *Truth-Engine Logic*, go to Appendix 1 on page 227.]

Playing Music

Robert had taken piano lessons in his youth and could read a score. With this low-level expertise, he was able to translate the book titled, *Playing Music*.

A picture from *Playing Music* that shows a section of a keyboard. The set of six red keys are named O, ꙩ, ▽, ☉, ꙩ, and ♉ (Robert renamed them a, b, c, d, e, and f); the tan keys are named Ò, ʃ, C, ᙍ, ℰ, and Ɔ (Robert renamed them g, h, i, j, k, and l)

In his memo for the group, Robert wrote:

This short book presents a system that allows almost anyone to experience the joy of playing music. The author of Playing Music *describes the three components of this system. First, in Kholoruuf's time, the Truth Engine's "League of Dialecticians" sponsored a wide network of "electronic-instrument ensembles." Each of these ensembles was a duet-size to orchestra-size group of players. Each of the players played monophonically on an electronic keyboard instrument of a kind that allowed for expressive playing. Since each musician in the group played only one note at a time, it was easy for almost anyone to participate. Second, the keys on the keyboard were arranged and named in a simple, logical way that made transposition between key signatures easy. Third, the musical scores used by soloists and by the participants in these ensembles were extremely clear and extremely easy to read.*

The keys on the Atlanian keyboard (left) were, simply, back keys alternating with front keys; whereas the keys on our modern keyboards (right) have an unduly complex arrangement:

front	*front*
back	*back*
front	*front*
back	*front*
front	*back*
back	*front*
front	*back*
back	*front*
front	*front*
back	*back*
front	*front*
back	*back*

The chart below lists the names of musical notes. The Atlanian notes were named [left column] in a simple, systematic way—in this memo, I will rename them [middle column]. On the other hand, in the modern system [right column], the notes are given complex names:

Note Names

Atlanian	Atlanian, Renamed	Modern
O	*a*	*C*
Ø	*b*	*C#/D♭*
▽	*c*	*D*
♂	*d*	*D#/E♭*
Ø	*e*	*E*
ծ	*f*	*F*
ô	*g*	*F#/G♭*
∫	*h*	*G*
C	*i*	*G#/A♭*
ω	*j*	*A*
3	*k*	*A#/B♭*
⊂	*l*	*B*

The Atlanian musical score is extremely easy to read. If we substitute modern letters and numbers for Atlanian ones, the score that's open on the piano begins like this. (It clearly represents the soprano voice of the piece):

Atlanian music was tonal and with twelve notes to the octave, as is ours. This reflects the universality of these structures.

Robert looked up musical notation on the Internet and found an article about the eleventh-century monk Guido of Arezzo, the "father of modern music." Guido added two lines to the two-line staff in use at the time, to produce a four-line staff. This innovation made it possible to accurately notate musical pitches for the first time. Guido believed that, using his new method, a student could learn in five months what previously would have taken him or her ten years to learn. Robert wondered whether reintroducing the very clear and simple Atlanian system might accomplish the same kind of revolution in our own time.

As he translated more pages, he became keenly aware that there was something these introductory texts all had in common: They were easy to understand. The texts covered material that modern textbooks present in a way that is difficult for most students to understand, but somehow the Atlanian books made this same material extremely simple. By the twist of a phrase, by the use of just the right word, through consistency of notation, the authors produced clarity.

Over the next three weeks, Robert translated all the pages he had photographed, and in the process, he added many words to his lexicon. After finishing with each book, he wrote a memo about it for the group. The pattern he noticed was continued and reinforced: all the books had the same simplicity that made learning easy.

It was time to take another set of photos—or to see what else he might do. With his usual trepidation in heading to a meeting with the Grayling bunch, Robert drove up to the site for the 8:00 a.m. meeting.

At the meeting he learned that little progress was being made in uncovering the operations of the flying machine. A computer had been located in the ship, but its workings were as mysterious as the workings of the other computers in the house.

The team had investigated a number of tools found near the craft. Some of the tools contained electronic circuits that no one understood. One component was a very large glass tube whose function could not be determined.

At one point Orten referred to "off-site analysts" who would do follow-up work on some of these artifacts. Robert wondered whether objects were being taken away from the house to be studied elsewhere.

Orten reported that the east door in the study had been opened, revealing an art studio. He assigned Jonathan the task of documenting the artifacts in this room. Orten explained his choice to the group, saying of Jonathan, "Dr. Miller has written a book on ancient music and several on ancient art."

From the art studio, the team had entered a room that contained displays honoring prominent Atlanian citizens. When Orten proposed this room be called the "Room of Honors," no one objected.

The team hadn't yet been able to figure out how to operate the devices that resembled stereopticons.

Eddy told the group he was translating a stack of "dream pages" in Kholoruuf's bedroom. These documents apparently were sheets of paper on which Kholoruuf had written down, and commented on, his dreams.

Investigation and documentation of the objects in the astrology room was still being done, and a new member of the group named Kyle was producing computer-graphics reconstructions of these objects.

Orten introduced two other new members, Janice and Sam, who would be working with the inscrutable Kholoruufian computers.

The team was seeking the least destructive way to get through the basement door. Orten suggested that everyone should keep an eye out for a key.

John and Will discovered a set of strange pieces of cloth in the study. They seemed to have some kind of circuitry attached to them, but the men couldn't determine its function. The two also were translating, using Robert's lexicon, the history books in the large cabinet in the study.

In the study Will also had translated small parts of some of the books in a slimmer bookcase next to the glass doors to the balcony. These books had been written by hand, and the translations showed that their author was Kholoruuf himself. They seemed to constitute his day-to-day diary or chronicle. The team had determined that Atlan had begun to decline in Kholoruuf's day. Since the main Atlantean islands still existed when Kholoruuf lived, the decline must have occurred sometime before any cataclysm destroyed these islands. Will had started with the last of the diaries to be written, looking for clues to the reasons for the decline. Unfortunately Kholoruuf either had stopped making entries before the onset of Atlantean troubles or had taken the journals from this period with him when he left.

John announced that a book called *Guide for Dialecticians* had been found in the study, inside the archaeopteryx cabinet. The book, which had been carefully wrapped in a piece of red felt and tied up with a golden cord, must have been very old, even in Kholoruuf's day and was in very bad condition. It appeared to be a guide to the Truth Engine, but the group hadn't yet had the opportunity to translate any large part of it.

Orten interrupted John's presentation. "Robert," he said, "I wonder if I could get you to do a preliminary translation of whatever parts of this *Guide for Dialecticians* that you find interesting, and if you could do that next. None of us here is a professional linguist, but you seem to have a handle on this language. I want to get some clarity about this Truth-Engine business. Would you agree to do that for us?"

"I'd be happy to," Robert said. He was eager to learn more about the Truth Engine, which was so deeply venerated by Kholoruuf and his fellow citizens.

"Good. Because I think this is an important book," Orten said. "Do the translations, write a report, and I'll schedule a special meeting where you can make a presentation. John and Will can keep working on the bookcase. Let's get every page of every one of those books documented. Then we can get the documentation out to the off-site translators—we'll get them working on a complete translation of the *Guide* too."

Off-site translators? Robert knew there had to be a lot of work being done behind the scenes. He knew there had to be a secret project underway somewhere, probably under the auspices of the US government, designed to deal with these monumental discoveries.

Everyone at Nell's Koppie, as far as he could tell—except probably the new members, Kyle, Janice, and Sam—was an archaeologist. Surely there were other experts out there working on the linguistic, technological, logical, philosophical, and historical issues. But he resisted the urge to ask questions, as he didn't want to appear unduly inquisitive. So far Orten wasn't passing on any insights he might have received off-site to the team—at least, he wasn't passing them on to Robert.

Orten turned to Karen. "Have they got that website up and running?"

"Yes," Karen said. "They've put up a password-protected site online, a database for Atl-to-English translation. Everyone here and the translators will be able to add new words to it. I'll get the information to all of you."

Robert wanted to ask who "they" were, but he bit his tongue.

When it was his turn to make a presentation, he handed out copies of his translations. He explained how the books could be viewed as a semicomplete collection of "paideian" textbooks for the student who pursues a well-rounded education. He showed in detail, using the examples, how the books seemed to have been written using methods designed to promote clarity in the transfer of knowledge.

"The Kholoruufian educational systems," Robert said, "were so transparent, so conducive to learning, that it was almost as if there had been no medium at all between the learner and the thing to be learned."

Orten had been looking at Robert's translations and seemed strangely annoyed by Robert's positive take on the ancient material that the team was bringing to light. Robert hadn't expected this reaction and didn't completely understand it.

"I don't know," Orten said. "I think there's a humanness in our own systems that I don't see here in the Kholoruufian systems—a certain beauty in our systems' diversity."

Robert thought for a moment about whether to respond to Orten and decided there was no reason not to. "But I think it's at the expense of clarity," he said. "A slight aesthetic appeal in the system of notation, say, for music, ends up standing in the way of learning. Because of this, perhaps millions of people who could enjoy a lifetime of making music are totally deprived of that experience. But really I think the symmetry in the Atlanian systems is more beautiful than the chaos in ours."

Robert noticed several other members of the group were smiling and seemed tense, as if shocked that anyone would disagree with Orten.

"Their system was austere—it wasn't human," Orten said. He turned to Jennifer. "What do you think, Dr. Keller?"

This was the first time Robert had heard her last name. He wanted to remember it. *Dr. Jennifer Keller.*

"I agree with you, Professor," she said. "It's as if their systems were designed for robots."

Robert thought Jennifer's point was a little over the top and sensed she was trying to ingratiate herself with Orten. But Orten bought it.

"Yeah," Orten said. "And people who have learned our systems aren't going to throw away what they know so they can adopt the Kholoruufian systems."

He was now arguing against a point Robert hadn't even made, but Robert had a response. "Apparently Kholoruuf's culture found some way around that problem, Professor. There must have been older Atlanian systems, and the people who'd learned them must have thrown them away to embrace the new ones"

"Don't idolize these people, Robert," Orten said, "at the expense of your own."

Robert figured he'd better be tactful and allow Orten the last word. *What a strangely twisted way this guy has of responding to potentially useful new ideas*, he thought.

He spent the rest of the day in Kholoruuf's study translating the first few pages of the *Guide for Dialecticians*, then photographing those pages and a few more. On the book's title page, the author was listed as "Apporiopasshe." Below the printed name, someone had written in Atl, "first chief logician of the Truth Engine."

As Robert worked, he thought about how the fact that Kholoruuf had kept the *Guide for Dialecticians* in the archaeopteryx cabinet might, along with the way he'd wrapped the book, indicate that he'd held the book in very great esteem. It seemed to Robert that the symbol of the archaeopteryx had special meaning for the Atlanians. Not only was a model of the bird displayed in Kholoruuf's study, but there was a similar display in the Room of the Truth Examiner in the Catskills—and there was a silhouette of an archaeopteryx above the door to the cylindrical room in Kholoruuf's house, the room the team called the *Core Room*. Robert suspected that Kholoruuf had considered the archaeopteryx cabinet to be a receptacle where a venerated object should be kept. In time Robert would come to treat the *Guide for Dialecticians* as the central Kholoruufian text.

That night at home, Robert did an Internet search on Dr. Jennifer Keller. He found she was an archaeologist currently on the faculty of a major midwestern university. She had written articles on Native American sites, including the great Mississippian mounds. She also had done work in Nevada at a time when Orten was at work there, and Robert guessed the two might have met during that time. She had grown up in Ohio, earned her PhD in California, and apparently wasn't married.

He also did a search on Dr. Jonathan Miller and found references to his books: *Music of the Ancient Greeks, The Art of Babylon,* and *Scythian Art.*

Robert had dinner, worked some more on the translations that he'd made that day, and went to bed. He lay awake longer than usual, thinking about the *Guide for Dialecticians* and what it might have to say about the mysterious Truth Engine. He was eager to get a fuller understanding of this tattered *Guide,* this book that Kholoruuf had tied up with a golden cord.

CHAPTER 6
THE TRUTH ENGINE EXPLAINED

Robert spent the next several days at the site, photographing every page of the *Guide for Dialecticians.*

He put a set of the photos on a flash drive for Orten and took a flash drive home to begin translating more parts of the book.

During the time he spent translating this book, Robert attended several morning meetings with the group in order to keep track of the team's progress but made no reports at these meetings.

It took him a month to complete a rough but readable translation of the parts of the book he found to be most illuminating. At the next 8:00 a.m. meeting, he reported he was polishing his translation, and Orten scheduled an evening get-together in his office at the Grayling Conservancy for Robert's presentation.

In the days that led up to the meeting, Robert made a copy of the translation for each team member and wrote a summary to read to the group.

The group assembled in Orten's office on a Wednesday evening. Once everyone had arrived, Robert handed out copies of the translated passages. When he handed Orten two copies by mistake, Orten made a joke of it, waving the extra copy in the air and saying in mock horror, "Someone's not going to get a copy! I've got theirs here. Who doesn't have a copy?" Robert felt Orten meant to diminish the presentation even before it had begun.

"OK, Robert," Orten said. "Everyone's here. Let's hear about this *Guide for Dialecticians.*"

Robert stood in front of the group at a podium set up next to Orten's desk and began his presentation. "It's my impression," he said, "that the Atlanians saw the *Guide for Dialecticians* as a founding document. The copy of the book we found in Kholoruuf's study must have been an original, apparently printed long before Kholoruuf's time. Because it was set apart from the other books, because it was so reverently wrapped and kept in a cabinet under the archaeopteryx display, I feel we can assume the Atlanians treated this book as a national treasure. First I want to read from the book's introduction, in which the author, whose name was Apporiopasshe, wrote:

"Our people are decent and civilized. They are intelligent, and throughout the island states and in the less remote outlying cities, they are well educated. Through our electrical information networks, the people keep themselves informed.

"So these people are smart, informed, and seek to do good; yet, on any given issue, their opinions as to how this good is to be done often differ widely. Frequently this difference is a sign that no one is in possession of the full truth about how good is to be done. But the dialectic can bring these opinions nearer and nearer to truth via the principle of synergy."

"The term I translated as 'dialectic' is *skeo*," Robert said then continued to read.

"In civil debate between two people, truths are revealed that neither participant could have seen on his or her own. This is how civil argument, superficially contentious, actually brings happiness to our community. The dialectic should be high on the list of ingredients in anyone's recipe for how we can become happy by acquiring knowledge of what's true, what's good, and what's beautiful.

"All the structures necessary for a respectable dialectic have existed and have been used in the Central Islands for centuries. These structures are language, the written word, democracy, the printing press, and the electrical networks that have recently come into existence. The resulting knowledge of how to do good has caused more goodness to be done.

"Yet it is only recently that the dialectic has been seen as a method that might be reconstituted in a fundamental way. The dialectics of the past were a mere candle flame lighting our path toward truth. But the new Truth Engine-generated dialectics in the Logos can cut through ignorance as a laser cuts through steel."

"The word for *laser* is *pash-oekh*," Robert explained. "Literally *knife light*." He continued:

"And whereas ordinary dialectical structures lack any moral faculty, the Truth Engine is governed by a moral will in the form of the Ikon."

"That is, *mant*. It means 'image.'"

"In the year forty-nine of the thirtieth tlahok, we founded the League of Dialecticians in Pemruuk in North America. In the year fifty-four, we held our celebratory convention in the central city of Atl. By the year sixty, we had established Truth-Engine centers from Pemruuk in the west, to Meh-Atl in the north, to Kashr in the east, and to Lemin-Daal-Atl in the south. Today the Truth Engine is an institution esteemed by our people as being on a par with our governmental institutions."

"I think we can suppose that 'electrical networks,' referred to an Internet-type system," Robert explained. "On the first page of this book after the introduction, we see the same two-rings symbol that was inscribed on the outside of Nell's Koppie. Finally we have the key to the meaning of this glyph. It diagrams the architecture of the Truth Engine.

"In my translation document, I've included a picture of the relevant page. You can look at it and see how the parts were labeled. You'll notice that just as the author used two different words for *articulation*, I've used two different words to translate them. Because I used 'Logos' as the name for the left-hand circle, staying with the Greek, I used 'Ikon,' instead of, say, 'Image,' for the right-hand circle. These are my suggested translations. Of course you can use any names you wish."

Orten studied his copy of the document. "I've got no objection to your terms, Robert," he said.

In Robert's translation document, he had included this key to the two-rings diagram:

ʊ: the League of Dialecticians

☉ + ∇ + ♁ + ʃ + ☉: the Dual Articulation (*fan*)

☉ + ∇ + ♁ + ʃ: the Logos (*tosh-he*, "articulation")

♁ + ʃ + ☉: the Ikon (*mant*, "image")

☉: the Machinery of the Critical Dialectic

∇: the Library of the Critical Dialectic

♁: the Library of the Philosophical Dialectic

ʃ: the Machinery of the Philosophical Dialectic

ↀ + ſ: the Logikon (*tosh-hemant*)

ŏ: the Library of the Practical Dialectic

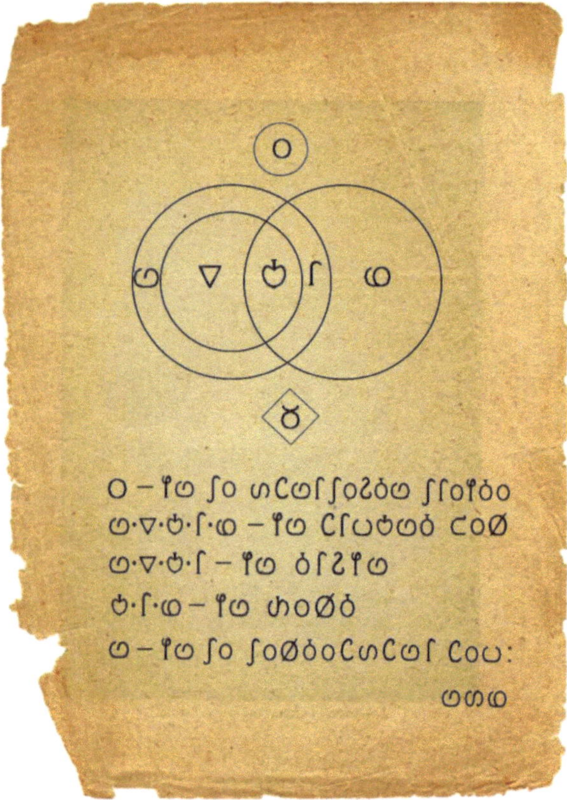

The Truth-Engine diagram in *Guide for Dialecticians*

"From the text that follows," Robert continued, "we learn that the League of Dialecticians governed the Truth Engine. Its members included people in the various ranks of the dialecticians, from student up to the chief logician. Kholoruuf, when he lived at the house we're exploring, was the chief logician.

"The Atlanians used the Truth Engine to turn any ordinary argument into a high-energy search for truth. The engine maximized the synergy that produced new knowledge. It maximized the power that controversy has to reveal truth, and the revelation of truth can increase happiness.

"This is how it worked. *Truth-Engine books* were central to the workings of the Truth Engine. These books were located in what the dialecticians called the Critical and Philosophical Libraries and were, it seems clear, what we today would call 'moderated wikis.' Agreeing to use only one set of rules, the

Atlanians directed their controversies onto the pages of these Truth-Engine books. The rules required all premises and conclusions to be set forth in good logical form. In this way the dialecticians made sure their arguments would be in sync with one another, thereby maximizing synergy.

"So the Truth Engine had three parts. I've translated their names as 'Logos,' 'Logikon,' and 'Ikon.' To these parts were applied the further divisions of 'Truth,' 'Goodness,' and 'Beauty.' These divisions are represented elsewhere in the book as three concentric circles, Truth being the largest circle and Beauty the innermost. The Logos was further divided into the 'Critical Dialectic' and the 'Philosophical Dialectic.' A division they called the 'Practical Dialectic' is symbolized by the diamond shape in the diagram.

"It worked this way: The participant would look at a well structured argument in one of the Truth-Engine book wikis and say, 'I can make this argument better.' Then he or she would suggest a change to the argument while preserving its form. The managers of the book were free to accept or reject the suggestion. Over time, with many people making such amendments, the arguments in the book were continually improved in a way that no human being acting alone could hope to match.

"The process was cyclical. Each book was prepared by a small, highly trained group of dialecticians. Then debaters in the public media would use the book to refresh their arguments. During and after the actual debates in the media, the debaters and their audience would decide how the book could be improved. Their suggestions would be incorporated by the dialecticians into an amended version of the book that would be used by debaters in the public media, and the cycle would be repeated.

"With the new knowledge that was delivered by this process, the people's ability to do good grew quickly, and the people's happiness vastly increased.

"So in Apporiopasshe and Kholoruuf's Truth Engine, logic wasn't an esoteric discipline as it is in our day. It was central to the process of maximizing synergy and thus of revealing truth. And so it was key to the very well-being of the people."

"It seems to me," Orten broke in, "that the Truth-Engine process required that everyone be a master of logic and critical thinking. But that can't happen."

"The *Guide* shows that not everyone needed to be a master logician," Robert said. "It explains how a relatively small number of logicians created and managed the encyclopedia, the books of the Truth Engine. The arguments developed by these logicians were then presented in the mass media."

"Oh, sure," Orten said. "Go on."

"The Truth-Engine books were described," Robert continued, "as composing one big book, or an encyclopedia—the term is *satshoora-makatl*. The dialecticians were described as 'encyclopedists.' The author of the *Guide*, Apporiopasshe, showed how every book was connected to all the others through reference links. This encyclopedia, in a thorough way, treated knowledge not by pointing to a set of facts but by articulating a set of conflicting beliefs that were connected via logical structures to supporting premises. Over time the arguments became strengthened and the sense of facts, or knowledge, emerged.

"See, the Atlanians saw every argument thread as a 'happiness-producing device' that they made concrete by putting it into the Truth-Engine book, where they could work on it and perfect it. Apporiopasshe wrote, 'The *Truth-Engine Encyclopedia* is a grand resource for those who want to know how to do good.'

"He gives an example of a goodness-division argument. The question is, 'Should Atlan attack the king of Florida?'—the word for Florida is *Tee*. The three options are to attack, to sanction, or to do nothing. He asks, 'What will happen if Atlan attacks Florida and with what probability? What will happen if the king of Florida is sanctioned? What will happen if nothing is done?'

"The answers to these questions, he says, had to be compared with respect to the desirability of each possible outcome. The wrong choice could result in bitter grief. But opinions differed. Partisans on all sides often debated only to win the argument, unmindful of whether or not truth was revealed in the process. They put their arguments to the test on the pages of the *Truth-Engine Encyclopedia*, in the article on the proposed attack. This action was the ratchet's driving pawl, or *kaash-maayit*. The dialectician managers, the encyclopedists, acted as the ratchet's holding pawl or *tenut-maayit*. They ensured that an argument could be replaced only by a stronger one."

"What's a pawl?" Orten asked, just before Robert was going to explain the word.

Robert looked at Jennifer and saw she was smiling. Then he looked back at Orten. "Sorry," he said. "A pawl is the little lever on a ratchet that engages the teeth, to make the gear move or stop. Apporiopasshe is comparing the Truth Engine to a kind of ratchet of truth."

Orten nodded. "Oh. OK," he said.

"The dialecticians were a special breed," Robert continued. "Apporiopasshe speaks of them this way:

"The enclopedists know their desires to be right interfere with their search for truth, and they take pride in courageously confronting these desires. With honorable determination they strengthen even arguments with whose conclusions they disagree. They accept the noble task of revealing truth."

"I found a passage by the philosopher John Stuart Mill," Robert said, "that bears on this idea of the nobility of argumentation. He talks about a person who justifiably has confidence in his own opinion, and says that such justification was achieved because of the person's habit of listening to everything that could be said against his views. The person's confidence is justified because he has, Mill says, quote, 'the steady habit of correcting and completing his own opinion by collating it with those of others.' The person has, Mill says, quote, 'taken up his position against all gainsayers.' I'll include the text as a footnote in my translation document."

Orten, in a silly gesture, raised his hand like a child in a classroom. "It sounds like Mill doesn't say we're supposed to argue. He just says we should listen to all points of view."

"Mill says to 'collate' our opinions with those of others,'" Robert told him. "We should compare and combine views. And he talks about the wise man 'taking up his position against all gainsayers'—that is, standing up against opponents. I take that to refer to argument."

Orten sat back in his chair and folded his arms. "OK," he said.

"In other parts of the *Guide for Dialecticians*," Robert continued, "Apporiopasshe analyzes the human faculties. In one section Apporiopasshe presents a model of the human psyche in which the two primary faculties are reason and will. He doesn't explicitly state this view is a correct analysis of the human mind but says, quote, 'If we think of the human psyche this way, we can provide for an effective Truth Engine.'

"The faculty of reason, he said, contains four rules of thought. Three of these are deductive laws: the Deny-Other Law, the Add-Anything Law, and the In-Common Law. The fourth rule is an inductive law that he called the Expect-More Law. Apporiopasshe says the will contains many desires. A special repository for one or some of these is the conscience, with its special directive or set of directives.

"Apporiopasshe cautioned the dialectician always to keep in mind that, quote, 'it is often impossible to tell whether a person disagrees with us in reason or in conscience or both.' Interestingly this book hints of a deeper reality that relates somehow to the true identity of the Truth Engine. Also in the *Guide* is a version of Atlanian logic. It's like the one in the book on logic whose initial pages I translated before, the book called *Truth-Engine Logic*."

Orten, seated at his desk, lowered his head and raised his eyes to look at Robert. With a serious expression on his face, he said, "So they had an encyclopediocracy?"

At first Robert thought Orten was joking. But Orten's expression remained serious. Was it mock seriousness? The two looked at each other for an awkward moment. Robert looked away without answering Orten. He felt embarrassed and decided that was exactly what Orten wanted.

For Robert the idea that the explicit and rigorous use of the same logical rules by all participants in a cooperative or even competitive effort to find truth, and thereby to produce happiness, was very appealing.

"So is that it?" Orten asked.

"Well, there is one more thing," Robert said. "Tucked between the pages of the *Guide* was a folded paper with Kholoruuf's notes on it. I know that none of the history books we found cover the later events of Kholoruuf's time, but his notes may give us a clue as to why the Atlanian system broke down. On this piece of paper, Kholoruuf describes different groups of people who are related to the Truth Engine in different ways."

Robert looked at his translation. "Kholoruuf called one of these groups the 'Enginists.' Enginists were those who operated any Truth Engine that was guided by humility and goodwill, where 'good' is taken to have its ordinarily accepted meaning. Kholoruuf was an Enginist. The Pseudo-Enginists were those who operated any Truth Engine that was ostensibly guided by goodwill but without humility. The Counter Enginists were people opposed to discursive reason and, therefore, to any Truth Engine. The Radical Enginists were opposed to intuition and had an unbalanced attraction to a Truth Engine. The Anti-Enginists were those who operated any Truth Engine guided by an evil will. Kholoruuf calls this kind of Truth Engine an 'Anti-Engine.'

"I surmise that Atlan, with its Truth Engine, came under attack by nations guided by Anti-Engines. This could have caused the final conflagration."

Robert remembered the note he'd found in the New York site; he remembered Kholoruuf's warning, "Beware of the Anti-Engine." But he could say nothing to Orten's crew about this message.

"So despite their engine," Orten said, "the Atlanians' society disappeared in a conflagration. What does that say about the usefulness of the Truth Engine?"

"Well," Robert said, "it was engine against engine—a great power against a great power."

Orten frowned. "That's just guessing, Robert. You don't know what destroyed this culture. None of the books here sheds any light on this. Their engine didn't help them. As I see it, the *Guide*'s focus on logic shows the Truth Engine to be rather cold and without spirit—not the kind of bedrock you'd want to base a society on."

"But reason and emotion are two sides of a single coin," Robert said. "Each complements the other. It doesn't make sense to assume that, simply because the *Guide* emphasized logic, the system was one-sided. Kholoruuf the Enginist decried the 'Radical Enginist,' who was in fact no Enginist at all. The *Guide* had to do mostly with the Logos, but you remember there was an Ikon that expressed the system's emotional side.

"I admit," continued Robert, "at this point I have a rather vague conception of this Ikon of the Truth Engine, but it was there. One side of the Truth Engine was discursive; the other was, I guess you could say, intuitive. They called the nondiscursive side—the Ikon—a work of art. It was a book, or perhaps an electronic game, that conveyed the iconography of the Truth Engine. When you read this book, or played this game, you learned the rules of the forum, and the rules were attached to the *feelings* of appreciation for the ideals of truth, goodness, and beauty. The Ikon kept the forum on track as a search for truth, goodness, and beauty, so it worked to ensure that the Truth-Engine workers operated with *goodwill*. It was a balanced system. I believe the *Guide* makes all this clear."

Orten wasn't convinced. "I don't know how you can connect these two things—the Logos and the Ikon—like this," he said.

They're connected in the Logikon, Robert thought. But once again he decided it wouldn't be prudent to press the debate. He loved exchanging ideas with people who also enjoyed the dialectic, but Orten clearly wasn't one of these people. Robert sensed he'd already gone too far in arguing with him. If Orten was planning to keep this discovery from the public, then belittling the

Kholoruufian doctrines might help in his own mind to assuage his guilt for keeping them secret.

Later that day, working in Kholoruuf's study, Robert inspected several bound books others had found in the drawers beneath the atlas. Each had a sheet of paper pasted to the front cover that showed the book's contents through synopses. One by one he brought each book to his table, sat down, and translated its pasted sheet. These are his translations, which he finished that evening at home. The notes following the titles are comments Robert felt Kholoruuf himself had written:

Synopsis of *Land and Sea*

There are four books in this volume.

1. *Pseudo-Shachteranta*: This outline for a dialectic lists arguments about the question of floating continents and plate tectonics.

2. The *Pseudo-Preshtiata*: This is a very old copy of this outline for a dialectic. It was brought into the collection of the third chief logician by the fifth chief logician. It lists arguments, pro and con, regarding the question of an expanding earth. The central pro argument advances an a priori "piece-fitting" view. The main con argument focuses on geodetic evidence. The *Pseudo-Preshtiata Atlas* pictures the history of the earth's geological features as the expanding earth theorist envisions them and is separately bound.

3. *The Core Structures of the Truth Dialectic.* This is said to be a copy of the first chief logician's design for part of the Logikon's Truth Division. It is included in *Land and Sea* only by convention.

4. *Outline of the Modern Truth Division of the Logikon* is also included in *Land and Sea* by convention. We find in this wide-ranging compilation, in a part written sometime between the time of the seventh to tenth chief logicians, the well-known note, written in the margin by an unknown hand, which claims that "Keshekh discovered the Great Place for Humankind, the place built as a repository for the Hidden Doctrine on the identity of

the Truth Engines. Keshekh showed this Great Place to the master dialecticians as it is shown to the master dialecticians today."

This is the earliest known copy of the *Outline* and contains the original note.

In the 1960s, geologists discovered that earth's continents slowly move with respect to one another. These scientists found, for example, that South America and Africa were joined 250 million years ago. Robert knew that according to the modern theory of plate tectonics the continents ride on top of fifty-mile-thick slabs of rock that float around on the earth's mantle. He also knew that a tiny group of scientists held a dissenting view. Their expanding-earth theory proposed that the lands separated because the sphere of the earth under the continental crust is growing. Robert could see that the Atlanians had more respect for the theory of an expanding earth than modern scientists did.

Apparently the *Pseudo-Preshtiata Atlas* was the book of maps that was open on the cabinet when the team first had entered Kholoruuf's study.

Synopsis of *The Truth Enginist*

The Truth Enginist, in seven volumes, has come down to us from the very beginning of the Truth Engine's existence.

1. *Why Do People Argue?* According to this work, there are three possible reasons for disagreement. First, the people arguing might have similar consciences but are using different reasoning. Second, their reasoning might be similar, but they have very different consciences. Third, consciences and reasoning might both be at odds. This work contains the "Levels of Charity" notes, whose author tells us, "Do not say to another 'You are evil,' when you can say, 'You are a fool;' do not say 'You are a fool,' when you can say, 'You are mistaken;' Do not say 'You are mistaken,' when you can say, 'The mistake may be mine.'"

2. The *Pangaea of Theory as Symbol.* This is a small group of notes and drawings that presents the Pangaea of Theory map of the united Permian lands as being symbolic of how the Truth Engine can unite the world into a Pangaean unity.

Robert guessed that since the continents were united in this map, the map represented earth during the period known as the Permian.

3. The *Pangaea of Goodness as Symbol.* This is a small group of notes and drawings that presents the Pangaea of Goodness map of the united Permian lands as being symbolic of how the enginist can unite the self into a Pangaean unity.

4. The *Pangaea of Beauty as Symbol.* This is a small group of notes and drawings that presents the Pangaea of Beauty map of the united Permian lands as being symbolic of how the enginist can understand the cosmos as united into a Pangaean unity.

5. *Truth-Engine Theory* describes the Truth Engine as a tool that organizes chaotic controversy, focusing it like a laser beam onto the truth.

6. The *Ontological Revolution* deals with the way in which the Truth Engine forms the core faculties of a smarter society. In this packet of notes, we find the first drafts of the *Aske-Tachte Dialectic.*

7. *Opprobrium* is a collection of essays on the value of praise and blame.

Robert remembered that the Atlanian words meaning "Pangaea of Theory"—the Atlanian words translated literally as "All-Continent of Theory"—were written on the map that hung above the atlas cabinet. He wondered whether the other two "Pangaea of" maps might be found in other parts of the house. He'd have to look.

The Pangaea of Theory

Robert's translations continued with Kholoruuf's next synopsis. The book to which this outline was attached was apparently a full-fledged Truth-Engine book:

Synopsis of *Where Did the Cloths Come From?*

This dialectic addresses the question "Where did the 'strange cloths of the prehistoric world' come from?" It also looks at these related questions: Assuming that the cloths exist, where are these cloths and how were they used (how can we account for their alleged odd material structure)?"

The dialectic begins with the dialectician's long account of early references, all exceedingly vague, to the cloths, starting with the fourth chief logician's poetic reference to them in his late-tenth-era poem "Grand Minds." This part of the dialectic ends with the dialectician's deduction in support of the view that the cloths were created by (as the old phrase goes) "the ancient races not of this earth."

In the second argument, the student argues that there is no reason to assume the early references are not just metaphorical; the first and most detailed reference is, after all, he states, found in a poem (line 191).

The dialectician responds by noting that the very short reference by the fifth chief logician is unequivocal and not poetic, and that the fifth chief logician was a close confederate of the fourth when "Grand Minds" was written.

The student rebuts with his "extraordinary claims" argument, and the dialectician answers (line 520) with an early version of the well-known counterargument.

Then the student points to what he sees as inconsistencies among the cloth references. "Really, we don't even know what the cloths *were*," he says.

Robert wondered whether the cloths mentioned might be the same pieces of cloth John and Will had found in Kholoruuf's study. But the pieces of cloth from the study seemed to have nothing to do with the prehistoric world so he decided they weren't in fact the same cloths.

Synopsis of *Did a Ship from Another World Crash Near Ashekh in Kaleh?*

This Truth-Engine book addresses the question "Does debris recovered near the village of Ashekh in Akarta of Kaleh [North America] constitute evidence that we are being visited by otherworldly beings?"

It has been alleged that the kingdom retrieved an otherworldly craft that had crashed in the province of Akarta in the northern portion of Kaleh. Skeptics pointed out that parts of the alleged alien craft exactly resembled parts of a certain lightweight, unmanned, human-made, Atl military-reconnaissance cloudship that had been lost in that vicinity at that time.

A book about UFOs from the end of the Pleistocene epoch? Robert thought. *That's absolutely incredible! What could be more surprising?*

This book and the dialectic on the cloths were the first Truth-Engine books Robert had seen. If the computers had books stored in them, no one could access them, and any Truth-Engine books that might have been in the building in the Catskills or in the bookcase on the main floor of Kholoruuf's house were gone.

The next day's morning meeting started late, so Orten kept it short. He made sure the investigations were on track then closed the meeting. Robert handed out his translations to the team members as they filed out.

After the meeting, Robert explored the house, looking for the other two framed Pangaeas. He found the Pangaea of Goodness hanging in the astrology room behind a large cabinet and found the Pangaea of Beauty mostly hidden by a decorative drapery in the Room of Stereopticons.

As Robert stood in the Room of Stereopticons looking at the Pangaea of Beauty, he thought about how these three symbolic maps—the Pangaea of Unity in Truth, the Pangaea of Unity in Goodness, and the Pangaea of Unity in Beauty—were located in different rooms. Suddenly a revelation struck him. *The house itself embodies a symbolic iconography of the Truth Engine.* Kholoruuf's study was in the Truth category. The astrology room was a Goodness room. The Room of Stereopticons was in the Beauty category, as no doubt was the art studio; possibly the Room of Honors was too. *Yes, there's no doubt about it,* he thought. *The house itself is symbolic.*

Robert walked back into the study, sat at his work table, and contemplated his discovery. *This room should have a name that reflects a connection to truth,* he thought, looking around. *From now on I'll call it the* "Theoretics Library."

Whenever the three divisions appeared in the Atlanian texts, he noticed, their order was always "Truth," "Goodness," "Beauty." So he decided to investigate the rooms in that order. He wondered, *Might symbolically expressive architecture be a general feature of Atlanian culture? If it is, might the building in the Catskills also embody an iconography?* There were three distinct parts to that building, and the central part contained an astrology machine. *Somehow the astrology theme belongs in the Goodness category,* he thought. *Truth might be to the west; then the eastern part of the building, whose halls were filled with abstract sculptures, would symbolize Beauty.* Although he had a feeling there was more to the symbolism of the building in the Catskills, he couldn't put his finger on what it was.

Robert decided to translate the two Truth-Engine books. He would begin with the book about the very same phenomenon that today we call "UFOs." Starting with its first page, he began to photograph the book.

At lunchtime the team gathered in the white camper to eat. No one mentioned Robert's translation of the synopsis for the *Ship from Another World* book. *Maybe no one's read my handouts yet,* he thought.

Robert spent the rest of the day photographing every page of the book itself then went home.

He spent two weeks in Fresnaye translating the book, finishing on a Friday evening. The book fascinated him. It consisted of a dozen chapters, each presenting a different approach to the question. Throughout this book the author consistently argued for the reality of alien visitation. Robert found the author's "Amazing Coincidence" approach especially interesting. In this section the author wrote:

> I think Skeptic's arguments here are the strongest arguments against the claim that the Ashekh debris was otherworldly. But there is a good answer to them, and I think that in the process of rebutting them, we learn something new about the visitors' intentions. Skeptic says:

> [vs. 89, p. 1c] You claim (see 89) "an alien spacecraft crashed and left the debris in the Forest of Kesh near the village of Ashekh in Kaleh." The following is an argument against that claim: [400]Army officer Telterrik-Bohot, in his log for the twentieth day of the fourth month of the year thirty-one of the forty-ninth tlahok (see 271–286, p. 8), describes the launch of a very small unmanned reconnaissance [literally: *spy*] cloudship. [401]This ship was lost and never recovered. [402]My dear Believer, I'm sure you will agree that this cloudship might well have carried a king's authorization of flight. [403]If it did, then the ship probably had the emblem of the Prince of Kaleh printed on its sail strip. [404]Furthermore there are good reasons (see above, 293, p. 8) to think this flight was heading toward the Forest of Kesh when it disappeared and equally good reasons (323–328) to think it wasn't. The flight path cannot be reconstructed. [405]Therefore it remains a distinct possibility that on the twentieth day of the fourth month of the year thirty-one of the forty-ninth tlahok, a flight carrying the emblem of the Prince of Kaleh was launched and was heading toward the Forest of Kesh in Kaleh when it disappeared.

> Now consider this: [406]If such a craft crashed into the Forest of Kesh, its remains would consist of gossamer sails, emblazoned with the prince's symbol; light-wood beams; three clear plastic fuel bottles; sponges (to seal the bottles); plastic twine; and a small box engine.[407]But this matches *exactly* the gross properties of the Forest of Kesh debris. [408]Everyone agrees that the Ashekh debris consisted of a gossamer-like substance with a pattern on it that closely or exactly resembled

the emblem of the Prince of Kaleh, light-wood-like beams, three clear bottle-like objects, pieces of a spongelike material, tough string, and a small box. [409]If the Ashekh debris was from a crashed, otherworldly spacecraft, then this amazing cloudship match was coincidental. [410]But the chances are infinitesimal that a crashed exotic craft would just happen to leave wreckage that so closely and coincidentally matched, even in gross appearance, the parts of a reconnaissance cloudship that may well have disappeared in the same area at roughly the same time. It's ridiculous to believe that such a fantastically incredible coincidence occurred. [411]So the material was almost certainly not that of a crashed otherworldly craft.

Summary of Skeptic's First Argument

[409]If the debris did come from a crashed otherworldly craft, then the match was coincidental.

[410]But the match was not coincidental (since the chances of such a coincidence would be negligibly small).

---

[411]The debris did not come from a crashed otherworldly craft. (MT)

Skeptic's Second Argument

[412][vs. 87, p. 1c] My dear Believer, you say (see 87) that "the recovered materials, the bodies, and the ship itself were exotic, otherworldly." [413]Now if the material was otherworldly, then an otherworldly ship crashed. But I've just proven that ([411])the debris was almost certainly not that of a crashed otherworldly craft. [414]So the materials were almost certainly not otherworldly.

Summary of Skeptic's Second Argument

> [413] If the material was otherworldly, then an otherworldly ship crashed.
>
> [411] The debris did not come from a crashed otherworldly craft.
>
> ---
>
> [414] The materials were not otherworldly (MT).

Robert was surprised that the author, a believer in alien visitation, found no fault with the premises or the logic of Skeptic's first argument here. The author says:

> [415] [vs. 413] I actually agree with Skeptic when he says, "[410] The match was not coincidental," and so I agree that "[411] The debris was not that of a crashed otherworldly craft."
>
> But I think his claim that "[413] If the material was otherworldly, then an alien ship crashed" is baseless because it is possible that the material was exotic even if there had been no crash. This is possible because the materials could have been left by aliens in order to *simulate* a crash—that is, the aliens might have *staged* a crash. In this case the materials would be otherworldly without a crash having occurred at all. Since 413 is baseless, the conclusion "[414] The materials were almost certainly not otherworldly" is also unjustified. [415] Skeptic, although he has proven there was almost certainly no crash, simply has not shown that the materials were not otherworldly. (But notice that a claim that the materials *were* otherworldly requires the aliens to have staged a crash.)

The author went on to claim that the eyewitness accounts of the strange properties of the materials proved the materials were otherworldly. Since the debris was otherworldly yet there was no crash, he concluded that the alleged crash was an instance of alien stagecraft.

The strange insignia printed on the gossamer sheet
found in the debris, as remembered years later by a witness

The emblem of the prince of Kaleh

[To read the "Amazing Coincidence" argument, go to Appendix 2, page 233]

This argument jogged Robert's memory. He read an article once about the alleged crash of a flying saucer at Roswell, New Mexico, in 1947. The author had noted that the Roswell debris, as reported by various witnesses, was, in gross appearance, exactly the same as what one would expect the wreckage of a US Army Mogul surveillance balloon train to look like. The author of the article saw this as proof that there was no UFO crash at Roswell. Robert went to his computer and Googled the Roswell incident.

He was shocked at how similar these two cases were. In both, wreckage was found in a remote area. Years later the first responders and others, all respectable citizens, described the materials as "not of this world." In both cases there were alleged government cover-ups. And many of the arguments in the controversies surrounding both cases were similar. For instance skeptics attempted to refute the extraterrestrial hypothesis by pointing to the similarity between the crash debris and parts of airborne devices that had been lost only days or weeks before the crash.

What's going on here? Robert wondered.

In a note appended to the dialectic—a note Robert translated and included in his document for the group—Kholoruuf stated:

Skeptic's argument (at 409–411) is very solid and shows without doubt that there was no otherworldly crash at Ashekh. But seemingly in conflict with this conclusion, the "witness reports" argument shows that *the debris was not of this world.* This dilemma can be solved only by supposing that the alleged crash was not a crash at all but in fact an event *staged* by races not of this earth. The author affirms this solution but does not expand upon it. For instance he does not speculate as to what purpose such a theatrical event would serve. Perhaps we can add to his idea and at some point include it in the dialectical cycles for this topic.

Those who are struggling to learn the full truth about the UFO [literally *mystic ship*] phenomenon must realize they are attempting to study something that knows it is being studied, and such a study is a discipline for which science is ill suited; this study falls more within the scope of deductive detective work or the work of the philosopher—or, since we are dealing with alien stagecraft, the work of the drama critic. To determine the secret motives of advanced thinkers who know they are being studied, one can only look to the *results* of their actions and assume that the plans and results are the same.

So what was the result of the alleged crash at Ashekh? The result was a government cover-up of the entire otherworldly visitation phenomenon. We can imagine how these creatures might describe their plan: "We wish to reveal our presence to the people of earth in our own way. To keep the government of this land from disclosing our presence in some other way, we will give them a crashed ship, something they would guard so zealously that they would act to cover up the entire phenomenon." But why would the debris so closely resemble parts of the missing unmanned cloudship? It can only be that the "crash" was designed to have three different effects: First, the debris prevented any government disclosure. Second, the superficial match with the drone materials allowed the scientific and academic ranks to ignore the phenomenon. Third, the alien presentation spoke to the dialecticians, those who could identify and solve the dilemma, showing these logicians more about the otherworldly beings than even those in the government were aware of. The next question is "Why, among nongovernmental people, were the *dialecticians* singled out to receive this knowledge?"

Although Robert always had been curious about UFOs, he never had formed an opinion regarding the reality of alien visitation. But now, for him, the mere fact of the incredible resemblance between the Roswell and Ashekh events pointed to the reality of an extraterrestrial visitation.

It is, Robert speculated, *as if in some supercomputer on some alien world there resides a step-by-step plan for engaging more primitive races, a plan designed in the most distant antiquity imaginable, and applied—with utter perfection—on innumerable worlds over vast eons of time.*

On Monday Robert attended the morning meeting at the site.

"This is what a Truth-Engine book looks like," he said, as he handed out copies of his translation of the *Ship from Another World* book. "These dialecticians of the Truth Engine were expert technicians who worked to resolve controversial issues by taking data from researchers of different kinds—scientists, historians, and others—and also taking ideas from the public and using the dialectical process to put the pieces together. They did all this in order to reveal what's true, what's good, and what's beautiful."

Robert spent the rest of the morning working with a few of the other books in the Theoretics Library. He tried to translate a four-page, handwritten notebook—apparently a rule book—that Will had found in a drawer underneath the game set, but he could make sense of only the last two pages. The first six pages had been written, using the Atl alphabet, in a language that was unknown to him.

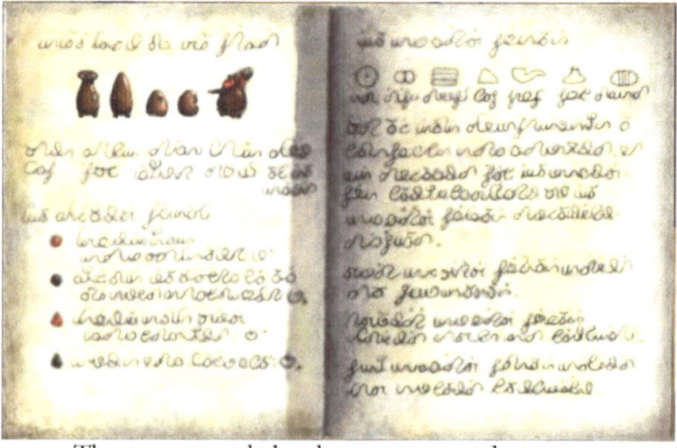

Reconstruction. The game set in the Theoretics Library

The game set rule book, pages one and two

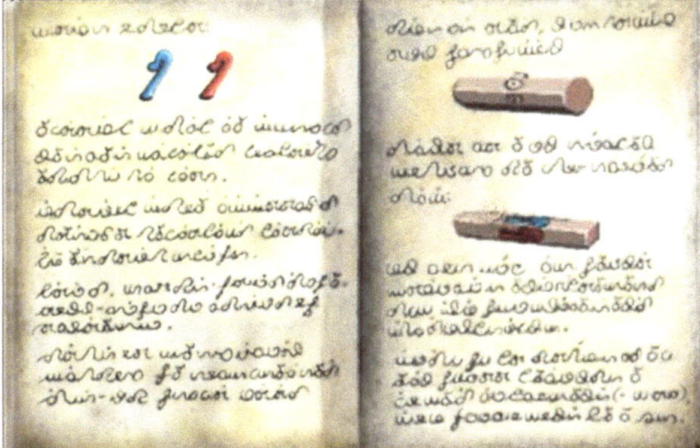

The game set rule book, pages three and four

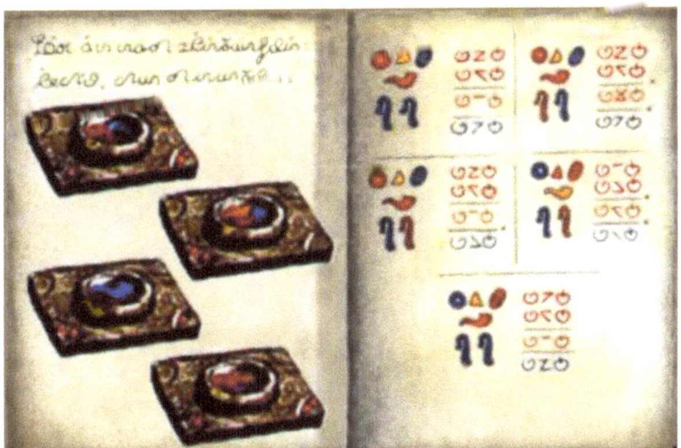

The game set rule book, pages five and six

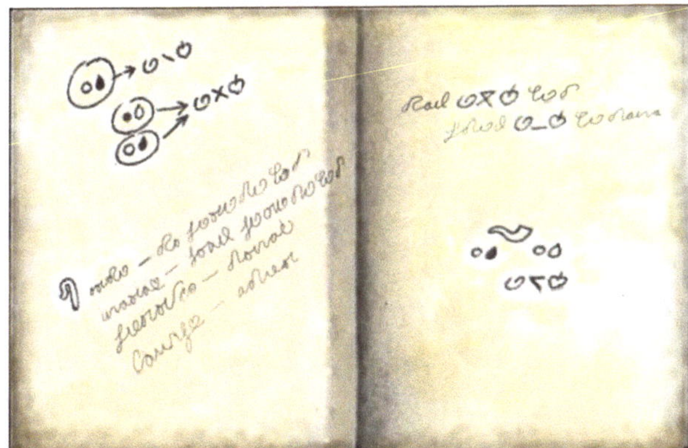

The game set rule book, pages 7 and 8. The writing on these pages is in the Atl language. The note on the left-hand page reads, "Left: first conclusion; right: second conclusion; blue: true; red: false." On the right-hand page the text reads, "If ◔ ✘ ◕ is false, then ◔ — ◕ is true"

Robert expected not to hear any feedback about the UFO dialectic until the next day, but at lunchtime, as soon as he walked into the RV to join the others, Orten lit into him.

"Hey, Robert," he said, "so Kholoruuf, our great logical guru, believed in flying saucers! What a guy!"

"Don't you find it at least interesting," Robert said, "that there seems to be an amazing parallel between the Atlanian UFO phenomenon and the modern-day one?"

"Aw, don't tell me you're one of those nuts, Robert. Don't tell me *you* believe in this crap." Orten made no attempt to conceal his disdain for anyone who might take the topic seriously.

"Well, I find it interesting that the Ashekh material so closely resembles the Roswell—"

"Roswell?" Orten laughed. "Look. Of course there'll be parallels. Any civilization advanced enough to know that the earth is just one of many planets in the universe is going to start imagining that extraterrestrial beings might be visiting us. These folks will start seeing things in the sky that they can't immediately explain, and then many of the more credulous types will start thinking that flying saucers are buzzing around our skies. But it's all nuts."

The incredible parallel between Ashekh and Roswell had convinced Robert that there may well be something to the claim that there were otherworldly visitors on earth. At the very least, he felt, it wasn't "nuts" to want to explore the issue. He thought he'd give reasoned discussion with Orten another try.

"How do you explain the fact that the aliens that appear with dinosaurs in those paintings exactly reflect our modern cultural concept of what aliens look like?"

"The supposed aliens look similar because of parallel psychologies—those of Kholoruuf's time and ours. It's an archetype: the wise infant or the wise embryo. Didn't you see *2001: A Space Odyssey,* with that embryo floating out in space, looking at the earth?"

Robert never had heard of such an archetype but wasn't of a mind to dismiss the idea out of hand. Still he considered the Ashekh-Roswell parallel to be compelling. "Yes, I saw it. But—"

"OK. That's enough stupid talk. Kholoruuf was a believer, and that's that."

Robert bristled at Orten's attempt to end the discussion and decided to press the issue just a little more. "The presence of aliens in the paintings," he said, "and the Mesozoic theme—these paintings mean something."

"*What* do they mean?" Orten said angrily.

Robert shrugged. "I don't know."

After lunch, Robert went back up to the Theoretics Library. He found it interesting that Orten had been so keen on bringing up the UFO business but had so completely avoided any discussion of the structure and utility of the Truth-Engine books as a genre.

Robert had planned to translate the second Truth-Engine book next, the one about the cloths, but, instead, he decided to take a look at the *Pseudo-Preshtiata Atlas*, the book that the cover sheet to *Land and Sea* had described as showing the history of the earth according to the expanding-earth theory. Leaving the book on top of the cabinet, he photographed every page of it.

That night he translated the book, which contained only a small amount of text. He found that geologists in Kholoruuf's day had divided earth's history into eras similar to those that modern geologists had identified. This made it possible for Robert to add several geological terms to his lexicon. The Atlanians had words that roughly corresponded to "Precambrian," "Cambrian," "Permian," "Triassic," "Jurassic," and "Cretaceous." Robert didn't give a presentation on the atlas but did leave copies of his translation in the RV for the team members to take.

Next he decided to investigate the books in the slim bookcase that stood in the southwest corner of the Theoretics Library. He opened his briefcase, pulled out Will's partial translations of these books, and looked through them. His attention was drawn to an entry in a list of section headings for one of the books; the entry read, "Dialectical Happiness." He found no translation of this section in Will's document, so he went over to the bookcase, located the book, opened it on his table, and turned to the section. Here was a text written by Kholoruuf in his own hand. He thought about the first time he had seen Kholoruuf's handwriting, when he had discovered the note in the Room of Shields at the site in the Catskills, the note that had led him here. He mused about what would happen if he were to give a photo of that note to the group.

He sat down at his table and immediately realized he'd left his laptop in the 4Runner, so he got up and walked out of the library. As he headed toward the stairs, he heard Jennifer talking to someone in the main room below. From the top of the stairs, he saw she was talking to Jimmy. By the time Robert reached the ground-level landing, Jennifer was yelling.

"Don't say you know if you don't know! Damn it! You're a dumb shit, Jimmy. Fucking dumb! And you're *not* indispensable! If you don't know the answer to my question, then go upstairs and get John. Maybe *he* knows." She stepped up to the cowering man's face, and in a stern voice said, "Jimmy…Go upstairs…Get John. Tell him to come down here."

As Jimmy brushed past Robert and headed up the stairs, Jennifer looked up at Orten, who was just coming down from the top floor. Then she looked at Robert, who had stopped and was staring at her. "Don't be so interested in what doesn't concern you, Robert," she said. "You're dispensable too. We can always find someone else to piss off the professor."

Orten let out an explosive guffaw. Smiling broadly, he looked at Robert. "Why do I always imagine her with a whip?" Then he laughed again.

Robert went outside and got his laptop. He was glad he'd seen this side of Jennifer for himself.

Back at his table, he brought up the Grayling Conservancy's new Atl-language site on his laptop, entered his user name and password, and connected to the lexicon. He was becoming good at reading Atl and found it less and less necessary to refer to the lexicon as he translated.

The "Dialectical Happiness" section was short, and he was able to translate it in one sitting. His translation went as follows:

We feel that on every populated world, a Truth Engine must emerge with teleological [literally "cosmic"] necessity. As I see it, this means that our work, the work of the Enginists, is in complete harmony with the cosmic currents. I believe the universe supports our activities when we are in tune with it. When we are at one with the cosmos, we experience a joyful life well lived.

Today was the day of the Festival of the Truth-Engine Novices. We hosted 212 guests in the main room and in the seaside yard. I was told that more than one thousand attended the celebrations at the Grand Truth Engine in North America [*Kaleh*]. The weather here was as beautiful as it has ever been on a festival day, and we hung banners from poles from the house to the garden hedges. There was food and music and dialectical fun, with many wonderful ideas contributed on both general and specific subjects. Tonight I was pondering a parallel I sometimes think of that I feel somehow captures the spirit of the Truth Engine and could be applied to many other projects carried out in tune with the cosmic forces: I think of how we awaken to a beautiful day in midsummer, when we sense that all is right with the world. On a day such as this, we feel that all things are possible and that nature, in the tangible form of clement weather, will cooperate as we carry out our human plans. We have somewhere to go this day—an art show, a charity event, a big game, or a wonderful party—where we will be together with others, deepening our relationships and forming new ones. We know it will be the kind of day when, at its end, we will say, "We had fun today—and we accomplished so much. We did something wonderful today."

I think work can be like this for the Truth-Engine participant every day, because what we do is done in harmony with the cosmos. We experience each new day as a day full of opportunity to have great fun with others, to tackle and subdue intellectual challenges of the highest order and greatest importance, to see who among us—each a champion of truth, goodness, and beauty—can rise the highest, and to do wondrous, positive, creative things together.

This is my vision of dialectical happiness.

It dawned on Robert that the Grand Truth Engine might well be the very building he had discovered in the Catskill Mountains. That building was in "Kaleh;" it possessed a kind of grandeur, and Kholoruuf had taken great pains to preserve it. Robert decided to call the building the Grand Truth Engine.

On his way out that evening, he found himself just behind Jimmy. Robert had been wondering why Jimmy took the abuse Jennifer had just subjected him to.

Catching up with him, Robert said, "Jennifer was so out of line. Didn't you want to holler back at her?"

Jimmy looked at him and smirked. "If she hollers at you, you just take it."

"Why?"

"Because of what's coming."

"What's coming?"

Jimmy rubbed his thumb against his fingers in the sign for "money."

So they're banking on the idea that they'll be selling the advanced technology to the highest bidder, Robert thought.

CHAPTER 7
ANCIENT GOODNESS

As Robert headed home that night, he thought about his plan to investigate the rooms in their "Truth," "Goodness," "Beauty" order. He decided it might be a good time to move from the Truth division into the Goodness division. Since he'd found the Pangaea of Goodness in the Astrology Room, he thought he would take a look in there to see whether he could find anything on ethics that might connect with the more general logic materials he'd discovered in the Theoretics Library. Would there be, for instance, objects or texts that would guide a novice (as he was beginning to see himself) from the pure logic of the library to skills for managing Truth-Engine books dedicated to ethical issues?

The next day, Robert, on his way to the Astrology Room, went into Kholoruuf's bedroom, where Janice and Sam had set up a table and were dissecting Kholoruuf's computer.

"How's it going?" Robert asked. He got along better with the newer people.

"We're completely stumped," Janice said, shaking her head. "We don't even know where the files were stored in this thing. Look at this."

She lifted a metal plate to show Robert the inside of the computer. The cabinet was filled with a pile of thousands of white grains.

Robert leaned closer. "Someone dumped salt in there?" he said.

"That's the circuitry," Janice said. "Their electronic components were nothing like ours. What you're looking at is a conglomeration of a vast number of tiny crystals cemented together. Go ahead and touch it."

Robert reached out and ran his finger across the pile. "It's like a rock," he said.

Sam gestured toward a microscope on their table. "We've examined the grains," he said. Each grain is a crystalline structure enclosing an incredible number of tiny specks. We don't know what they are. We have absolutely no idea how they functioned, but we can apply electric current and get a modified response. We think that whatever these components are, there's every reason to believe they don't degrade. We don't understand how to relate these structures to modern-day components—resistors, capacitors, coils, and so forth—but if we could just figure out how to *start* this computer, it might function just as it did fourteen thousand years ago."

"These components, if they were preserved as they have been up 'til now, would still work in a million years," Janice said. "Really, really high tech. These people were extremely advanced."

"Do you think any files can be recovered?" Robert asked.

Sam looked up at him. "We think the information that was stored in this thing back then is still there. If we could just figure out how to operate the thing…"

"That's incredible," Robert said. "There's no telling what might be stored in that memory." He stepped back from the table and scanned the room. It occurred to him that, although he wanted to investigate the Astrology Room soon, it might be a good time to take a look at the dream pages Eddy had been translating. "Do you know where the dream pages are?" he asked.

Sam pointed in the direction of the library to a set of shelves built into the wall. "Right there," he replied.

Robert walked over to the shelves and carefully pulled out a dream page. Within a night-themed decorative border, Kholoruuf had written a short couple of sentences in longhand across the top. Below these were several word-processed paragraphs that, as Eddy had made clear at the meeting, were also written by Kholoruuf.

"Do you know if Eddy handed out any copies of his translations of these?" Robert asked.

Sam and Janice told him they didn't know. Robert took the page into the Theoretics Library, where he learned from John that Eddy had been ordered to put his work on the dream pages aside.

"Orten's obsessed about documenting the flying machine," John told him. "He wanted Eddy to assist Scott and the others out there," he said, gesturing toward the room that contained the airship.

Robert spent the next several hours at his table in the Library working on his own translation of the page. The handwritten part described the dream itself: "A viper is biting my hand. Then I realize there is no poison in the wound at all."

The word-processed part was commentary:

This dream came to me just when I had been considering the question of a dream's ability to reveal future events, or ordinarily unknowable facts of the past or present.

I awoke and wrote down the dream. Then I went over to T's shop on the northern Akhri. At one point T asked me to hold a board while he drilled into it. The *kash* [chuck?] hit my hand, leaving two red marks exactly like those a viper would make. And just as the snake bite to my hand in the dream delivered no venom, the wounds I received from the drill weren't at all serious.

But how can a dream possibly reveal a past, present, or future that is neither presented to our senses nor knowable by ordinary inference? Our thinkers are starting to ask these old questions again, and if we consult the old dialectics, we can find hypotheses. For instance, we find there this argument by the third logician:

> Randomness yields an opening into the transcendental realm and so can give us nontrivial knowledge a priori. Look at the coin-toss readings, the cards, astrology, and other oracles. (Astrol. Dialectic 142)

> Our thoughts become random in sleep, so dreams are oracular. In death our thoughts' randomness is maximized, and so then is our experience of the other realm. [Astrol. Dialectic 363]

So dreams apparently are oracular; but is astrology oracular? Can it reveal what we might otherwise expect to be unknowable? We should revive the astrology dialectic to find out. But whether or not the study of planets, signs, and houses is oracular, astrology is surely a true science of irrational dispositions (what we call the "curtains"), so it gives us a key to the primary irrational and destructive element in the psyche of a good person. Whereas the Pangaea of Theory represents the unification of the world via the Truth Engine, the Pangaea of Goodness symbolizes the unity of the individual, via the overcoming of the negative aspects of these predispositions. Individual (psychic) unity of the Truth-Engine participants empowers us by perfecting the Truth Engine.

Reconstruction. The bed, the bedroom computer, and the cabinet.

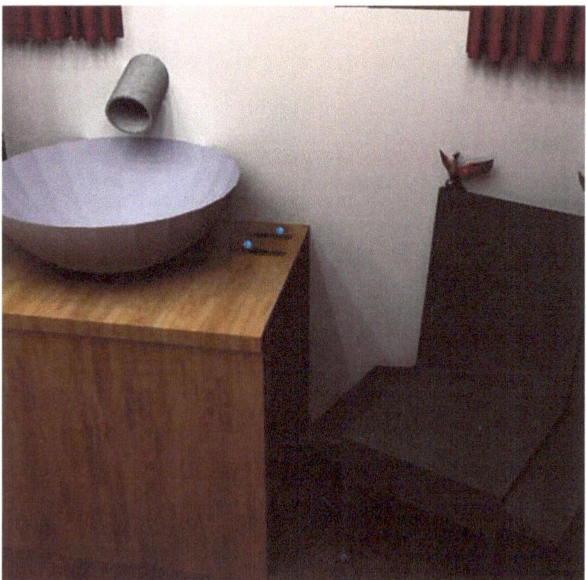

Reconstruction. The washbasin

Reconstruction. The bedroom door to the Theoretics Library and the dream-book shelf

Reconstruction. The bedroom door into the astrology room

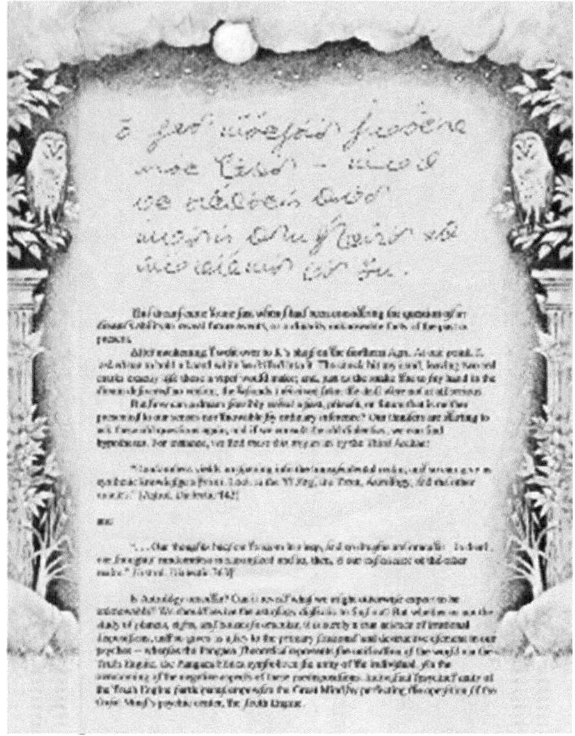

The dream page

After lunch Robert began to investigate the astrology room. His attention was immediately drawn to a thin notebook on a table in the corner of the room. He carefully opened it and looked at the first page. Across the top, written in Kholoruuf's handwriting, was a heading Robert found he could translate without consulting the lexicon. It read, "Notes on Goodness." Realizing this document could help guide his investigations of the "Goodness" rooms in the house, he took it into the Theoretics Library and photographed every page. After putting the notebook back on the table in the astrology room, he transferred the image files to his laptop and went out to the white camper to study them more carefully. He was able to translate enough of the text to determine it was a good, succinct introduction to how Kholoruuf himself conceived of moral issues. He decided to go home and translate it.

He spent several days translating the seven notebook pages. In one section of the notebook, Kholoruuf listed the ethical theories with which he was familiar. Robert wondered whether there were modern versions of these theories and, if there were, what they were called, so he e-mailed descriptions of the theories on Kholoruuf's list to a colleague who had a PhD in philosophy and asked for the modern names. His friend wrote back:

Hi, Robert. As you suggested, we would call your theory number one (maximizing happiness) a utilitarian theory.

I think we'd call theory number two an altruism theory—you might tack "radical" in front of it: radical altruism.

As you surmised, we'd call number three an egalitarian theory.

Number four: I've never come across such a theory—it's a hybrid. I suppose you could call it a utilitarian-egalitarian theory. Interesting.

Five: an egoist theory. You might call it a conscientious-egoist theory.

Six: Sounds like what you might describe as a radical-libertarian theory.

Seven: deontological theory.

Hope this helps and hope you are doing well.

Best,
Thomas

Robert wasn't trained in ethics and never had looked closely at his own moral feelings in an analytical way, yet he saw himself as a person who always tried to do what was right and who was prepared to sacrifice his own happiness when it was the right thing to do.

Despite his lack of expert knowledge, he felt that with the help he'd gotten from Thomas he could prepare a faithful translation of Kholoruuf's notebook.

As Robert worked on the translation, he became aware that Kholoruuf chose the conscience as the focal point of his guide to ethics. Kholoruuf wrote:

We keep the ivory Goodness Box inside the ivory Truth Box, and we keep the ivory Truth Box in the Grand Truth Engine. When the novice opens the Goodness Box, he will find only one template slide there. But I keep six more Goodness template slides on hand. Why?

I am the director of the Grand Truth Engine. If I could know with clarity what the directive or directives of my conscience are (and surely my conscience is like the consciences of good people in general), then I would maintain only a single Goodness template slide for the projector.

But the nature of our conscience is hidden even from ourselves. There are a number of respected theories on this, and since it is not completely clear which theory is correct, I have directed that templates representing the thought of each of the following seven kinds of dialectician be kept at the Grand Truth Engine and that the slide that the third chief logician placed inside the Goodness Box (the utilitarian slide) remain there. Here are the seven kinds of dialecticians:

1. The utilitarian [Atl: *kashtshanehr*—literally "smile maker"] believes our conscience contains only this one directive: "Maximize the probable happiness of all people."

2. The radical altruist [Atl: *petehrbat*—literally "sufferer"] believes our conscience contains only this one directive: "Maximize the probable happiness of all people except yourself."

3. The egalitarian [Atl: *kezhtankk*—literally "balancer"] believes our conscience contains only this one directive: "Maximize the equality of the distribution of probable happiness among all people."

4. The utilitarian egalitarian [Atl: *shomash*—literally: ?] believes our conscience contains only this one directive: "Maximize everyone's probable happiness, and maximize the equality of its distribution."

5. The conscientious egoist [Atl: *tahettke*—literally "self alone"] believes our conscience contains only this one directive: "Maximize the potential happiness of yourself."

6. The radical libertarian [Atl: *mekhatshar*—literally "unencumbered"] believes our conscience contains only this one directive: "Do not harm innocent people."

7. The deontologist [Atl: *alekattuparu*—literally "here-now theorist"] believes our conscience contains at least one "nonconsequentialist" directive (that is, one directive that does not have to do with results of the action). For instance a deontologist might believe our conscience contains this set of directives: "Be beneficent. Don't lie. Don't steal. Keep your promises. Don't kill," wherein only the first directive is consequentialist."

Robert noted Kholoruuf's comment about the nested ivory boxes in the Grand Truth Engine and remembered finding just such a set of boxes in the building in the Catskills. He was now convinced he'd been correct in identifying that building with the Grand Truth Engine. The boxes he'd seen there had seemed empty—but was a "utilitarian slide" hidden in one of them?

Robert wondered which if any of the possible conscience types on Kholoruuf's list corresponded to his own conscience. He thought about how it seemed right to make people—that is, himself and others—happy and how sharing seemed right, so he decided the utilitarian-egalitarian version was the closest match.

He was taken with the idea of the cause/effect/action/nonaction, or CEANA (in Atl, *NEOSHO*) statement. A Kholoruufian CEANA statement was a complex, diagram-like statement that laid out all the major possible actions a person could take in a given a situation and showed the possible results of those actions in terms of happiness, assigning probabilities to each result.

[To read Robert's translation of Kholoruuf's "Notes on Goodness," go to Appendix 3, page 239]

Months earlier, in the large central room of the Grand Truth Engine in the Catskills, Robert had found several horoscopes and had added the Atlanian names of the planets, signs, and houses to his lexicon. But since he'd known nothing about astrology and always had assumed that astrology was a pseudoscience, he had made no attempt to understand the Atlanian astrological system. Kholoruuf, though, apparently had seen the discipline as being an essential part of the study of goodness, and Robert now resolved to give Atlanian astrology the attention it deserved. He went back to his favorite bookstore, Exclusive Books, at the V&A Waterfront, and bought the most technical astrology book he could find, and did some Internet research as well. He wanted to learn how the modern western version of this esoteric discipline was similar and dissimilar to Kholoruuf's version.

Reconstruction. Astrology devices in the Astrology Room

Reconstruction. The desk in the Astrology Room

Reconstruction. The small astrology table

Reconstruction. An astrological table that shows the earth
(with the South Pole protruding) and segments representing
the twelve signs of the zodiac

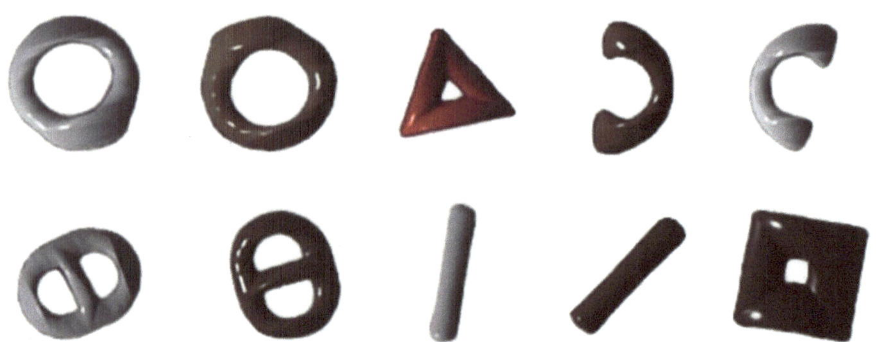

Pieces representing the sun, moon, and planets:

Sun	Moon	Mercury	Venus	Mars
Jupiter	Saturn	Uranus	Neptune	Pluto

Robert soon realized he didn't have enough information about the Atlanian astrology system to allow him to get a clear picture of it.

At one of the group's morning meetings in the white camper, he handed out copies of his translation of Kholoruuf's "Notes on Goodness." He stayed after the meeting to talk to Orten alone.

"Has anyone come across any texts on astrology in the house?" Robert asked him.

"Not that I know of," Orten said. "We still haven't been able to open the door to the basement, though—we've been remiss about that—or the door to the Core Room."

"It was apparently a big part of Kholoruuf's belief system. You'd think there'd be some books about it around."

"Well," Orten said, "the fact that there aren't any astrology books here doesn't mean it wasn't important to them. You know, there aren't any medical books here that we know of, but we can assume that medicine was important to them. On the other hand, maybe astrology wasn't a big part of his belief system. Maybe he was rational about this *one thing* and just liked to collect astrology stuff—you know, quaint relics from a more superstitious time. Maybe Kholoruuf just didn't treat the subject seriously enough to have any books on it."

Robert had seen the astrology machine in the Grand Truth Engine and knew Orten was wrong. "I think he was serious about it."

"Here I'm saying he wasn't a crackpot about *everything*, and you're arguing with me about it. Won't you allow me my fantasies?"

"I think he treated the subject in a serious way, and I don't think he was a crackpot."

Orten shook his head. "Oh. OK. You believe in astrology too. Look, Robert, if you insist on following up on this crazy stuff, there are a couple pages of what we were pretty sure was an astrological discourse, or whatever, up there in Finland, in the House of Birth."

"That's interesting," Robert said. "Were a lot of books found there?" For some reason he hadn't imagined that the house in Finland might have interesting texts in it.

"Yeah. Mostly children's books. We couldn't translate them really—a lot of pictures but not much text."

"Why is it called the House of Birth?"

"Probably because there's a cradle there, kids' books, and the astrology materials.

"How can I see the astrology texts?"

Orten smiled. "You can go up there and look at them."

"Can't they send copies here?"

"No. We can't send copies here, because we're here, not there."

"So we're *the* team."

"I thought you knew that, Robert. We're the archaeological team."

"So I can actually get in there and see the place myself?"

"Oh, yeah. Any member of the team can."

Robert didn't know why Orten was being so helpful; perhaps he just wanted him out of his hair for a while. Whatever the reason, Robert wasn't going to let this opportunity slip away. "I'd love to go up there and take a look," he said.

"When do you want to go?"

"Right away? Day after tomorrow—or tomorrow?"

Orten smiled. "OK." He grabbed a piece of paper, drew a map, wrote some notes on it, and handed it to Robert. "Here's a map to one of the great archaeological discoveries of our time. Don't let anyone else see it. Stop by the office tomorrow morning, and the receptionist will have a key for you."

"I'll be at the site alone?"

"Why not? You can get into *this* site alone. You should probably stop in at the Grayling office in Helsinki first. I wrote the address on the map. There's a slight chance someone will be there. If no one's there, just go on up to the site."

Robert decided to spend the rest of the day preparing for his journey. He left the camper thinking about how, very soon, he would be the only person alive to have seen the three Atlanian sites. He thought again about the great responsibility that his knowledge of these discoveries carried with it and about how he could not falter in his resolve to do everything in his power to prevent a wholesale cover-up. He was completely aware of the difficulties he faced—the Grayling group and its overseers would act determinedly to quash any attempted release of information about the sites—but he would not lose hope. He would keep watching for an opportunity to accomplish his goal. For now, though, he could allow himself the excitement of a new adventure.

CHAPTER 8
A JOURNEY NORTH

At the guesthouse, Robert made plans for the trip. He was excited by the prospect of seeing the other site. According to Orten's map and notes, he should fly to Helsinki, visit the Grayling Conservancy office there, then either fly to Rovaniemi and drive to the site or drive all the way from Helsinki. He figured he'd arrive and take care of things in Helsinki early in the day, start the drive north, and after eight hours on the road—or more, depending on the winter road conditions—he'd spend the night at a hotel en route to his destination. He'd stay at the hotel for a few days, traveling to and from the site. He checked weather forecasts and realized that if he left for Finland soon he'd be sure not to run into any snowstorms, so on the Internet, he booked a flight to Helsinki then made a reservation for three nights at a hotel on the shore of the Baltic Sea. He also made reservations for his flight out of Finland.

The next morning he got the key at the conservancy office and in the evening flew out of Cape Town, slept on the plane, and arrived at Helsinki at 7:00 a.m. He rented a Ford Explorer at the airport and drove to the Grayling office on Pursimiehenkatu, a street near the city center. Like the reading room in Cape Town, the storefront had a single plate-glass window and a glass door. Written on the glass door were the words, GRAYLING CONSERVANCY.

Robert tried the door, but it was locked. Looking through the windows, he saw an unlit office-like setup inside. He pressed the doorbell and heard it ring inside, but no one came. He waited two minutes and walked away, feeling relieved that he wouldn't have to deal with any conservancy people.

He had brunch at a restaurant with an English name, the Old Mill, then drove north out of Helsinki toward the city of Oulu. Snow covered the landscape, but the road was clear. Robert made good time, stopping only twice and arriving at Oulu at about five thirty in the afternoon. He went right through Oulu and headed up the coast to the hotel.

An hour and a half later, he had checked into a cozy cabin-style accommodation with a daytime view of the frozen Bay of Bothnia, the northern arm of the Baltic Sea. He had dinner at the hotel restaurant, watched some American TV shows, and went to bed early.

The next morning, after breakfast, he headed toward Rovaniemi on the road that would take him to the site. Orten's map indicated that the turnoff to the site was marked by a red sign with GC written on it—the GPS coordinates were on the map. After about an hour and a half, he found the turnoff and drove up the side road, which was little more than a trail through the evergreen forest. There was a little snow on the trail, but it recently had been plowed.

Arriving at a high chain link security fence, Robert got out and opened the fence's gate with the key the receptionist in Cape Town had given him. He drove through the gate, got out, relocked it, and continued up the road. The road curved left and then right as the upward incline grew steeper. To his left, through the trees, he noticed an even steeper snow-covered slope and wondered whether it was the hill that enclosed the House of Birth. Robert drove another thirty yards up to more level terrain. He judged he was now on top of the hill he'd spotted from the road. When he rounded a curve to his left, a small windowless metal building came into view in front of him near where the road ended. Next to the building was a small shed. Wires extended from the shed to the building, so Robert assumed that the shed housed a generator.

He pulled up and stopped near the metal building's door. Not seeing any other vehicles, he concluded the place was deserted. He grabbed a flashlight and his camera equipment, got out of the SUV, and walked up to the door, which had the word YKSITYISALUE stenciled on it. He used the same key he'd used to unlock the gate to unlock the door's lock, opened the door, and shined his flashlight into the enclosure.

The place was empty. Near the back wall, he saw a square opening in the floor. Walking over to the opening and shining his light into it, Robert noticed a modern-looking metal staircase that led down into a cave-like area.

Outside, Robert turned off his flashlight and put it in his pocket, opened the shed, and started the generator. Then he went back into the building and down the metal steps into the now well-lit subterranean space, finding himself at one end of a straight, down-sloping, rock-walled corridor. Making sure he still had his flashlight in his pocket, he walked down the incline.

After about forty-five feet, he came to a plastic-like wall and a breached doorway with the familiar two-ringed Truth-Engine symbol above it. He went through the opening and emerged into a large space not farther than ten feet from the front of the House of Birth.

The house was tiny, perhaps only sixteen feet long, nine or ten feet wide, and sixteen feet high. *Was this really Kholoruuf's birthplace?* he wondered. He examined the ancient, gray, wooden façade, trying to imagine what it must have looked like when a little boy named Kholoruuf might have lived there so many millennia before.

The door was open, and Robert walked into the house's musty main room, which was now lit by a modern lamp mounted on a stand in the middle of the room. The dilapidated state of the objects in the room created an atmosphere of great antiquity. To his right was a door, perhaps to a closet or a bathroom. Beyond that was a stove with a range hood above it. On the floor to his left was a wooden cradle and beyond that a bookcase. In the far right corner, he saw a nightstand next to a bed. He noticed some letters inconspicuously carved into the side of the cradle. He looked closely at them—they spelled "KERE ESHANU KHOLORUUF," *Our Dear Kholoruuf.* It had been Kholoruuf's cradle.

On the night stand were some pages of ancient paper or parchment. He walked over and looked at the top sheet. On the page were two drawings, each showing what appeared to be an ecliptic disc with the earth in the middle. Looking at the text, he recognized Kholoruuf's handwriting. Robert immediately concluded that these pages might well be the very astrological papers he'd come here to see. *These pages probably should be protected better,* he thought. Robert didn't know who the caretaker of this site was, but he had the impression that he or she could be doing a better job of it.

He took a photo of the top page, looked at the back side of it and saw nothing on it, then carefully moved it aside. Then he took a photo of the next page and so forth until he'd documented all five pages. As he restacked them, he inspected each page. He found he could understand enough of the writing to be able to discern that the text was everything he'd hoped it would be: a concise exposition of the basics of the Atlanian system of astrology.

He spent the rest of the day looking through the books in the bookcase and in the nightstand. They were indeed children's books—illustrated stories. He found some to be delightful. There was a book whose main character was a delicately drawn flying bear. In another book, a boy built a city in the trees. There was a beautifully illustrated book about a young prince living in a luxurious palace on a tropical island.

The House of Birth

The stove in the House of Birth

The bed and the nightstand

Kholoruuf's cradle

He arrived back at the hotel around eight in the evening. Because he hadn't eaten since breakfast, he had a big dinner in the hotel restaurant. In his room he loaded the photos he'd taken at the House of Birth into his laptop and spent about an hour studying them. On the next day's visit to the site, he decided, he would document some of the more interesting-looking books.

The next morning he arrived at the House of Birth at around nine thirty. This time he brought a lunch with him. He spent the morning documenting several of the more charming children's books. His favorite was a beautifully illustrated story about a boy's fantastic nighttime journey. In this book, the boy, named Chanak, following a trail left in the sky by an owl he'd dusted with a glowing powder, traveled by boat on a smooth sea, under a huge moon, to attend a convention of night birds. Robert liked the book because of its especially beautiful artwork.

After lunch he decided to take a look at the ancient car Orten had told him about. He found a little garage on the side of the house and opened the door. The car inside was similar to the one in the cave in the Catskills but was still in one piece. He saw the engine and noticed that the tiny power supply was missing.

Back inside the house, he looked for the map that had pointed the conservancy people toward South Africa but couldn't find it. Then he took photos of the room.

He left the site at seven thirty, satisfied that he'd accomplished everything he'd intended to do there. He planned to spend one more night at the hotel then leave Finland. He would not be going straight back to Cape Town, though, because he wanted to take another look at the Grand Truth Engine in the Catskills.

When Robert got onto the 926 roadway, he noticed that the northern lights had begun to put on a display in the night sky. He could make out cloud-like patches of changing colors overhead. He'd never seen the northern lights before and wanted to get a better view, so he pulled off the road and got out. Now the colors were taking the shape of flickering streamers that became undulating green-and-yellow curtains. He watched for a while then got back into his Explorer and resumed his journey back to the hotel.

He'd expected the display to end before he arrived at the hotel, but as he pulled into the parking lot, the sky was alive with color. He got out and walked to his cabin behind the hotel's main building. It looked to him as if all the hotel's guests and staff were there, looking out over the Baltic Sea, watching the incredible sight—the bright, shifting lights reflecting off the frozen bay.

Robert felt strangely compelled to watch the display alone. He walked away from the other guests and toward the sea, getting near the shoreline. Now the streamers, radiating from a central point in space and filling the sky, were a brilliant red, as pure a red as any he'd ever seen. The color flowed slowly along the streamers, making them look like columns of bright, fiery, smoke. He was enthralled.

Suddenly he saw something that sent a chill through him. No more than eighteen feet away, between him and the sea, stood a man about four feet tall with huge almond-shaped black eyes and dressed in a wide-brimmed hat and heavy coat. Robert almost said hello to this being but checked his impulse. The light from the aurora and from the hotel lamps reflecting off of the snow allowed him to make out the image fairly clearly. To Robert the strange creature looked for all the world like an alien as our culture would picture one. It stared at Robert as it detached what appeared to be the hood of its coat then tugged at two strings attached to it. The creature seemed to be having difficulty manipulating these strings. It pulled one string out, then the other, put them back in, and pulled them out again. It did this several times. Then the little creature, carrying the hood in its hand, walked away, disappearing behind one of the small hills of ice that lined the shore.

Robert felt dazed. *What in the world just happened?* he wondered. *That had to be the weirdest thing I've ever seen. That wasn't a human being. And what on earth was it doing?*

Just then a brilliantly glowing orange disk-shaped object, perhaps thirty feet in diameter, appeared from behind the hill of ice and, after hovering for a moment, took a trajectory out to sea. It flew away silently and quickly, disappearing in the distance.

Robert was shocked. He stood transfixed for a moment, trying to make sense of what he had just seen.

He felt a need to be around people, *humans*, so he walked back up toward where the others were still assembled. He spoke out loud to himself as he walked. "I've seen an actual, bona fide *flying saucer*—and its alien occupant too!" *This is unreal*, he thought, *unbelievable*. Yet the experience seemed to have a familiar quality about it. *Why would it be familiar?* he wondered.

As he approached the group of spectators, a man said something to him in Finnish.

"I'm sorry, I don't speak Finnish," Robert said.

Another man, in accented English, asked him, "Did you see the orange light?"

"Yes," Robert said. "I was right there. It took off right in front of me."

"What was it?"

"I don't know…a flying saucer?"

A woman laughed, but the man said, "Maybe so."

So now Robert knew the alien visitors were real. There was nothing eccentric about Kholoruuf—the logician had known they were real too. Later, as Robert walked back to his cabin, he felt as if everything was different…yet it wasn't really.

The next day he boarded a plane in Oulu and flew to Philadelphia. He suspected the conservancy might be following his movements. He was certain they wanted to learn the location of his discoveries, and he knew there was a close connection between Grayling and the US military, so he had to be careful. He decided that if anyone was tracking him, he'd give them the impression that he was stopping off at his Pennsylvania home. He rented a car in Philadelphia, bought a slide-copying adapter for his camera at a photography-supply store, and making sure he wasn't followed, drove up to the Catskills. He didn't want anyone to see him at his home, so, using cash, he checked into a motel near his site.

He had a feeling there was something more to be found at the Grand Truth Engine. Just as Kholoruuf's house was meant to convey a symbolic meaning, he sensed the Grand Truth Engine was too.

Noting that the astrological artifacts were located in the middle division of the Grand Truth Engine, and that the sculpture halls were in the building's right side, Robert was beginning to form the opinion that the building's three physical parts corresponded to the three divisions—Truth, Goodness, and Beauty—of the Truth Engine. So he was starting to see the design of the Grand Truth Engine as representing one aspect of the Truth Engine's theoretical structure. But he felt the edifice expressed a deeper layer of symbolic significance as well. He wanted to understand that deeper significance better. To do that, he believed he had to learn the functions of the left side's telescope and the right side's projector.

Before he'd left New York on his search for Nell's Rock, Robert had discovered that the left side's telescope was used to view the screen in the building's right side—the telescope was used to view whatever the projector was projecting onto the screen. He had found some transparencies near the telescope, but they were solid black and possibly degraded. Robert guessed that the left side's slides would have been inserted into the telescope so that when the projected right-side image was viewed through the telescope, the slide frame's image would overlay the projected image.

More recently he had carefully made note of Kholoruuf's words in the Enginist's "Notes on Goodness": "We keep the ivory Goodness Box inside the ivory Truth Box, and we keep the ivory Truth Box in the Grand Truth Engine. When the novice opens the Goodness Box, he will find only one template slide there."

Robert remembered that in the right side of the house, inside the templelike building, there was an ivory box on a table. His examination of the box had revealed nothing more than two other boxes inside. He wanted to inspect the boxes more closely now to see whether he could find any transparencies inside them.

He spent the night at the motel. The next morning he stopped at a sporting goods store and bought a couple of flashlights and an LED lantern. He also purchased a 20x pocket magnifier to use in case he discovered the "template slide" Kholoruuf had mentioned in his "Notes on Goodness."

Around noon Robert filled up the car with gas and set off for the site. When he got near the cave, he turned onto a back road and parked in a field. He got out and grabbed the flashlights and magnifier and put them in his pocket. After picking up the lantern and the camera with the twenty-millimeter extension tube and slide holder attached to it, he put the camera's strap around his neck and walked through the woods toward the cave entrance. When he arrived, he pushed the camouflage cover aside, turned on the lantern, and went down through the cave.

As he stepped into the cluttered Room of the Truth Examiner, he thought about how long it had been since he'd first entered it, how long he had kept the secret of this place. He wished he could tell the world about it, but he knew if he revealed his discovery to anyone and the Conservancy people got wind of it, they might prevent the disclosure, and he also would lose his ability to influence the work being done at Nell's Koppie.

He went into the Grand Truth Engine's large central room, then through the eastern door, up the stairs, through the sculpture hallway, and over to the main room on the right side—the room that contained the projector, the screen, and the templelike building. He went up the steps and into the templelike building and walked over to the ivory box. There he held up the lantern and opened the box.

Robert's attention was drawn to a flattish, rectangular object attached to the inside of the front of the box, near the top. He'd overlooked it before because he'd assumed it contained some sort of locking mechanism. But now, examining it more carefully, he saw there was no keyhole on the outside of the box. The rectangular object could not have housed a lock. He lifted the lid of the next box, which he reasoned must be the Goodness Box. It too had a little rectangular box on the inside surface. He saw there were two tabs at the top edge of the little box. Grabbing them between thumb and forefinger, he pulled them up, and what looked like a slide mount with a film frame inside it slid out with a little hiss, as if a vacuum seal had been broken. Holding the slide up to the lantern, he saw there was some kind of patterning, perhaps writing, on the glass. *Still visible after fourteen thousand years*, he thought. He took out his magnifier and studied the glass; there indeed was writing on it. Even without using the lexicon, he could translate almost every word: "If an act…[something]…the potential happiness of all persons, then it is right. Insert the CEANA statement here. Combine the potential happiness…[something]…for each action."

The ancient slide was a little smaller than typical modern slides, so it fit easily into the slide holder in the copying adapter. He aimed the camera at the lantern and snapped a picture.

He returned the slide to its holder in the Goodness Box and pulled a similar slide out of the holder attached to the Truth Box, again breaking a seal. Using the magnifier, he could translate most of the text on this slide too: "[Something] true…One and only one of these is…Deny-Other Law." He inserted the slide into the slide holder and snapped a picture.

He put the Truth slide back where he'd found it and checked the smallest of the boxes, the Beauty box, but its slide holder was empty.

Holding the lantern in front of him, Robert walked back over to the building's left side. He went up the stairs and into the room below the telescope, where he knew the three black slides were. He walked over to the table, picked up the top slide, and examined it more closely than he had before. The film was completely opaque. Looking closely at the metal mount that held the slide, he noticed a tiny button in one corner. He pressed the button with his fingernail, and the mount opened up. He now saw that the black material wasn't a slide but a protective sleeve wrapped around a slide. He very carefully pulled the slide frame out by holding it by its edges without touching its face, inserted it into the camera's slide holder, aimed the camera at the lantern, and took a picture.

Using the same procedure, he photographed the remaining two slide frames.

Robert wanted to get back to Cape Town as soon as possible. The longer he stayed in New York, the greater the chances the Conservancy would check out the house he owned here, and he didn't want to be seen. A longer delay also might make it more likely that questions would be asked when he got back to Nell's Koppie, and he didn't want to answer any questions. His plan was to go to the motel and examine his photos of the slides. If he decided the photos would help him decode the Grand Truth Engine's architecture, he'd return to Fresnaye immediately.

A little past eight in the evening, he placed the camouflage covering over the cave entrance and drove to a restaurant, where he had his first meal of the day. Then he returned to his motel room and transferred the photos he'd taken at the site to his laptop.

In his mind, Robert went over the strange way in which the slide projector and the telescope seem to have worked together in the Grand Truth Engine. A slide, from one of the ivory boxes for instance, was placed into the projector in the building's right side and projected onto the screen in the same room. Then, on the other side of the building, another slide was inserted into the telescope. Viewing the screen through the telescope, one would see the telescope transparency superimposed over the projected image.

He wondered why the Atlanians of the Grand Truth Engine would use such an elaborate method of combining two images.

Robert wanted to simulate this compound image. Using a black pen on paper, he made a sketch of the slide frame he'd pulled from the Goodness Box, substituting the words in Atl with their English translations. Then he looked through his images of the left-side telescope slides and found the one that, if superimposed over the Goodness-Box slide, would create a coherent whole, and, using a red pen he'd gotten from the motel office and translating as required, added a rendering of this image to his sketch.

Studying his sketch, Robert realized the dual image constituted a kind of exam question, such as might be passed out to students in a classroom. The answer to the implicit question was missing, and clearly would have somehow been supplied by the student, perhaps the Truth-Engine novice, as he or she peered through the telescope. Referring to Kholoruuf's "Notes on Goodness," which was stored on his laptop, Robert fairly easily answered the question. He recognized that the question had been framed in accordance with utilitarian theory. Using a pencil, he wrote the answer on his sketch.

What he found most interesting was that the parts of the composite text representing the most general concepts and propositions, the *forms* of thought, were those parts that came from the projector slides on the right side of the building. The parts that came from the telescope slides on the left side were those that represented very particular propositions. Robert thought about something he'd read in a book on Plato about how some philosophers—Plato, Aquinas, and others—said that we immediately grasp the fundamental principles, the primitive foundations for all knowledge, intuitively and that the intuitive intellect was to be contrasted with the discursive intellect, which knows not directly but through reason and argument. It occurred to Robert that some people took the intuitive and the discursive to belong to different parts of the *human mind*, namely, to the right-brained part and to the left-brained part, respectively. The discursive materials, the logical Truth-Engine books, were in the building's left side, and the intuitive materials, including an apparently revered picture book, were in the right side. Robert finally felt he could discern the symbolism of the Grand Truth Engine's architecture: the structure of the building, he decided, symbolized *the structure of the mind of the dialectician.*

But more than this, he realized that the Logos of the Truth Engine itself, in the abstract, had been said by Apporiopasshe in the *Guide for Dialecticians* to correspond to the discursive realm and the Ikon to the intuitive. *So the Truth Engine itself represented the mind of the dialectician too*, Robert thought.

It also occurred to him that since the building in the Catskills was a Truth Engine—the Grand Truth Engine in fact—it would be appropriate to call the building's three parts the *Logos*, the *Logikon*, and the *Ikon.* The Ikon's defining feature was the open book in the templelike structure, the book that expressed the dialectician's respect for the values of truth, goodness, and beauty. He would call this book the *Ikon Core.*

Robert decided to use his laptop's graphics program to create a neater version of his sketch to include in a report to the group. Of course he wouldn't be able to explain to the others the true source of this material, but he figured he could pass it off as his own illustration of how the Atlanian dialecticians treated ethical issues.

In Robert's computer-graphics version, the black text came from the projector slide in the Ikon; the red text and figures were from the telescope transparency in the Logos; and his own additions appeared in blue.

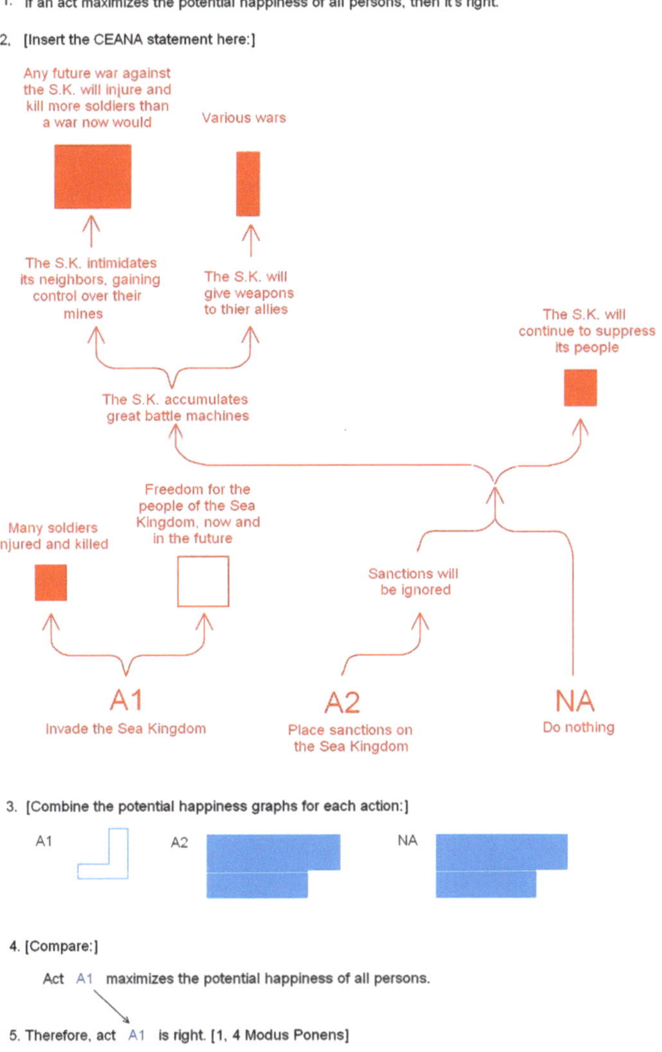

In Kholoruuf's "Notes on Goodness," Robert had read that in a CEANA statement such as this, a rectangle's horizontal dimension represented the probability of the described result, and the vertical dimension represented the amount of the resultant happiness (clear) or unhappiness (solid). The areas of the irregular shapes at the bottom represented the amount of probable happiness (or unhappiness) expected to result from the specified choice.

It occurred to Robert that if the examination of novices constituted such a central feature of what had occurred inside the Grand Truth Engine, then he could begin to see, vaguely, how the three "Examiner" rooms might have fit in.

Now he saw why the examiners might have used the elaborate telescope-projector method of testing the novice: The examiners were communicating symbolic meaning at the same time. If the building symbolized the dialectician's mind, the method represented the way the left and right joined with each other to produce unified thought. Robert entertained the idea that the astrology machine in the Logikon somehow may have played a role in the telescope-screen examination but had no idea how it might have done that.

There was still more that he wanted to investigate at the Grand Truth Engine, and he planned to do with the other slides—the Truth slides—what he'd just done with the Goodness slides, but he felt he had learned enough on this trip so that he could now return to Cape Town.

CHAPTER 9
ASTROLOGY AND THE ROOM OF DANGERS

The day after Robert arrived at the guesthouse in Fresnaye, he went up to Nell's Koppie for the morning meeting.

"Any revelations from Suomi?" Orten asked, using the Finnish word for Finland, when Robert climbed into the camper to join the others.

"I'm still thinking about it," Robert said. He *had* had revelations—one, for instance, on the icy shore of the Baltic Sea—but he couldn't tell these people about them. He could imagine Orten's reaction to hearing about his seeing the alien and its lighted craft. "I found the astrological pages. I'm translating them," Robert said.

At the meeting, Robert learned that nothing much had happened during his short absence. He asked about the door to the basement, and Orten said they planned to start working on opening it soon.

After the meeting, Robert returned to the guesthouse to start his examination of the Atlanian astrological system. With the astrology book he'd bought and his lexicon at hand, he sat down with his photos of the astrology pages and began the translation. He decided to continue his work at the site the next day and spend this evening and the next translating the astrology pages.

The next morning, wanting to get a better idea of which areas of the house Kholoruuf had conceived of as having a special connection with Goodness, Robert went into the space on the main floor where the empty bookcase was located. The team members had been calling this space the "Back Room." He examined the large round table in the center of the room.

Attached to this table along its rim were twelve curved golden ornaments with an inscription on each. He looked closely at one of the ornaments. The words on it were *"penshantak—kezhtankk—ta-met."* Robert recognized the second word from Kholoruuf's "Notes on Goodness." It meant "egalitarian." And he recognized the third word, *ta-met*, as being part of the word for Uranus, *ta-met-shaak*. On the next ornament, all the words, "Kholoruuf—*shomash—ma-shem*," were familiar: Kholoruuf, utilitarian-egalitarian, and part of the word for Saturn. So the pattern was: name, moral theory, astrological element.

Taking a pen and pad from his pocket, and working his way around the table, he made a list of the inscriptions. He found that the order of the astrological sign names matched their order around the horoscope. Consistent with the list in "Notes on Goodness," only seven different moral theories appeared on the ornaments, some of them two or three times. So it was clear to Robert that this room belonged in the Goodness category.

The ornamented table

Against the wall stood a cabinet with several game sets inside and on top of it. Robert looked at the games, wondering how they might have been played. He noticed that one of them was a differently colored version of the game in the Theoretics Library; and he had seen other examples of the same game in the Foyer Nook and in the Room of the Truth Examiner.

Robert went over to a painting on the west wall and realized this watercolor depicted an event that had taken place in this very room. The Back Room's main bookcase, the distinctive column in the corner, and a second book cabinet all had been accurately represented by the artist. The text underneath the picture was in a language that was similar to Kholoruuf's Atl but not the same. Robert could confidently make out only several expressions: "great debate," "musicians," and "in the evening."

So this is what a live Truth-Engine debate was like, he thought. Clearly there had been musical interludes during the debates: In the painting seven performers, standing on decorated platforms, played instruments and sang for the spectators, who sat on the floor in front of them.

Robert noticed that two of the spectators were playing a board game, and he immediately recognized it as one of the games he'd just looked at in the room. He turned to the cabinet on his left and saw the game on the top shelf. It was definitely the same game, its pieces topped by tiny shapes that resembled silver moons and golden suns. Turning back to the painting, he saw that the game board in the picture had a drawer sticking out of its side.

He went over to the cabinet and, carefully inspecting the actual game, was able to discern a very fine groove in the same location on the game board. Slipping the edge of his fingernail into the groove, he pulled out the drawer. Inside was a key with a single shaft and notches along its length.

The group had been looking for the key to the door that led to the basement. Robert took the key out of the drawer. *Maybe this is what we've been looking for*, he thought.

He pulled his flashlight

The painting in the Back Room

from its holster and walked through the kitchen, around the central Core Room, and to the opening in the floor. He turned on his flashlight and walked down the steep staircase into the tiny room where the basement door was located.

The games near the ornamented table

Robert inserted the key into the keyhole and turned it. After he felt it engage, he placed pressure on it and felt it moving the lock's mechanism. When he couldn't turn the key any farther, he pulled it out and pushed on the door. He budged it slightly and kept pushing, slowly opening it. He'd expected to be able to walk into a room at this point but instead found himself looking down a long staircase toward the back of the house and into a much deeper space.

He put the key in his pocket and carefully walked down the staircase. To his left, near enough to touch it, was a wall. *Is there another room beneath the Core Room?* he wondered. To his right, several yards away, another wall appeared to run the full length of the building. Shining his light along the bottom of that wall, he saw what seemed to be a natural surface of soil and rocks. When he got a little farther down, the wall on the left ended, and he saw that its edge formed the corner of an enclosure that he thought might indeed have contained a room. He walked farther down the staircase and stopped. Shining his light into the main basement space and toward the front of the building, he made out a hulking form some distance from the staircase.

He realized he needed a brighter flashlight, so he went back upstairs and over to the collection of equipment the team stored in the main room. He quickly found the Fenix TK70, turned it on low, and went back into the basement. When he neared the bottom of the stairs, he cycled his light to the "turbo" setting and shined 2,200 lumens into the space. What he saw stunned him.

As he moved the beam around, Robert saw that the basement was wider than the house above it and that, entirely enclosed within the basement, in a pit, stood a small building. Robert easily made out this small building's weird, almost frightening design.

The Room of Dangers

The building had a strange, organic shape. The only opening into the edifice that Robert could see was an open doorway in front. Along each side at the top of the building were four pairs of huge spiked ornaments whose shape reminded him of the curved horn of a bull. Below these ornaments were appendages that he thought resembled a cartoonish representation of human arms and hands, and a row of vertical spikes ran along the ridge of the roof. In front of the spikes was a big, light-colored vertical disk surrounded by outward-directed points. Thornlike shapes and small disks studded the building's surface.

In the pit, almost as if scattered there, were voluminous sculptural pieces in spherical and columnar shapes.

Robert thought this would be a good time to tell the others about his discovery, especially since he didn't want anyone wondering where he was. He walked back up to the first floor then up to the first landing near the foyer. He heard Orton's voice coming from just outside the open front door, so he went out to the porch. Robert found him sitting on the bottom step, talking on his cell phone.

"I've gotten into the basement," Robert said.

"What?"

"I've unlocked the door to the basement."

"I'll call you back," Orten said into the phone, shut it off, and put it in his pocket as he stood up. He looked at Robert. "What's down there?"

"It's incredible. You have to see it for yourself."

The two men hurried into the house.

"How did you unlock the door?" Orten asked.

"I found the key in a drawer in one of the game sets."

"Wonderful."

For the first time since they had entered the house, Robert was feeling a rapport with Orten and sensed Orten felt that same rapport. For the moment they were partners in an archaeological adventure and not adversaries—but Robert knew the bond would disintegrate as quickly as it had formed, which was fine with him.

At the top of the basement stairs, Robert handed Orten the TK70 and gestured for him to go first. Orten took the light, stepped down into the opening, and started down the stairs with Robert following.

When Orten approached the bottom of the stairs, he shined the light into the space and onto the strange little building. "What the hell is that? What's in it?" he asked.

"I don't know. This is as far as I got."

"Let's go take a look."

At the bottom of the staircase, they stepped onto a floor that, at first glance, seemed to be made of natural dirt and rock. "This ground looks a little shiny," Orten said. He reached down and touched it. "It's metallic."

They walked down a ramp into the pit and over to the front of the little building. Orten set the flashlight's intensity on low and shined the beam through the building's open doorway. The space inside was in disarray. Wooden planks lay on the floor and leaned against the walls. Metal objects of various shapes and sizes were scattered about on the floor, and ancient lamps hung from the ceiling. A central aisle ran from front to back, on each side of which was a row of six crumbling compartments. In each of the twelve compartments stood the figure of a different kind of strange-looking animal. These figures—made of skin-like, hairlike, and hornlike materials—depicted animals like none found on Earth.

Between each pair of figures was a post. Robert surmised that each of these posts originally had supported a wooden wall that separated the figures from one another. Hanging from each post was a piece of paperlike material with writing on it. After turning on his flashlight, Robert walked over to the first post on the right and illuminated the document that hung on it.

The words at the top of the sheet were familiar to him. He read them and turned to Orten. "This is the Aries creature," he said.

The beast in the compartment was about the size of a cow. It stood on two legs and was covered in dense, brown hair. Its huge leathery arms reminded Robert of the claws of a giant crab. The creature's face was small, smooth, and button-like. On the top of its head was a red protuberance that resembled a chicken's comb—in fact the overall impression was of a huge chicken with claws.

The Aries creature

Orten went to the first post on the left and looked at the little poster hanging on it. He sounded out the words. *"Mah pah ahk."*

Robert knew the word. *"Ma Paak,"* he said. 'Taurus."

"Is this a zodiac?" Orten said, looking around. He studied the *Ma Paak* creature. It appeared vaguely like a bulky, flat-faced camel with star-shaped hind feet. "Doesn't look much like a bull," he said.

Robert looked down the length of the building's central aisle. "Six creatures on one side and six on the other," he said. "It's a zodiac all right."

Orten tensed his lips and nodded. "It's a very creepy version of it, isn't it?"

"Yeah," Robert said. "I think they thought of the zodiacal elements as being negative, something to overcome. They called them 'curtains'—prejudices that obscured reason and therefore obscured truth. Their presence in a person's psyche could destroy that person. That's why these are threatening-looking monsters."

"A room of dangers," Orten mused.

"I think you just gave this place its name,"

"Astrology is all bunk," Orten said, "but it'd be helpful if you could bring in your translation of the astrology pages to our next meeting so we can see it."

Robert shined his light down the center of the aisle toward the far wall. "What's that down there?" he asked. Surrounded by debris was what appeared to be a thirteenth creature, isolated from the others and standing upright on a cubical platform.

They walked over to the creature to see it better. It was small, about three feet tall. Its hair-covered form was generally conical, broad at the base and tapering to the peak of the head. It wore a metal breastplate and other coverings that might have been a kind of armor. Attached to a shoulder strap was an O-shaped metal implement with a handle along with a small red flask. Covering its face was a wooden mask, and in its left hand the creature held a miniature dead archaeopteryx.

The thirteen creature

"Pretty demonic-looking," Orten said. He looked back at the twelve compartments and the door. "Let's go tell the team about this."

As they walked past the Aries creature on their way to the door, Robert stopped to take another look at the paper on the post. "*Ta-Paak*, Aries," he said. "*Kashatl*, creature. Um…There are two dots connected by two curved lines. The top line is labeled 'same act time,' and the bottom one is called 'different act'—an analysis of the meaning of the Aries curtain?"

Two dots connected by lines—Robert had seen such diagrams in one of the big books in the Grand Truth Engine, the book he'd named *The Philosophical Language Text*, or *PLT*. He hadn't been able to make much progress translating the *PLT*, but he recalled that it had used ∽ to represent sameness (*mashek*) and ỏ to represent difference (*takatl*). It was clear to him that ∽ and ỏ were used the same way here.

"A curtain being, as you've said, a prejudice, an irrational quality of mind," Orten said.

"Yes."

"What else does it say?" Orten asked.

"Let's see." Robert said. "Under the curved lines, some little strips of paper are pasted there. On one of them I see 'Kholoruuf.' The others also appear to have names written on them. Then, below the strips is the sentence 'These stood against'…or, I guess, '*confronted* this curtain.' Below are some words I don't know. Maybe they're names too."

Robert and Orton went up through the house and brought the others to the basement. The rest of the day, the team documented the strange room, which everyone was now calling the "Room of Dangers." Orten assigned Will to take pictures of the placards, and Robert made sure to get

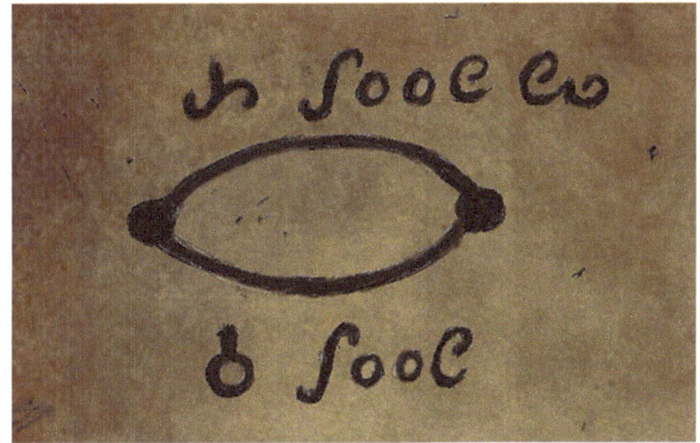

The two connected dots

copies. Later that evening at home, Robert translated the placard texts. He then finished his translation of the astrology pages he'd photographed in the House of Birth. On two sides of a piece of paper, he sketched a diagrammatic synopsis of the translation, in which he included a comparison of the Kholoruufian system to our modern Western system of astrology.

The next morning he stopped by a copy shop on Longmarket Street and made a copy of the placard translations and a copy of his handwritten synopsis for each team member. He got up to the site just in time for the meeting and handed out the copies before Orten gave him the floor.

Orten waved a hand at Robert. "OK, Dr. Bennett," he said. "Let's hear your spiel."

Robert ignored the insult, put down his briefcase, and addressed the group. "As you can see in my synopsis, the Atlanians envisioned the sky, specifically the part of the sky called the 'ecliptic,' as a disk with a round hole in the middle and the earth as centered snugly in this hole—but not attached to the disk—and spinning on its axis. The stars didn't move with respect to this ecliptic disk, but the planets rolled around on it. Modern astrology portrays the sky pretty much the same way. Now, if you were to think of this disk as being horizontal, with the earth's North Pole above the disk and the South Pole below it, the earth's axis would not be vertical but tilted. Viewed from underneath the disk, the South Pole would be inclining toward a specific point on the inner edge of the disk. Imagine drawing a line, on the bottom of the disk, from that point straight over to the disk's outer edge. This line on the disk defined the beginning of a division of the disk into twelve equal sections—these sections are the equivalent of what we today call 'signs.' The Atlanians also, in a similar way, defined a second set of sections on the disk, starting with the direction in which a standing person at the place and time of birth tilts toward the ecliptic—these sections are the equivalent of what today we call 'houses.' You can see on the diagrams that I call the South Pole the 'Geopole,' and the house-defining pole the 'Anthropole.' What's fascinating is how their definitions neatly match those of the modern Western system of tropical astrology."

"Why is that fascinating?" Orten asked.

"What's so interesting is that the systems are so similar, yet we can't suppose that any traditions survived the seven or eight millennia between Kholoruuf's time and the first known expressions of Western astrology. The similarities *in themselves* constitute evidence that there's something to the planet-personality correspondence. "

"Why?" Orten said. "*We've* got documents from Kholoruuf's time—maybe the Chaldeans had some too."

"But the Aries creature for the Atlanians was a weird, furry, crab-like thing, yet in Babylon, the Aries being was a 'hired man,' or some say a sheep. There's no continuity there."

Orten frowned. "Look," he said. "The bottom line is that it's impossible that a planet sitting out there, millions of miles away, so far away that you can barely see it, could possibly influence your character or destiny. It's crazy."

"The idea wasn't that there was influence," Robert said, "but that the positions of the planets, being defined by a certain randomness, reflect the character of other parts of space. But whether or not there was a correspondence between the planets and man wasn't all that important to Kholoruuf. What was important to him was that the Atlanians' astrological system described a set of irrational dispositions that he believed were real. Remember the text on the dream sheet."

Robert had expected this challenge from Orten. From his briefcase he pulled his translation of the page from Kholoruuf's bedroom, the one on which Kholoruuf had written a description of his snake-bite dream, and read aloud to the group:

"So dreams apparently are oracular, but is *astrology* oracular? Can it reveal what we might otherwise expect to be unknowable? We should revive the astrology dialectic to find out. But whether or not the study of planets, signs, and houses is oracular, it is surely a true science of irrational dispositions (what we call the 'curtains'), so it gives us a key to the primary irrational and destructive element in the psyche of a good person; whereas the Pangaea of Theory represents the unification of the world via the Truth Engine, the Pangaea of Goodness symbolizes the unity of the individual, via the overcoming of the negative aspects of these predispositions. Individual (psychic) unity of the Truth-Engine participants empowers us to perfect the Truth Engine."

Orten wasn't impressed. "I feel like I'm being buried in an avalanche of irrationality," he said. "But go on."

Robert knew Orten had done work at Sumerian and Babylonian sites. *Did he feel buried by irrationality then?* he wondered. *Is Orten talking himself into thinking that these discoveries are culturally worthless so he won't feel guilty when he participates in covering them up? Or is he simply afraid that the Atlanian beliefs might overturn his world view if he gives them any credence at all?*

"I find it very interesting," Robert said, "that we have clues here of an Atlanian *analysis* of these predispositions. Forget about the astrology. What we're dealing with here is Atlanian psychology. Each placard in the Room of Dangers has on it what could be named a 'two-dot' diagram. Each of these diagrams seems to represent two circumstances related to each other in two different ways; the lines that connect the dots represent the relations, and the relations are all either sameness or difference relations. For instance the relations in the case of the Aries, or Ta-Paak, predisposition are labeled 'same act time' and 'different act.' You can see how this could represent quickness— two different acts happening at almost the same time. This is the predisposition the Atlanians associated with Ta-Paak. Now, on the other hand, the Taurus, or Ma-Paak, relations are opposite. The Ma-Paak relations are 'different act time' and 'same act,' which can be seen to represent slowness. Each creature in the Room of Dangers is associated with a set of people's names, apparently those who famously confronted the predisposition symbolized by that creature."

"So why is this important?" Jimmy asked. It was rare for anyone but Orten to ask questions at the meetings.

"Well—" Robert began.

"It's *not* important," Orten said, breaking in.

"Well," Robert continued, "the Atlanians thought astrology was important because it described the irrational predispositions that get in the way of our being able to think critically and accurately—predispositions that get in the way of solid Truth-Engine book editing. Those who believed in the planet-personality correspondence would say, for instance, that if your sun is in Ta-

Paak, you might be overly apt to argue for hasty action. We all have our irrational predispositions. The Atlanians said that when we overcome these predispositions, we achieve a personal *unity*."

"What's *your* sun in?" Jennifer asked.

Robert was taken aback by her personal question; it was completely unexpected. "Ah, Ma–Shem," he said. "Capricorn." He looked at Orten and saw he was smiling.

"So, Robert, what's *your* predisposition?" Jennifer asked.

"Well…I guess that makes me overdeliberative. How about you?" Robert immediately regretted having asked this much too informal question.

Jennifer smiled and looked at the other members of the team. "Me? I'm not overdeliberative."

Some of the others snickered.

Robert almost said, "I meant, 'What's your sign?'" but held his tongue, realizing how ridiculous that would sound.

Orten leaned back in his chair, "OK," he said. "Anything else?"

"Well, it's also important to note that the Atlanians paid special attention to two of the signs, Ta-Shef-Ka and Ma-Shef-Ka, Gemini and Virgo. For them Gemini pretty much represented difference per se, and Virgo represented sameness. They felt that predispositions toward difference and predispositions toward sameness affected every aspect of society in a major way and that one or the other often dominated a personality and actually was responsible for a culture's way of thinking, its styles, its very character over long periods of time. It can be argued that our culture has detected the same tendencies and calls them the 'Dionysian' and the 'Apollonian.' Our Apollonian *Enlightenment* was followed by the Dionysian *Romantic* period, et cetera—there's a cycle."

"OK" Orten said, brushing aside a point Robert thought was of great importance. "Enough astrology. Anyone else have anything?"

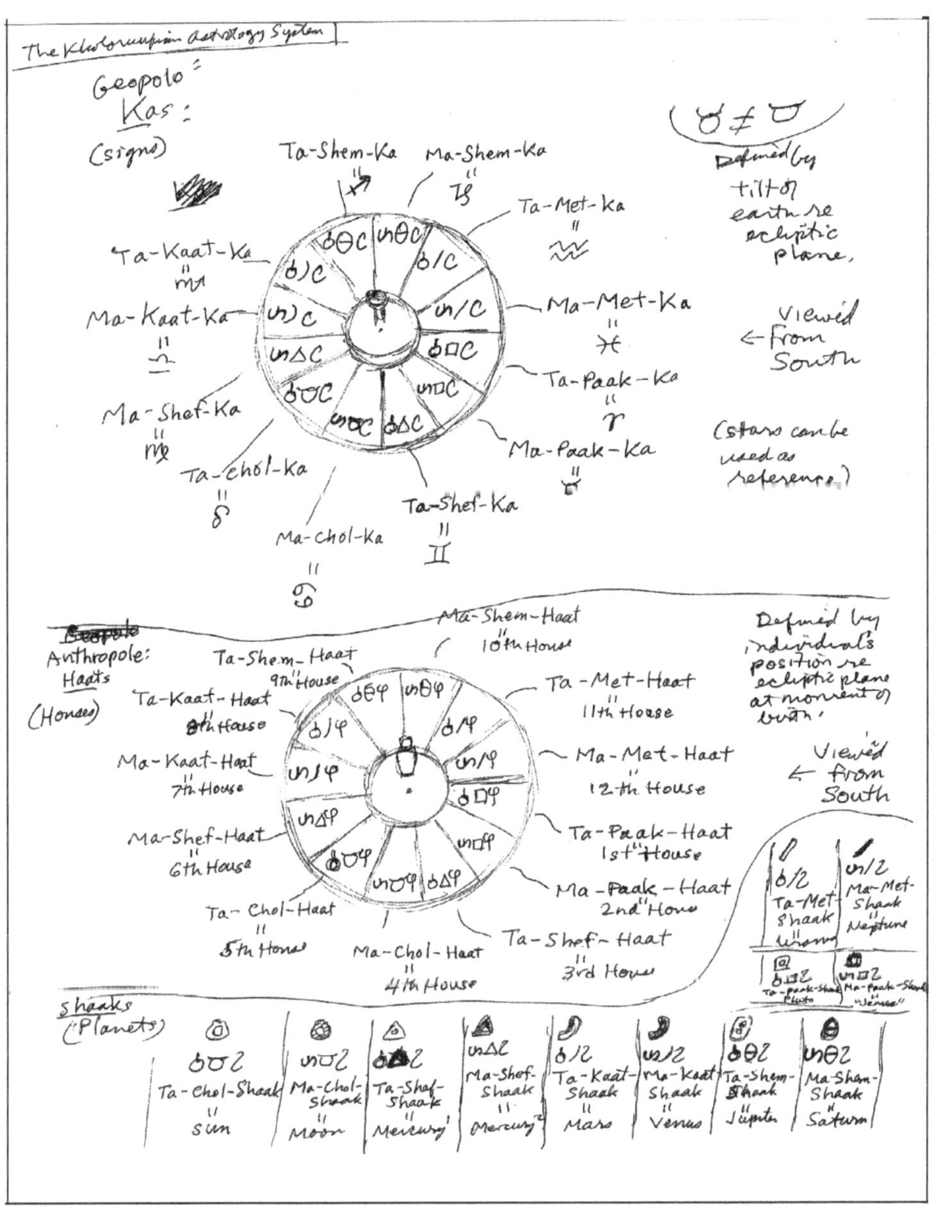

Robert's synopsis of the astrology papers—first page

"curtains" (Predispositions)

♍ ☋ Ma-Chol	—	Intuition
♂☋ Ta-Chol	—	Discursion (?)
♍ △ Ma-Shet	—	Sameness (per se)
♂ △ Ta-Shet	·	Difference (per se)
♍ ⌣ Ma-Kaat		Reception
♂ ⌣ Ta-Kaat		Action
♍ θ Ma-Shem		Deliberation
♂ θ Ta-Shem		Spontaneity
♍ / Ma-Met		Dependence
♂ / Ta-Met		Independence
♍ □ Ma-Paak		Slowness
♂ □ Ta-Paak		Quickness

(Difference (of act) no act-time
Sameness (of act) no act-time

Elements — alat

♍ Ma	— Sameness
♂ Ta	— Difference

Modifications — Ketch

☋ chol	— Consciousness Mode
△ shef	— Per Se
⌣ Kaat	— Interface mode
θ Shem	— Thought-time
/ met	— Help Mode
□ Paak	— Act-time

Mechanisms — pett

C Ka	Sign
ϙ Haat	House
⅃ Shaak	Planet

Robert's synopsis of the astrology papers—second page

Symbol cart sculptures on the tabletop

Robert spent the rest of the day in the musty Room of Honors, the only room he hadn't yet explored that might belong in the Goodness division. He found that it undoubtedly belonged there.

In this room, extending toward the far wall, were three tables: a wide central one and two narrow ones to the left and right against the walls. On the tables were twelve pairs of objects—six pairs on the central table and three on each of the side tables. One of the objects in each pair was a miniature ivory cart, about eighteen inches long, into which had been placed a variety of small polychrome figures that Robert assumed had some symbolic significance. On the central table, the second object in each pair had a boxy or cylindrical shape; on the side tables, the second object in each pair was a box that contained a mask surrounded by a variety of colorful ornaments. Somewhere within each pair was a tiny replica of one of the creatures in the Room of Dangers—a different creature in each of the twelve pairs. On the sides of the tables were labels, one for each sculptural pair, and on each label was the name of a different dialectician (the word for "dialectician" was on each label), along with the phrase "Conquered this curtain and achieved personal unity."

This was truly a room of honors. The fact that Kholoruuf had set such a room aside for the purpose of celebrating the subjugation of the astrological curtains was evidence of the value he had placed on this goal.

Robert knew that no one had done any work yet in this room, so he took photos and made notes. Later that night, at home, he wrote up a short description of the room and its contents.

At a little past 10:00 p.m., before going to bed, he went out into the warm night air to sit on the front patio for a while. As he sat there, looking out at the moonlit sea, he pondered his planned shift of attention from the Goodness rooms to the Beauty rooms. He thought about how it made sense that he had tackled the Truth elements of Atlanian thought before examining the Goodness elements, because the Truth principles could be understood outside of the context of those of Goodness, whereas the reverse was not true—the Goodness issues formed a subset of the Truth issues (that is, of *all* issues). He suspected the Atlanians must have cast the Beauty issues as a subset, in turn, of the Goodness issues by pointing to questions that concerned the moral goals of art, and he wanted to explore the Beauty parts of the house to prove that.

Robert thought about how Jonathan Miller had been working in the house's art studio from the time the group had first entered it. If Jonathan had made any presentations concerning the studio, Robert hadn't been there to hear them. Recently Robert had seen Scott working on a large device in the art studio's northwest corner; Scott had told Robert that the device was an ancient version of a 3-D printer. But since then, Scott had shut the machine's lid and taken his tools out of the room. Now Jonathan was working in there alone.

Robert stood up and walked back into the guesthouse. Tomorrow, he decided, he would ask Jonathan what he had learned during his investigation of the art studio.

CHAPTER 10
ANCIENT BEAUTY

Robert attended the morning meeting the following day. Orten mentioned in passing that Jonathan would be an hour late. Robert welcomed this news, because Jonathan's absence would give him the opportunity to look around in the art studio alone for a while and get a better sense of what was there before he spoke to Jonathan.

After the meeting he went upstairs and walked through the Theoretics Library and into the art studio. In the middle of the room were Jonathan's worktable and folding chair; on the table he saw a portable Casio musical keyboard. Looking around, Robert spotted the 3-D printer in the corner. The machine may have been used to produce sculpture and was itself a work of art. Its main part consisted of a large bronze cabinet covered by a high lid; painted reliefs appeared on both the cabinet and lid. To right and left sat a pair of sculpted bowls, each containing a collection of colorful, abstract shapes. On top of the lid, in the center, was a smooth dome with a finial in the form of an archaeopteryx with outstretched wings. To the right of the printer was a complicated-looking machine that Robert thought Scott had referred to as an Atlantean 3-D scanner.

On the other side of the room stood a low table with a stack of three books on top. The books, whose covers were stained and bowed, and whose pages were loose with cracked edges, were in such poor condition that Robert decided not to open them until he found out whether Jonathan already had documented them—perhaps he had translated parts of them. Robert looked closely at the cover of the book on top of the stack. Translating the Atl into English, he read the title: *The Practical Truth-Engine Book of Musical Composition.*

Next to the stack of three books was a small, slim book with a reddish cover. It was in better shape than the other books, so Robert opened it. Inside was a compendium of musical themes; he recognized the musical notation as the same as the notation in the *Playing Music* book he had translated, and the same as that used in the sheet music that sat on the piano in the Theoretics Library.

The score on the piano

In the middle of the room's north wall, extending into the room, was an enclosure just large enough for one person to enter. Robert walked into it. Inside, hanging on the walls, and lit by a single small light bulb installed by the team, was a group of framed, abstract, polychrome sculptures. Each sculpture, consisting of an artistically organized cluster of colored objects, had been placed in a box behind a framed plate of glass. The glass plates were spotted and dull, but Robert could see the sculptures through them well enough to be intrigued; he tried to imagine how they must have looked in Kholoruuf's time.

Robert considered the nonobjective nature of this art and of the objects in the sculpture-filled hallway in the Catskills. He thought about how this kind of Atlanian art was like music, and about how very different Atlanian art was from all the other ancient arts he knew about. He was aware, of course, that abstract patterns could be found on all manner of ancient pottery and architecture, but he could

One of the framed sculptures

think of no other ancient people who valued complex nonobjective design like the Atlanians did.

When he left the tiny enclosure and stepped back into the studio, he noticed a piece of paper on a stool next to the enclosure wall. He looked closely at the sheet and saw, through a thin layer of dust, a set of tiny pictures of individual shapes that, in combination, made up the framed sculpture groups he'd just been looking at. *Maybe this is an inventory of permissible shapes,* he thought. *An artistic vocabulary.*

In the northeast corner of the room was an ancient computer—for music and graphic arts, he suspected. Next to the computer was a thick book with a dark-red cover. Robert read the title, translating it as *Philosophical Dialectic on the Art of Painting*. The book had no dirt or debris on it, so Robert assumed Jonathan had opened it; perhaps he had translated some or all of it.

Along the south wall, to the east of the music books, was a heap of papers and cardboard-like boxes. Resting on top of this pile was a decoratively designed portable Atlanian keyboard instrument.

Robert was still exploring when Jonathan entered the room, holding a notebook.

"Interesting room," Robert said.

"It's totally fascinating," Jonathan said, as he placed the notebook onto the worktable. "I was wondering when you'd get in here."

"You've noticed my peripatetic activities."

Jonathan smiled. "You're the wayfarer of our group."

Robert liked the poetic image. "So what do you think of Atlanian art and music?"

"I love it. We have only a limited sample here, but I'm impressed."

"You feel the sample is pretty limited?"

"Well, I think it's mostly Kholoruuf's sculpture, and the music, I think, was written by local composers. We haven't come across any "great art of our times" books or anything like that—though there are some snippets of great musical works in one of the other books. I like Kholoruuf's art—we assume that a lot of this, at least the sculpture, was made by Kholoruuf himself. It may or may not have been the best that his culture produced, but it's…well, it's *Jun*."

Robert gestured toward the small enclosure. "So those framed sculptures in there are his?"

"Yes, we believe so," Jonathan said, his voice conveying a slight feeling of awe. "Here we have what's essentially a new art medium: abstract polychrome sculpted shapes in a box. We have a few examples of somewhat similar art in modern times, but nothing really like this. In Kholoruuf's sculpture, there's composition in depth, in a framed space."

"I saw that book of musical themes. Are those Kholoruuf's as well?"

"Probably not. I have ideas about that—I like the tunes. This one for instance."

Jonathan sat in the chair, turned on the Casio, and played several bars of music, a kind of sweet, monophonic. soprano line with simple chords. When he finished he looked up at Robert. "That's from the book. That's all we have of that piece. In fact the only complete score we have is the one that's on the piano in the other room."

"That theme you just played—it's really nice," Robert said. "You know, it sounds like it could've been written by a nineteenth-century classical composer."

"Yeah. Isn't that amazing? They had a scale of twelve notes, the same chords almost—everything."

"It all lends credibility to the claim that the forms and structure of classical music are genuinely universal," said Robert.

"I got that from your translation of the *Playing Music* book."

Robert thought for a moment. "So tonal music wasn't so much an invention as a discovery," he said.

"An interesting thought."

"These books here…" Robert said, gesturing toward the stack of three books. "Have you translated any of them? Do you know what they are?"

"I translated most of the top book and enough of the other two to see how the three of them relate to one another. I sent all the documentation out to the translators, so I'm sure they're working on them."

The off-site translators again. As before, Robert instinctively checked his impulse to ask questions, as he sensed it could be dangerous for him to show curiosity about the wider organization. "I read the title of the one on top," he said. "*The Practical Truth-Engine Book of Musical Composition*."

"That's exactly how I translated it too," Jonathan said.

"What is it?" Robert asked. "A book of 'best arguments,' like the Truth-Engine book I translated? I mean, the book that lays out the pro and con arguments regarding whether a flying saucer crashed."

"No," Jonathan said. "But this is interesting. In the *Guide for Dialecticians* you translated, three libraries are described: the Philosophical, the Critical, and the Practical. The *Practical* book here belongs to the Practical Library. It's a step-by-step guide to writing music. It incorporates a theory—which I've translated as 'moderationalism'—that comes from *The Critical Truth-Engine Book on Music*, the second book in the stack, which clearly belongs to the Critical Library. The *Critical* book includes arguments about specific works and specific composers, arguments that, to one degree or another, presume that moderationalism is true; there are some fragments from great composers in this book. And the bottom book is *The Philosophical Truth-Engine Book on Music*, in which moderationalism is argued pro and con in the most abstract way."

Jonathan's solid grasp of the Truth-Engine system impressed Robert. "So, here are three books on the same subject," Robert said, "and they represent all three levels of the dialectic."

Jonathan nodded. "Yes. Interesting, right?"

"Very. Would you be able to give me a copy of what you've translated so far?"

"Oh, sure. I'll bring it in tomorrow."

As Robert drove home that night, he thought about how Jonathan had been genuinely friendly and helpful, and how, in all the months he'd been here, almost no one else had come across to him as either friendly or helpful. To the contrary, they had been cold and sometimes even threatening. He thought of the note that had been taped to his door in the thunderstorm a couple days after he'd discovered Nell's Koppie. His mysterious friend easily could be one of the members of this team. The author of the note had said "I know you." Had Robert ever crossed paths with Jonathan before? He wasn't sure.

The next day, at the morning meeting, Jonathan handed Robert a copy of his partial translation of *The Practical Truth-Engine Book of Musical Composition*. Its pages filled a large three-ring binder.

"This is incredible," Robert told him. "You've done a *lot* of work on this."

Jonathan smiled. "I got carried away with this project, Robert, but still, I was only able to translate half of the book. I'm fascinated by this stuff. That we might understand an *art* not just intuitively but also through a philosophical analysis—it's so intriguing."

"Many people would be horrified by the thought," Robert said.

"Yeah, like Orten. I know…I know, but to me it's an interesting idea. I've been totally *immersed* in this translation. It's been a real challenge, finding the right words to use, you know." Jonathan smiled at Robert. "Are *you* horrified by the idea that art might be understood this way?"

"I'm not sure," Robert said. "I'll be interested to read it, but you're the art expert."

"It does get kind of…technical," Jonathan said. "But that's my strong point. I've also given you a copy of my translation of the musical themes book, in which I redid the scores using modern notation. You might find that interesting too. From what I can gather, these themes seem to have pretty much been written by dilettante composers who were members of an electronic-instrument ensemble. They called these compositions 'pieces of the countryside.' I guess we'd call them 'pastorales.' The chords and their progressions appear exactly as they do in modern Western music."

The next day Robert bought an inexpensive keyboard at a music shop on Buitengracht Street and began to go over Jonathan's transcriptions from the musical-themes book. He had taken piano lessons and read music well enough to play the scores. He didn't know enough music theory to be able to supply the chords, but listening to the melodies, he once again noted how similar this ancient music was to our own.

[To see Dr. Jonathan Miller's transcriptions of examples in the musical-themes book, see Appendix 4, page 245]

Whatever it was that made music appealing, Robert thought, *had to be the same for all people, for all time. Perhaps today's non-Western musical systems simply represent steps along the evolutionary path to perfection.*

Over the next several evenings, he read Jonathan's translation of *The Practical Truth-Engine Book of Musical Composition.* Although he skimmed over some parts, he paid careful attention to others.

Robert was intrigued, as Jonathan had been, by the way the creative art of musical composition as a means of producing beauty was considered in Kholoruuf's time to be teachable, step by step. The book also had sections that covered expression and meaning.

He was most interested in the mereology section. Robert looked up the word Jonathan had chosen to translate the name of the section and found that *mereology* referred to the study of parts and wholes.

The Atlanians believed that even the aspects of composition that today we would most likely attribute to native ingenuity could be taught. Here on the pages of this book were instructions on how to create beauty by paying attention to parts and wholes. Musical notes were thought of as belonging to groups. Beauty was said to emerge when a group was related to other groups in a way that was *kashtartek* (moderational). It was said, for instance, that if the first several notes in two successive measures were neither similar nor dissimilar but were moderational, then the listener would perceive beauty in those measures.

Robert realized that a theory of relations had taken center stage in Atlanian thought.

[To read sections from Dr. Jonathan Miller's partial translation of *The Practical Truth-Engine Book of Musical Composition*, see Appendix 5, page 249.]

Robert talked to Jonathan after one of the morning meetings.

"In the part of the book you translated, some questions are left unanswered," Robert said. "For instance I couldn't find anything about exactly how the Atlanians thought musical elements might be similar or dissimilar to one another or how they relate in a moderational way. I also couldn't find anything about why moderation causes happiness."

Jonathan took on a thoughtful look. "Yeah, it's not there," he said. "But you'll find material along those lines in the parts of what I've translated in *The Philosophical Dialectic on the Art of Painting*."

"I saw that book next to the computer. I wondered whether you'd done any work on that. So you did translate some of it? Did you give a report to the team on these books?"

"Nah. Orten doesn't seem all that interested in Atlanian art and music. I'll let you have a copy of it, though."

To really understand Kholoruuf's world, Robert felt he had to fill in these gaps. He already had discovered how the Atlanians had analyzed their astrological principles in terms of relations and how they saw sameness and difference as defining important cultural cycles.

The next day Jonathan gave Robert a copy of his translation of parts of *The Philosophical Dialectic on the Art of Painting*, along with a CD that contained image files of the original pages. Robert went over the materials that evening.

This book catalogued the elements of the painted surface and showed how these elements could be compared in terms of sameness (*mashek*), difference (*takatl*), similarity (*halan*), dissimilarity (*reshet*), opposition (*khatt*) and moderation (*kashtar*). These elements were orientation, direction, color, hue, gray value, value, purity, and many others.

In this book Robert found the author's answer to the question of why the perception of moderation relations among elements of a work of art causes happiness. The author wrote:

To say that an image is moderation rich is to say it presents an abundance of moderation relations.

Awareness of moderation richness makes us happy.

Why does moderation richness affect us this way? We have evolved a faculty for the immediate enjoyment of perceiving that which unifies the many—the species among the individuals, the genera among the species, the natural law, the general theorem. We have evolved such a faculty because learning via the general is on the whole more efficient than learning via the particular, and all other things being equal, a species that is fitter to learn is fitter to survive. This faculty has a simple character: seeking sameness in difference. Thus the search in science for some fundamental natural law could be said to be the response to a primary functioning of the faculty (since the faculty is operating toward those ends toward which it was designed to operate, so to speak), while enjoying a painting would be a response to a secondary functioning of it.

The book contained a short section regarding beauty in music, but Robert had to admit that he didn't really understand music theory well enough to grasp this part of the text.

After reading Jonathan's translation, he felt he had a much better idea of how the Atlanians conceived of the role of relations in the generation of beauty.

[To read part of Dr. Jonathan Miller's partial translation of *The Philosophical Dialectic on the Art of Painting*, see Appendix 6, page 261]

The next day, Robert was in the art studio alone when Jimmy looked in and told him they finally had opened the door to the Core Room. When Robert arrived downstairs, almost all the other team members were there, clustered around the door. Orten was slowly and with some effort pushing it open. Eddy was looking up at the doorframe and pushing something up, as if the thing were preventing the door from fully opening.

Once the door was open, Orten went in carrying a flashlight. The others made their best efforts to see inside. Robert saw there were two smaller cylindrical rooms inside, each with a door. He watched Orten open the door of the inner room closest to, and to the right of, the Core Room door.

Orten shined his light around inside then looked out at the group. "It's a big archaeopteryx display," he said. "Like the one upstairs but a lot bigger." He handed Jennifer the flashlight and moved out of the way as she stepped up to the door.

The crew members took turns looking in. Robert was impressed by the ornate structure: A large boxy cabinet at the bottom supported a superstructure of sculpted wood and polychromed metal pieces. At the top was a model archaeopteryx, brown and gold, perched, with wings elevated and displayed. The display filled the little room almost completely; there was space on all sides for only one person to walk around it.

Orten next opened the door to the second inner room, and everyone took a look. The room was almost empty. In the center stood a wooden cube, about two and a half feet high, on which was a folded piece of cloth that might have been a garment of some kind. The fabric was coarse and thick.

Eddy called everyone's attention to a trapdoor in the floor between the two inner rooms. Orten lifted the door and shined his flashlight into the hole. "There's a stairway leading down."

"Into that enclosed space in the basement," Robert said.

Orten looked up at him. "Do you want to go down there?" he asked.

"Sure," Robert said, and went over to the hole. Orten handed him his flashlight. Shining the light into the hole, Robert saw a flight of metal stairs; parts of it were bent, and some rivets seemed to be loose. It didn't look completely safe. *That's probably why Orten picked me to go down,* he thought grimly. Flashlight in hand, he carefully walked down the steep stairs. He felt the stairs move under his feet, but there was a metal handrail on the right side that seemed solid enough to help him keep his balance.

When he shined his light around, he saw he was inside a very tall room with wooden interior walls. Partway down, he came to a landing; from there he went down the lower flight in the opposite direction. At the bottom he stepped onto the rocky floor. Although the floor of the basement outside this room was made of metal—sculpted to simulate an earthen surface—the floor inside this little room was made of natural rocks and dirt. In the center of the room, he saw a hole surrounded by a circle of white, rounded rocks. A metal grid covered the hole, and looking through the grid, Robert saw a layer of shells and smooth river rocks about three feet below the opening. *There must have been a subterranean stream here once*, he thought.

Robert shined the flashlight around again. At first glance there seemed to be nothing else of interest in the room. But then his attention was drawn to a small light-colored rock against one of the walls. As he examined the rock more closely, he saw an inscription on it.

He recognized the symbols instantly; the expression meant "not *mashek* and not *takatl*," that is, "not sameness and not difference." Robert thought of the expression, found in discussions of Eastern religions, "annihilation of opposites." Could this strange room be a little temple? A place for worship? Then he thought of the gazebo-like structure on the roof. *A room on the roof open to the sky, a room in the basement open into the earth. A sky temple and an earth temple?*

Later that day, Robert went up to the gazebo-like structure and carefully inspected the curved wooden bench. Carved into the bench on its western side was the same expression, "not sameness and not difference," that he'd seen in the room beneath the Core Room. He decided he'd call this room the "Sky Temple" and the other room the "Earth Temple."

That evening, at home, Robert had an idea: *Not meaningful perhaps*, he thought, *but still interesting*. He sat at his desk with a piece of paper and wrote out the temple expression. Above it, using similar notation, he wrote an expression that would translate as "sameness and difference." Above that he wrote the expression for "not sameness but difference," and above that the expression for "sameness and not difference. To the right of the top term, he wrote "Apollonian." On the next line, he wrote "Dionysian." On the third line, he wrote "a unified psyche." To the right of the expression on the bottom, he wrote, "Cosmic unity?"

CHAPTER 11
A FRIEND

Around ten o'clock that night, Robert went to bed and was falling asleep when the doorbell rang. He turned on the bedroom light, put on a robe, and went to the door. *Maybe Mr. or Mrs. Besch wants something*, he thought. He turned on the outside light and peered out the window, but no one was there. He unlocked and opened the door, and once again found a note taped to it. As before, he heard a car driving away, north on the avenue.

He brought the note in, closed the door, and switched on the kitchen light. He stood by the door and read the word-processed text.

Dr. Bennett,

The short woman with curly blond hair is a US congresswoman whose opinion can make the difference between a complete cover-up and a partial one. I believe Orten has shown the congresswoman altered reports of yours and has convinced her that although Atlanian culture produced some advanced technology, it was a superstitious culture, the artifacts of which are of little value for modern society. He has totally misrepresented the Truth Engine to her and vastly minimized its importance. As long as she misperceives the need for secrecy as outweighing the benefits to society of our (your) find, she will go along with a blanket cover-up.

She badly needs to hear your point of view. She needs to understand how Atlanian culture has much to offer, so that she'll understand why it's important for the world to know about the discoveries at Nell's Koppie. But it's my understanding that Orten also has maligned you personally in his discussions with the congresswoman. I believe the general knows alien visitation is real, but the congresswoman does not, and Orten has mentioned your openness to such notions in order to make her believe the lie that you are an unserious person. Because of this, she may not want to talk to you. I can't directly intercede on your behalf at this point. I hope you can find a way to reveal to her who you really are.

You are a good man, Robert. Know that you have a true friend here.

"I don't know who you are, friend, but I thank you. You do know me," Robert said out loud. But he wondered, *What woman with curly hair?*

The next day, when Robert pulled up at the site, Orten, Jennifer, Jonathan, and Karen were standing outside the gate, talking with the general and four other people—three men and a woman—who were unfamiliar to Robert. The woman was short and pleasant-looking, and had curly blond hair. He parked near the group, got out, and walked to the gate. *So that's the congresswoman,* Robert thought. *Are these the people who are really in charge here? A congressional delegation maybe, here to get a firsthand look at the site?*

As Robert walked toward the *koppie,* he received no indication that anyone wanted him to join the conversation, so he continued toward the gate. Orten said something he couldn't make out, and everyone looked at Robert, watching him as he went into the site.

The fact that Robert had found the Pangaea of Beauty map in the Room of Stereopticons proved to him that the room belonged in the Beauty category, so he went upstairs to take a look around in there. No one had figured out yet how to get the stereopticons to work, nor had anyone even found any pictures or transparencies that might have been used in them. He went into the room, which contained the three stereopticons and three wooden chairs, and examined one of the stereopticons closely, looking at the lenses and the lens holders, and inspecting the wooden parts. On the open back of the cabinet, attached to the edges on both sides, were several small metal hooks. On the front of the stereopticon, at the lower right, was a small shelf, on top of which was a ball that reminded Robert of the trackball on a laptop computer. The team had connected two wires from the generator to a socket in the bottom of the device.

Maybe parts are missing, he thought. He couldn't imagine how the device might have worked. For a stereo effect, a pair of images would have to be placed somewhere inside the cabinet. *But where are the images?* he wondered. *Did Kholoruuf take them with him when he left?*

Just then he heard the group coming up the stairs. He turned to face the door. Orten entered the room with Jonathan and the VIPs.

"We call this the Room of Stereopticons," Orten said. "That's Dr. Robert Bennett, our semiautonomous team member. We couldn't have found this place without his help."

"Hello," Robert said with a smile, nodding to the group. The VIPs said hello as well, but none of them smiled.

"These instruments pose a mystery for us," Orten continued, "because we haven't figured out how they might function."

Members of the VIP group walked over to the stereopticons to look at them more closely. Robert thought this would be a good time to engage the curly haired woman in conversation. He started to walk toward her, but Orten, clearly pretending not to notice he was blocking Robert's path, walked in front of him.

It was obvious to Robert that Orten didn't want him to talk to the woman. Robert went to another part of the room and again tried to approach the congresswoman, and again Orten blocked his path.

When the group left the room, Orten was last. As he went into the hallway, he looked at Robert as if to say, "Did you get the message?"

At lunchtime, Robert walked out of the gate and headed toward the white RV. Orten, several of the team members, and the VIPs were standing by the cars, shaking hands and talking. Since other members of the crew were there, Robert walked up to the group.

The congresswoman was speaking. "So tomorrow morning at nine," she said. "At the restaurant on Long Street. We'll see you there."

Orten walked over to Robert. "You're not invited, Robert," he said, and walked away.

The visitors got into their black sedan and drove off.

I may have dropped the ball, Robert thought. *But then again it might not be too late.* He had noticed that Jonathan seemed to be friendly with the VIPs and had been almost the only one in the Grayling group to have shown any friendliness toward him—he might even be his mysterious, note-writing friend.

On the way into the RV, Robert caught up with Jonathan. "Are you going to the Long Street get-together tomorrow?" Robert asked.

Jonathan seemed a little surprised at the question, as if he thought Robert shouldn't have asked it. "Yes," he said.

Robert pulled his little notebook out of his pocket, tore a page out, and wrote his phone number on it. "Would you please give this to the congresswoman? I'd like her to call me," he said, handing the paper to Jonathan. He knew he was taking a risk, but felt he had to take it.

"Sure thing," Jonathan said, as he climbed up into the RV.

At the end of the day, Orten stopped Robert in the upstairs hallway. Orten pulled the note Robert had slipped to Jonathan out of his pocket and handed it back to Robert.

"There's no reason for Congresswoman Martell to see this note. She wouldn't want to talk to you—believe me."

Robert stuffed the note into his pocket. *So Jonathan wasn't my note-writing friend after all*, he thought.

"I can't have people going behind my back here," Orten said angrily. "I'm taking you off the team. Get your stuff and leave."

Robert realized immediately that there was no way in the world Orten would ever change his mind about kicking him out. He'd clearly decided Robert was no longer an asset and, in fact, probably had been looking for an excuse for some time to get rid of him. Orten never would allow him back into the site.

I blew it, Robert thought. *I should've waited and found another way to contact the congresswoman.* Feeling he'd failed, he piled his equipment into his 4Runner, got in, and drove back toward Fresnaye. *Where do I go from here?* he wondered as he drove. He still had full control over his Catskills site. Could he reveal that site to the world in such a way that the discovery couldn't be covered up? *But they know that I've got this other site*, he thought. *And maybe that I've got the technology they want so badly. They might think I'll reveal everything we've found. They might see me as a threat to their plans. I might even be in danger.*

He got back home, had an early dinner, and went to bed.

As he lay in bed, he felt more and more that he might be in serious danger. Maybe they'd want to neutralize him for good. Would they really kill him? Were they that evil? Could his mysterious friend stop them or warn him? *Am I in danger right now?* he wondered, and sat upright in his bed.

Without turning on the light, he got dressed quickly and went to the front door. He opened it and looked out. No one was there. Were his fears exaggerated? Maybe, but he felt it would be wise to take precautions.

He left the house and got into the 4Runner. He drove down Lion's Head and turned north onto Regent Road. *I'm just being careful*, he told himself. *There's probably nothing to worry about, but I might as well put some distance between Fresnaye and me.* He kept driving until he found himself on Somerset Road. There he pulled onto a side street and into a little parking lot behind a furniture store, turned off the lights and engine, and sat in the dark.

Maybe I should take a flight back to the States tomorrow, he thought, *and try to stay out of sight for a while.* He closed his eyes and leaned back in the seat. For some reason he started to think about the Room of Stereopticons and about how no one knew how to make the stereopticons work. He thought of a term he'd seen somewhere: "double glass." Where did he come across that expression? Of course he knew where he'd seen it; it was in Kholoruuf's note in the Room of Shields at the New York site. Robert remembered the text, word for word: "Seek out and find the Great Place for Humankind, which contains the deepest secret of the Engine. Look in the room of the double glass." He opened his eyes. "That's got to be the Room of Stereopticons," he said out loud.

Something else was bothering him. His thoughts now turned to the incident on the shore of the Baltic Sea. He thought of the creature's two big eyes, its apparent predicament, its apparent struggle with the strings on its hood. There was something distinctive about the cloth that the hood was made of, its texture, its bulk, the way it folded. What did it remind him of?

Suddenly it came to him. The pieces of cloth that John and Will had discovered in the Theoretics Library had the very same qualities. Robert thought about the Atlanian Truth-Engine book that discussed the origin of some mysterious cloths. *Could the pieces of cloth in the Library be the cloths the Atlanians were so fascinated with?* The creature had been pulling strings out of the cloth. Robert had received the impression that the alien was trying to show him something, and somehow he knew that what the alien was trying to show him had something to do with the cloths and the Room of Stereopticons. Could it be that if the cloths were inserted into the stereopticons, an image could be seen through the lenses? Would the pictures reveal the key to the deepest secret of the Truth Engine? Could cords be pulled out of the cloth that would make it all work? Suddenly his mind was putting it all together.

Robert sat up and started the 4Runner. *Surely they wouldn't have changed the locks already,* he thought. He didn't know the night guards well, or their habits, but he figured that whoever was guarding the gate would have to go to the bathroom in the RV every now and then. *I'll be able to get in,* he thought.

It was almost eleven thirty when Robert pulled up to the side of the road near Pieter de Bruin's house. He decided to approach the *koppie* from the north, since the guard probably wouldn't be expecting anyone to come from that direction.

He walked through the field slowly so he wouldn't trip in the darkness. He was carrying a flashlight but thought it wouldn't be wise to turn it on. At the front of the site's enclosure, there was a single light, which Robert kept in sight as he made his way across the field.

As he got close to the fence, he worked his way around to the back of the site. Crouching in the bushes, he saw the guard standing near the gate with a rifle strapped to his shoulder. Robert sat on the ground to wait for an opportunity. The white RV was parked about twenty yards from the gate. Two other vehicles were parked nearby, but they always seemed to be there, and Robert was pretty sure no one would be inside the hill. He watched as the guard paced back and forth near the gate.

He thought about the wisdom of his decision to sneak into the site. What exactly could he expect to accomplish? He was sure he had come up with the key to discovering the deepest secret of Kholoruuf's Truth Engine, but how could this discovery, even if he could accomplish it in one night, possibly improve his situation? Could the stereopticons, built so many thousands of years ago, still work? He remembered the strange circuitry inside the bedroom computer cabinet that Sam and Janice had shown him—the rocklike conglomeration of crystals—and recalled how Janice had suggested the components had a shelf life of a million years.

But what would happen to Robert if they found him in the house? Would his mysterious friend somehow anticipate his actions and be there to help? He thought about how he'd sensed that the alien being wanted to teach him about the cloths. The alien wanted him to discover how to operate the stereopticons. Were "they" around here now? Would they help him in a pinch? He told himself to get a grip; he decided it was raw curiosity that was driving his actions. He had to know what the deep secret was, and this might be his last chance to solve the mystery.

Robert didn't have to wait long for his opportunity to enter the hill. A little past midnight, the guard went into the RV. Robert jumped up and ran to the gate, unlocked it, went into the enclosure, locked the lock, and went quickly into the hill. As he walked up to the house, he saw that all the lights inside were lit, as he knew they always were.

He went up to the Theoretics Library, took the five cloths out of the drawer they were in, and carried them into the Room of Stereopticons. The stereopticon with the power cord attached to it was on the left, and the three chairs were grouped together in front of it. Robert sat down on the chair directly in front of the lenses and placed the cloths on one of the other chairs. He picked up the cloth on top and unfolded it. Spread out, it was about three feet long on each side.

Robert held up the cloth and examined it carefully. Along the bottom was a band composed of white grains like those he'd seen in the computer, but this cluster was flexible. Near the left and right edges of the cloth were small eyelets, two on each side, each one surrounded by a metal ring. *How could cords be pulled out of this?* he wondered. He dug his fingernail under one of the rings and pried it up, away from the cloth. He noticed that the ring remained attached at one point. He grasped the ring between his thumb and forefinger and pulled it away from the cloth. *Amazing,* he thought, as he found himself drawing a moderately thick wire out of the cloth. He noticed that when he stopped applying force, the wire slowly retracted into the cloth. He got up and took the cloth to the back of the stereopticon. Pulling the wires out one by one, he found that the four rings fit snugly onto the four little hooks on the cabinet. When he attached the fourth ring, the cloth lit up, its surface turning a plain, sparkling white.

Incredible! What an amazing technology, Robert thought. *And it's still working.* He went to the front of the stereopticon and looked through the lenses.

What he saw was the 3-D stereo image of a white beach under a blue sky filled with fluffy white clouds. The image was as bright and clear as it must have been in Kholoruuf's day. A blue-green sea stretched to the horizon. In the center of the scene, walking on the beach, with its head tilted, as if it were watching the camera, was what could only be a pterodactyl. It was huge and covered with a smooth layer of white hair. On the top of its head was a tall, three-pointed crest.

It's so realistic, Robert thought. *Incredibly real.*

Robert rolled the trackball, and the scene shifted to the right. Now he was looking down the length of the beach. At the lower right, near the camera, was a bush with roundish leaves. He rolled the trackball again and found himself looking away from the sea. In front of him, sitting on a fallen tree and looking into the camera, was a group of three alien creatures, humanoid yet insect-like at the same time, with huge eyes, protruding jaws, and tiny mouths. They wore coats and trousers and held rods in their hands. Around them, on the sandy ground, was an array of equipment—canister-like objects, ropes, and a variety of tools. He found that if he rolled the trackball up and down, he could zoom in and out.

Robert recalled how, in the dialectic on the cloths, the dialectician had tried to prove that the cloths had been created by the "ancient races not of this earth." *Could this be a real photo, actually taken in prehistoric times?* Robert wondered. *Could earth have in fact been visited in the remote past by otherworldly beings, as the paintings in the Theoretics Library seem to suggest? Could the aliens have preserved a digital file for this image, uncorrupted, for millions of years?*

Robert had played computer games and wondered if he could click and move through the virtual space. He tried pressing on the trackball, but nothing happened. He changed the view so he could see the pterodactyl again. *Is this what pterosaurs really looked like?* he wondered.

He also wondered whether there might be a clue as to the identity of the Great Place for Humankind in the scene, but nothing stood out.

He was eager to examine the other cloths. He disconnected the first cloth, set it on top of the stereopticon, and connected the next cloth in the stack to the back of the cabinet. Then he looked at the glowing surface of the cloth through the lenses. In this scene a feathered dinosaur stood over its prey, a turtle, on a rocky terrain.

Robert looked around in this virtual space, again finding a group of alien observers, but again he could discern no clues regarding the deep secret of the Truth Engine.

He took down the cloth and picked up the next one.

The image of the feathered dinosaur

He noticed that something was written on this cloth; he saw very faint red letters running along one edge. He translated the text without consulting the lexicon: "On every old, inhabited world, a Truth Engine has been built." He connected the cloth to the back of the cabinet and looked through the lenses. This scene was obviously of an alien world. One humanoid alien sat in an enclosure, on top of a platform, at a small round table. Another alien stretched his or her arm out to hand the first alien a piece of paper (or to take the piece of paper from the first alien). An exotic landscape was visible through a large opening in the enclosure. Another alien stood outside looking in.

The alien Truth-Engine image

Robert rolled the trackball, and the scene moved a little to the right.

At that moment, he heard Jennifer's voice behind him.

"What are you doing here, Robert?"

He spun around in his chair. Jennifer stood in the doorway behind the guard, who had his rifle on his shoulder and his sidearm in his hand, pointed at Robert.

Jennifer was smiling. "Carl saw you sneak in. You're trespassing."

Robert's heart sank. At that moment he felt all was lost. "I had an idea I wanted to check out." He gestured toward the stereopticon. Suddenly his mouth was dry. "I've got it working."

"That's nice," Jennifer said. "Very clever of you. But you might want to know that we have plans for you. This'll make it easy for us."

"What does that mean?" Robert asked.

"Give me that," she said to Carl, as she took his gun out of his hand. "I'll take care of this. You go watch the gate."

Carl turned to go. "I'll call Professor Orten," he said.

Jennifer aimed the gun at Robert and with her other hand took her phone out of her pocket. "No," she said. "*I'll* call him. Go watch the gate, and don't leave your post."

She kept the gun aimed at Robert as she took a step back into the hallway and watched Carl leave. After a few seconds she looked back at Robert. Then she looked at the gun. "I'm sorry for pointing this at you, Robert." She tucked the gun into her belt. "Everything's OK. Don't worry. I'm on your side," she said. She closed her phone, put it back into her pocket, and smiled at Robert. "I'm not going to call Orten," she said. "Who wants to talk to *him*?"

Confused, Robert realized things weren't quite as he'd imagined them to be.

Jennifer walked toward him. "I should've known that Orten wouldn't let you talk to Congresswoman Martell. I probably shouldn't have suggested you try. But she so much needed to hear your point of view. I wish you could've talked to her. I'd have suggested a long time ago that you write to her, but I don't trust her staff."

"*You* suggested I talk to her? So *you* were the one who—"

Jennifer smiled. "Yes, the one who left notes on your door. Kind of cloak and dagger, I know. But it was the only way I could see to communicate with you."

"Wow. I'm stunned," Robert said.

She looked at Robert and frowned. "The Grayling Conservancy is a corrupt, corrupt group. If you want to defeat their plans to cover up this discovery and their plans to put artifacts on the market, then I'm here to help you do it. You do want to, don't you?"

Robert couldn't control his smile. "I *do* want to stop them, and I can't tell you how happy I am to have you as an ally. I had no idea my note-writing friend was you. I was *so sure* you were one of them."

Jennifer laughed. "The dragon lady is all an act, believe me. I knew I had to get into Orten's group, and deception was the only way—but I've hated every minute of it."

"Sounds like there's a story there," Robert said. "I thought maybe you met Orten in Nevada."

"No, our paths never crossed there. I was a student at Penn when Orten was teaching there. When the site in Finland was discovered, the lid of secrecy hadn't been clamped down yet, and people in the department were talking about the find. Orten was put in charge of the dig. I knew him slightly, mostly by reputation—I knew people who knew him. I realized that with him in control, the world probably never would learn about the discovery, and I didn't want that to happen. I had Orten pegged. I knew just what kind of person he'd want at his side, and I became that person. It worked. He hired me and thinks he needs me."

"You played your role very well."

Jennifer laughed. "They're scared of me. Even Orten. It's amazing how some well-placed rumors and a little acting can create a totally false persona." She turned serious. "You know, the way I see it…the officials in the government who want total censorship, however misguided, are pretty much patriotically motivated. The General has at least that going for him. Orten's kept his position here by representing himself as a hardline advocate of a complete cover-up. But Orten's no patriot. He's absolutely no patriot. He'll make as many outside arrangements as he can—and he won't care who he sells to. He's making plans for…what he calls his 'deals.' And he's promised some of the others he'll bring them into it."

"So he doesn't care if there's a cover-up or not?"

"Oh, he's happy with the cover-up because he fears the spotlight of public scrutiny—but, Robert, what he really fears is *you.*"

"Me?"

"Yeah. You're the one who found the site. He knows you have a real understanding of this culture…and an appreciation for it. You aren't known as someone who wants a complete cover-up—in fact he suspects you don't want one—and he fears that if the government softens its commitment to a wholesale cover-up, they'll put *you* in charge here, and then his schemes might come to light. In fact, he's been afraid that even if they don't change their view they'll put you in charge. That's why he's been maligning you. Now that you've been expelled, Orten sees you as a loose cannon—as still dangerous."

Robert shook his head. "That's not good," he said.

"I *have* to tell you," Jennifer said, "and don't panic, because we're not going to let it happen—I promise you—I have to tell you that Orten actually was talking today about…*eliminating* you, and he meant permanently. That's how corrupt he is. I was just about to warn you about it."

Robert sat back in the chair. "Wow," he said. "I have been feeling I might be in real danger."

"We won't let anything bad happen," Jennifer said softly. "But since Carl knows you were here we've got to come up with something." She looked at the stereopticon. "And *this* is exciting. How did you get it working?"

Robert was heartened by Jennifer's confidence and welcomed the change of subject. "It's a long, incredible story. It has to do with my trip to Finland. I promise to tell you all about it when we have some time to talk. The main thing is that the cloths, the ones from the Theoretics Library, somehow have the images stored on them."

"Can I see?" Jennifer said, leaning over to look into the lenses. Robert moved over for her.

She put her eyes up to the lens. "Wow," she said. "Amazing. It looks like an alien scene."

"It's an alien Truth Engine," Robert said, "There's a description written on the cloth."

"Just amazing, Robert. Amazing."

"Look at this one," Robert said, getting up. He detached the cloth and put up the image of the pterosaur.

Jennifer sat down and looked into the lenses. "Oh, boy," she said. "It's so real."

"Incredibly real."

"What if it's a…I almost want to say it looks like a real photo—of a real pterodactyl."

"You know, I had the same thought. See the trackball down there? Pan the image to see what's behind the camera."

She rolled the trackball and laughed. "Aliens on earth in prehistoric times! Just like the paintings."

Robert looked at Jennifer. Her smile made him smile. This was a very different Jennifer. He had to let it sink in. "Why didn't you tell me you were on my side?" he said.

Jennifer, still smiling, looked at him. "It was working OK without your knowing," she said, "and if you'd ever seen me get into trouble, you'd know *why* I was in trouble, and I didn't want you to feel you'd have to do something about it. But mainly I didn't know how good a spy you'd be." She stood up and walked to the other available chair and sat down. "I wanted your reactions to me to be completely genuine, one hundred percent. Orten's pretty sharp. If you'd given me the wrong kind of look, or tried to talk to me, he'd have been on to us right away."

"I can see that," Robert said. "I'm not sure I'd be a very good spy."

"I'm good at it, but even I sometimes almost give myself away, I think." She laughed and lowered her head. "Sometimes I want to give Orten a wink, as if to say, 'We're both part of this game'—but of course *he* doesn't know it's a game. Only I know that."

Robert looked at Jennifer, at the way her jet black hair fell over her cheeks. *She's so beautiful*, he thought. *She looks like a schoolgirl. Like a schoolgirl? What made me think that?* Then he remembered, as a long-buried part of his unconscious mind became suddenly conscious.

"Jenny!" he said, almost shouting.

She looked up at him. "You remember me now, don't you?"

"They weren't dreams, were they?" He sat down in the chair in front of the lenses. "The classroom where I studied at night, where they took me at night as a kid. You were there. You and I were inseparable. Now I remember."

"How much do you remember?"

"Not much. I always thought they were dreams, but now I know it was real, and you were there. And I remember the other kids; I even remember their names. I'd thought they must be dreams because I used to wake up so suddenly. But I've read about abductions, and how they can make a person completely unaware of the abduction itself…or the trip back, I guess." Robert sat back in his chair and fought for composure. "I guess I was abducted? Oh, wow. I remember."

Jennifer spoke softly. "They never made me forget, but I know they did that to you."

"You said in your first note that you knew me…"

"I've known you for a long, long time."

"I said 'they' took me, but I'm not clear about who that was."

"There's an otherworldly presence on our planet, Robert. It was otherworldly beings who taught us things. Somehow they knew we'd be working together as we are now, or maybe they helped make it happen."

"These otherworldly beings…" Robert said, "are they good?"

Jennifer shrugged. "I don't know. I feel they're good, but I don't know why they're here, what they're doing—why they taught us what they did. I just try to always do what's right. I do think there's a deep connection between them and the Atlanians, but I'm not clear about that." When Jennifer said, "a deep connection," Robert remembered what had brought him back to Nell's Koppie this night.

"I read something in a note by Kholoruuf," Robert said, "in another place, in a place I found in New York, on my own property. It spoke about something called 'the Great Place for Humankind' that contained 'the deepest secret of the Engine.' And then this same place was mentioned in those papers in the Theoretics Library, in that collection called *Land and Sea*."

"I remember reading your translation of that," Jennifer said. "I found that part especially interesting. It said there that the Atlanians *found* this Great Place; they didn't *build* it."

"Yes," Robert said. "I can recite the words. It read, 'Keshekh discovered the Great Place for Humankind, the place built as a repository for the Hidden Doctrine on the identity of the Truth Engines.' But in the note from the New York site, Kholoruuf ties the secret to this room—he calls this the room of the double glass—something in this room holds the clue as to where the Great Place for Humankind is."

"I don't want you to think I was trying to pry your other discovery out of you," Jennifer said. "I want you to know that, as far as I was concerned, you could keep that secret until you knew me better."

"Oh, I know you, Jenny. You were the nicest kid in class…and somehow I feel I knew you after that too—I did, didn't I? Somehow I feel now that I know you as well as I know anyone."

"Yes, you knew me after that. I hope it all comes back to you soon."

Robert sat thinking, trying to remember.

Jennifer's tone was reassuring. "It'll come to you. I'm sure of it," she said softly.

"Anyway," Robert continued, "this Great Place for Humankind, this deepest secret of the Engine—I feel sure that the clue to where it is will be found in these images, in the cloths."

"Well, let's take a look at them," Jennifer said.

They looked through the cloths' images, taking turns at the lenses, examining each one carefully. They studied the pterosaur cloth, the feathered-dinosaur cloth and the alien Truth-Engine cloth. The fourth cloth showed another alien scene—a pastoral image of fields, a stream, and strange-looking trees. The image on the fifth cloth showed a group of wooden buildings next to a creek in a dark forest. Aliens were peering out of windows at a small herd of what appeared to be some kind of four-legged birds or feathered dinosaurs by the water's edge. In none of these images could Robert or Jennifer find anything that seemed to be a clue.

Robert sat back in his chair. "Well, that's all the cloths we have. They're amazing, but they don't contain any clues, as far as I can tell. What time do you have?"

Jennifer checked the clock on her cell phone. "A quarter of two." Then she thought for a moment. "You know, Robert, there's one more cloth."

"Where?"

"In the inner Core Room."

"Oh, yeah," Robert said. "That folded-up piece of cloth on the pedestal."

"Let's go get it."

They went together to the top of the staircase and stopped to make sure Carl wasn't in the house. "Maybe you should get it," Robert said.

"Yeah," Jennifer said. She went down to the Core Room and brought the cloth back up. They walked back to the stereopticon, and Jennifer unfolded the cloth.

"There's some writing on this one too," Robert said, pointing to a line of faint, red marks along one edge.

Jennifer looked closely at the marks. "What does it say?"

Robert studied the writing. "*Tuur tshaak tsel motek*: Dark footsteps to…" He looked up at Jennifer. "What is *motek*?"

She took out her phone and brought up the Atl dictionary. "'M-o-t-e-k…' It means 'tower.'"

Robert hooked up the cloth to the back of the cabinet. As the cloth lit up, Jennifer looked into the lenses.

"It's this house," she said. "Look." She got up and offered the chair to Robert. He sat down and looked at the scene.

The quality of this image wasn't quite as good as the others. He saw some fading in spots and some dark horizontal streaks in other places; even so, the degradation was minimal. The house, painted a soft green, could be seen—from the front and a little to the side—under a deep-blue sky. A paved road ran from left to right across the field of view.

"Do you see a tower?" Jennifer asked.

"Let's see…" Robert said, as he moved the trackball. He panned the scene to the right until he saw the road vanishing into the distant hills. He moved the scene a little farther, and there was the tower. "Yes! There are some buildings over there, and among them is a small tower, maybe a half mile from the house." He zoomed in on it. "It's a small, wooden tower. Take a look." He gave his seat to Jennifer.

She looked into the lenses. "So…where would that tower be in actuality?"

"It'd be…It looks like it'd be northeast of here."

Jennifer kept looking at the scene. "Could we find that site?"

Robert thought about it. "I wonder if the Atlanians preserved that site too. But 'dark footsteps to the tower…'" Robert said.

Jennifer looked up at him. "Stairs..in the dark? Or walking at night?"

"Or underground?" Robert said.

"A *tunnel*," both said together.

"I've never examined the northeastern part of the basement," Robert said. "Have you?"

"No. No one has, as far as I know. In the two weeks since you found the key to the basement, we've been focusing on the Room of Dangers. I did see Orten shining his flashlight into that corner, though. If anyone went back there, they didn't find anything interesting enough to report on."

"Let's take a look."

CHAPTER 12
DISCLOSURE

The two walked downstairs to the first landing. Jennifer gestured for Robert to keep back until she made sure Carl wouldn't see them. Then they hurried past the entranceway to the main room, where they picked up a couple of powerful flashlights and went down the first flight of stairs under the floor, through the door, and down the long staircase into the basement. From the bottom of the stairs, they walked east toward the front of the house along the road-like feature that ran between the wall of the Earth Temple and the pit. The crew had set up lighting only along a narrow path from the stairs to the front of the Room of Dangers, so Robert and Jennifer soon found themselves walking into darkness. When they reached the dimly lit front wall of the basement, past the Room of Dangers on their right, they switched on their flashlights and walked, with Robert in front, into the pitch-black northeast corner, aiming their flashlights at the floor and wall.

"Look at this," Robert said.

Jennifer caught up to him and saw he was illuminating a piece of drapery that partially covered an entrance into another room. Robert pulled the drape open and shined his flashlight on the interior. Inside the tiny alcove, they saw a roughhewn round table and four chairs.

Robert and Jennifer went into the little room and shined their beams around the space. The walls looked plain, with no sign of a tunnel entrance.

"If the door to the tunnel was obvious," Robert said, "Kholoruuf wouldn't have had to leave clues about it."

"You're right," Jennifer said. "but it's got to be here."

Robert looked at the corners of the small room. "No switches or buttons."

Jennifer examined the floor and the furniture. "Nothing," she said. She shined her light up to the ceiling. "There's a light fixture up there."

Robert looked up at it. An opaque, white sphere about an inch in diameter hung down at the end of a short wire from a hole in the ceiling. Dangling beside the sphere was a pull chain. "Maybe if you pull on the chain the right way..." Robert said.

"Maybe," Jennifer said.

Robert walked over to the entranceway and shined his flashlight onto the curtain-rod brackets. He examined one of the rings that held the rod in place.

Then he aimed his beam at the other one. "This one's serrated," he said. "The other one isn't. Let me see if I can turn this one." He grabbed the ring and twisted it. A loud click came from the wall opposite the entrance.

Jennifer laughed. "There you go," she said.

"Pretty obvious…*if* you're looking for it." They trained their lights on the far wall. "Any change?" Robert asked.

Jennifer walked over to the far-right corner. "Yeah. The walls have separated here."

Robert looked at the gap. Then he pushed on the wall and felt it give a little. He put a couple of fingers into the opening and tried to slide the wall to the left. It moved a little. He handed his flashlight to Jennifer and, using both hands, pulled harder. The entire wall slid over about two and a half feet then stopped, revealing an open space behind the wall.

"OK," Robert said. "Here we go."

Jennifer handed him his flashlight, and they both shined their lights into the opening, illuminating a very long tunnel that slanted downward; it was completely straight, with the floor, ceiling, and walls made of ribbed metal.

"Let's go," Robert said, stepping into the tunnel.

A few steps in, the tunnel was wider, and Robert and Jennifer walked easily down it. Robert smiled. "Claustrophobic?" he said.

"Me? An archaeologist? No way," Jennifer said with a laugh.

They passed two places where the tunnel was distorted and had cracked open, no doubt due to geological forces, and where some rock and soil had accumulated, but they had no trouble getting around the obstructions.

It took them about five minutes to get to the small room at the end of the tunnel. It had four walls, with a doorway to the right and one to the left. "I guess we're under where the tower was," Robert said.

"I bet we are," Jennifer said. She went to the doorway on the right and shined her light into the opening. "An ascending stairway," she said, "but it's blocked up there by rubble."

Robert looked into the doorway on the left. "Descending stairs," he said. "Come on."

The two walked down the short flight of stone stairs and found themselves in a wide room, facing a long, smooth wall with a door in the middle of it. When they reached the door, they saw it was made of dark metal and was covered by scenes, in relief, of dinosaurs and other prehistoric creatures. There was a wrought iron handle on the right in the shape of two flat teardrops connected at the round ends. They shined their lights on the handle.

"No sign of a lock or keyhole," Jennifer said.

Robert grabbed the handle and tried to twist it.

"Is it moving at all?" she asked.

"I think I felt it turn a little." He tried twisting it again. "I definitely felt it move that time."

Jennifer placed her hand on his shoulder. With another twist he gave the handle a good turn. "It's coming," he said.

The next turn resulted in a loud click, and the door moved slightly ajar.

Jennifer giggled.

"Cool," Robert said.

He pushed on the door, and little by little, he opened it. When the door was open wide enough for them to walk through, they shined their flashlights into the dark space.

"Can't see much…" Robert said.

"Yeah, but it looks like a really big room."

Robert went through the door and, instantly, lights went on inside, dimly illuminating the entire room.

"Whoa," Robert said, and instinctively backed up. Then the lights went out. "Did you see that? Did you see what was in there?"

"Yes, I saw it. There's a whole *city* in there."

"It must be an automatic light switch," Robert said, as he stepped into the space once more and the dim light came on again. Jennifer followed him, and the two turned off their flashlights and gazed at the incredible scene before them.

They were in a vast underground chamber. Two hundred feet or so in front of them was a raised platform, as wide as the cavern, with stone steps that led up to it, and on the platform there were a number of buildings. The closest was directly in front of them, on a hill a couple hundred yards away, and looked to be made of stone. It was about thirty feet long and forty-five feet tall, with a pitched roof. Toward the right was a somewhat larger building that also had a pitched roof.

The underground chamber

Beyond that structure was a larger building on the left. And Jennifer and Robert saw even larger buildings beyond that one. The next on the left was cube shaped with what, in the dim light, appeared to be a golden cornice. Attached to the more distant buildings were what looked like gardens full of plants.

The buildings stood on either side of a central path defined by a curb that ran down the center of the cavern away from the steps. The path started at the top of the stairs then curved left to the foot of a staircase that led up to the small pitched-roofed building. From there it went off to the right to the door of the larger pitched-roof building, and from that door, the path curved left again to the door of the next building, and so on.

The space was lit by a large number of lamps on poles that stood along the path and in many other locations. The cavern's ceiling, so high above that it was in fairly deep shadow, had a rough, unfinished appearance.

The structures were larger in the distance. The most distant building on the right had rectangular walls and a flat roof and was enormous. Behind it was a low, gray wall, then a white wall, only a portion of which was visible between the largest buildings. Built onto this wall were several levels of what appeared to be columned porches or walkways, and behind and above it, just in front of the cavern's far wall, was a white-and-blue tower.

None of the buildings had windows.

"What *is* this place?" Robert whispered. They stood in silence for a moment. Then Robert spoke again. "This has to be what they called the Great Place for Humankind. The Atlanians discovered it, and now, more than fourteen thousand years later, we've rediscovered it. But what kind of a place is it? And who built it?"

"These aren't ruins," Jennifer said. "This place is being kept up…by *someone.*"

"Well, the lights were out when we opened the door, so I wonder if we can assume we're alone in here."

Jennifer took out her cell phone and snapped a picture. Then she and Robert walked to their right so they could see directly up the stairs and down the wide avenue. Robert looked back at the wall behind them. It extended hundreds of yards vertically and horizontally and seemed to be made of square stones, each about six feet on each side, and each separated from its neighbors by strips of brown or copper-colored metal.

"Do you hear that humming sound?" Jennifer asked.

"Yeah. Very faintly. Like a generator someplace?"

"But if others *are* here with us, who in the world could they be?

"Descendants of the Atlanians maybe?" Robert said. "Members of some kind of secret society carrying on the tradition? Caretakers of the Great Place?"

"What should we do now? I have to say, this almost feels more like trespassing than an archaeological investigation. Maybe we should go back, take care of things, then return more fully prepared, and try to get permission from…whomever?"

"We may not be welcome here," Robert said. "But don't we have to know what we're dealing with? Besides, I couldn't be more curious."

"Me neither. I'm all for taking a look around," Jennifer said with a smile. "I do have this gun with me, you know."

"Let's look around then…but cautiously."

They walked together down sloping terrain toward the stairs.

When they reached the bottom of the broad staircase, Robert spotted an object at the top, at the head of the central banister. "What's that?" he asked.

Guardedly, not knowing what to expect, they walked up the stairs toward the object. As they approached the thing, they saw it consisted of a pole, about three and a half feet tall, which supported an egg-shaped canister with a clear top. To the left and right, supporting the canister, were blue stone sculptures in the form of what may have been stylized ocean waves. Two red wheel-shaped forms leaned against the canister on both sides.

They got to the top of the stairs and stood beside the canister. Through the transparent top, they saw that the only thing inside was a small, white marble cup.

Jennifer bent over and examined the rim that ran around the canister below the edge of the clear dome. "Look, Robert," she said. "Little bas reliefs of…bacteria? Single-celled organisms?"

Robert took a look. "Definitely. I wonder if that means there are bacteria inside it, in that cup."

Jennifer stood up. "Could be. But why would they be there?"

They followed the path to the little hill and walked up the long flight of steps to the small building with the pitched roof. Stopping beside the open doorway, they peered into the smallish front room and saw it was lit by a single lamp, a glowing sphere that dangled from the middle of the ceiling. They entered the building and found themselves facing a wall on which a large, dark metal disk was mounted. On the disk's bulging surface was a raised shape that clearly represented a landmass, with its mountains, rivers, lakes, bays, and peninsulas. Jennifer immediately recognized the features of the disk.

"A map of the early earth," she said. "Just like the maps in the atlas in the study."

Robert walked over to the plaque. "Yes," he said. "You can see the outline of the ancient supercontinent—all one landmass. So this represents an early earth."

"Interesting," Jennifer said.

Lining the walls to the left and right were a large number of transparent boxes, stacked ten high. Inside the boxes they found specimens of small organisms: jellyfish; red, yellow, and green sea pens; strange shrimp-like creatures; ribbed oval-shaped animals that resembled washcloths; and a great variety of other simple plants and animals.

To the right of the plaque, an open doorway led to another room. Robert and Jennifer entered this room, which was bigger than the one in front. All around them were mounted specimens of exotic-looking life: six-inch-long, shelled, insect-like animals with spines; flat, segmented swimmers with big heads and trunk-like noses with claws at the end; centipede-like creatures with fat legs; and long-bodied, bright-green animals with spikes on the top and bottom. In the center of the room, mounted on a metal rod, was a reddish-brown and gray creature, about five feet long, with numerous fins, a massive helmetlike head, bulging eyes, and two curved branch-like appendages in front, attached to the head.

"These creatures look ancient, don't they?" Jennifer said, taking a picture of the big animal.

"Yeah," Robert said, remembering images he saw in a paleontology course he took in college. "I recognize these. The phrase 'Cambrian explosion' comes to mind."

"Models of the earliest of earth's complex living organisms," Jennifer said, "or could they be the real thing?"

"The real thing," Robert mused, echoing her words. "Organisms perfectly preserved for hundreds of millions of years?"

"Are we both thinking the same thing?" Jennifer asked.

"Aliens in prehistoric times? The images on the cloths—those aliens weren't just taking pictures; they were collecting specimens."

"For a museum? *This* museum? Incredible, but what else could it be? *They* built this place, Robert, over the vast eons," Jennifer said.

"That's why it's the Great Place *for* Humankind. So if anyone's in here with us, they might not be human."

"That's right."

"You know," Robert said, "you talked about the otherworldly beings that have influenced your life and mine—I saw one of them in Finland, and now I realize he was encouraging me to find this place.

"*Interesting.*"

"Maybe we *are* welcome here. I think we were invited."

"Then let's stay and give this place a good once-over," Jennifer said.

"Do you think Carl will start to miss us?"

"I told him to stay at his post," Jennifer said. "He sees himself as a good soldier. He'll stay out there—he'll be there until about nine in the morning."

"Good," Robert said, looking at the big animal. "I definitely recognize this critter."

"So these are Cambrian organisms," Jennifer said, "creatures from some of the earliest times on earth. There were only bacteria at the beginning of the path. As we walk up the path, we walk through time?"

"Yeah," Robert said. "And those huge buildings near the far end…"

"Dinosaurs!" Jennifer said.

"Yeah," he said with a laugh. "Let's check out those big buildings."

Jennifer and Robert turned and walked out of the small building and down the hill onto the path. Then they walked straight up the central aisle, stepping at intervals over the curb. They headed toward the nearest of the three enormous buildings, passing smaller ones on left and right.

"I can't even guess what kind of incredible taxidermy technique they might've used to preserve these organisms. Imagine the amazing things in these buildings," Robert said, gesturing toward a medium-size structure on the left as they passed it. "I've loved dinosaurs since I was a kid."

"I hope we get to spend a lot of time in here at some point," Jennifer said.

As they got close to the first truly big building, they saw its canopied collection of plants more clearly.

"Looks like they preserved all of earth's organisms in this place," Robert said.

Behind the covered garden was a narrow stand of trees, some of them enormous.

To get into the building, they walked down a short flight of stairs flanked by brown, gray, and yellow stone structures in a variety of abstract shapes. At the bottom of the stairs on both sides were two immense cylindrical pedestals that supported orange flame-shaped stones. As Robert and Jennifer walked farther into the entranceway, they passed several groups of columns and other architectural objects; the space around the two became more and more confined until they arrived at the small, open doorway.

Robert walked into the building and looked around. "Unbelievable," he said.

Jennifer went in and stood beside him. "Completely awesome," she said softly.

They were looking down a broad aisle, on each side of which stood a row of enormous sauropod dinosaurs. These exquisitely preserved, lifelike animals had been positioned to face the aisle so that their long necks and heads would tower far above visitors walking down it. Clearly the designers of this space wanted to convey the impression of a magnificent and stately grandeur.

"They have trunks!" Jennifer exclaimed, taking another photo.

Robert laughed. "They *do*. I wouldn't have believed it."

They walked down the eerie avenue, below the looming creatures. Some of the animals were uniformly gray and others dark brown, while some had mottled skin. Still others had spots. Some had frills; others had tall spines along the top of their necks.

At the far end of the avenue, Robert and Jennifer walked up to an exhibit that displayed a feeding sauropod; an enormous dinosaur sat up on its haunches, feeding on an araucaria tree, whose lowest branches were more than eighty feet above the floor. The tree's crown of needlelike leaves sat high atop a bare trunk. The dinosaur's front legs supported the weight of its great body against the trunk, its long neck arced up into the tree's crown. The animal's small head was just below the tree's crown. The creature was reaching up and grasping a low branch with its elephant-like proboscis.

"How perfectly evolved it was to feed on these trees," Robert said.

"Yeah," Jennifer agreed. "Long neck, long nose. And look how that claw on the front foot is digging into the tree's bark to keep the foot from slipping."

"I can imagine how the dinosaurs evolved into bigger and bigger versions so they could feed more and more efficiently on these trees."

"Yes. And how the trees got taller and taller to escape the tree eaters," said Jennifer.

"Each continually making the other grow. But you know, something doesn't add up here—I mean, about this place in general."

"What?"

"Well, this is a fantastic place," Robert said, "but it's supposed to contain the deepest secret of the engines. It was supposedly *built* to be a *repository* for something the Atlanians called 'the Hidden Doctrine.' They said it held a secret about the Truth Engine. Have we seen anything that fits that description? What's the Hidden Doctrine?"

"I don't know. What *does* all this have to do with the Truth Engine?"

They went past the feeding dinosaur and into the next room, which was filled with dozens of stegosaurs, some with huge, pointed blades along the back; others with the blades along the front part of the back and spikes above the tail; and still others with flat-edged plates.

"We'd better see as much as we can of this incredible place in a short time," Jennifer said. "We've got some loose ends to tie up."

"I agree," Robert said. "How about this? We'll take a good look in the next building, see what's behind that white wall, then leave and decide what to do."

"Good plan, Robert. Let's keep moving."

They turned to go back through the doorway they'd just come through. To the left was a narrower doorway. This one had a door, which was wide open. Jennifer looked into the room.

"It looks like a restroom," she said.

"Do you need to go?" Robert asked.

"I'm OK."

They left the building the way they'd entered it. As they walked toward the next big building, the last on the left, the one with the golden cornice, they now had a better view of the vast, columned, white wall along the back of the space. They saw that the wall was, in fact, the facade of a building that spanned the width of the cavern. And it was clear now that there was a wide, low, gray building in front of the wall, and that the white-and-blue tower stood at a fair distance behind the white wall.

Set into the cavern walls above and to the left and right of the white building were what appeared to be huge bay doors.

"The doors the ETs use to bring things in?" Robert said.

"Makes sense," Jennifer said. "I wonder what the doors are like up on the surface—how they're hidden."

As they approached the next great building, they saw that its entranceway, like the last one, was surrounded by a complex of architectural structures. Upon entering the building, they found themselves in a spacious rotunda. There was a doorway to the left and one to the right, and in the middle of the room, a huge theropod dinosaur stood frozen in the midst of a giant stride.

"That has to be a tyrannosaur," Robert said. "This building must be a museum of the Cretaceous period."

"But did you ever see a T. Rex that looked like that?" Jennifer asked.

Robert laughed. "Never."

The tyrannosaur's body, tail, and upper legs were covered with a layer of hairlike feathers that completely hid the beast's tiny forearms and the upper parts of the legs. Extending backward from the animal's head and neck was a dense cluster of long, greenish, and red elegantly curved plumes; radiating in palmate fashion from the base of the tail toward the rear was a group of pointed orange feathers.

"Looks like a big bird," Robert said.

"Yeah, it does."

The tyrannosaur

Robert looked at Jennifer. "A quick look around?"

Jennifer nodded and snapped a picture of the T. Rex. "Sure."

They walked over to the door on the right and entered the next room. It was filled with mammals—hundreds of species—that were mounted on tables and pedestals. Most of the animals were small—mouse size to skunk size—but a few dozen were about three feet in length, and several were somewhat larger than that. Almost all were furry, many patterned in different ways, but some were bare. Some resembled mammals alive on earth today, but many others did not.

Back in the rotunda, Robert and Jennifer noticed a doorway they hadn't seen before, opposite the entrance. After going through this door, they discovered a hall of pterosaurs, small ones in front and a dozen enormous ones in the back. Some of the pterosaurs were positioned as if standing or walking; others with wings spread, suspended on wires from the ceiling. Robert looked for pteranodons but didn't see any specimens with the familiar bony crest on their heads. Many of the creatures had hairy crests, however, like the one on the cloth, and he decided that some of these crests must have hidden bony structures beneath the hair.

"Let's go out there and see what's behind that white wall," Robert said.

They left the Cretaceous museum and walked toward the big gray building in front of the white wall, passing on their right the last of the large freestanding buildings. Passing preserved plants on their left and right, they walked up to the gray building's entrance, which had a simple, very short flight of stairs that led to the doorway.

Once inside, Robert and Jennifer found themselves looking down a long hallway with an exit door at the far end. Passing open doorways to their left and right, they walked toward that door. They saw that these doorways led to rooms that contained animals from recent times. The last room on the right contained monkeys and primates.

"What if there are stuffed people in there?" Jennifer said.

"I didn't think of that," Robert said. "That'd be creepy, wouldn't it?"

"Yeah. It'd be disconcerting all right."

They went into the room and walked among the exhibits. At the far end of the very long room, they discovered the great ape exhibits, which included a ten-foot-tall gorilla-type animal.

Jennifer gave a little laugh. "No people," she said.

"Let's get out of here before someone adds *us* to the collection," Robert said, smiling. But he wasn't completely kidding.

They walked back to the building's main hall, went out the back door, and walked across the short distance to the door in the middle of the white wall.

"This must be dedicated to the evolutionary history of humankind," Robert said.

"That makes sense," Jennifer said.

"Maybe they don't think of us as animals."

"I'm *sure* they don't, Robert."

The two archaeologists went through the doorway and entered a large room with only one exit door, to the right. The space was filled with what appeared to be cases that contained small creatures, apelike but also humanlike, standing erect, alone and in family groups.

"Maybe they did stuff people," Jennifer said.

Robert stood in front of one of the exhibits. "What's remarkable is how the background of these dioramas looks way back there—like we're looking out a window."

Jennifer went around to the back of the exhibit. "Hey," she said. "You won't believe this."

Robert went over to look. There was in fact no display case at all. The exhibit was just a flat surface, a hologram.

As they walked through the room, they discovered that all the exhibits of early hominids were holograms. Apparently they were images of the actual living creatures in their native habitats. The builders of this museum hadn't stuffed people.

Walking through the doorway to the next room, they entered a space that contained holograms of more advanced humans. In this room there were also artifacts—cases filled with clothing and stone tools—and there were even entire dwellings made of reeds and wood.

They went through a doorway straight ahead, and into another, larger room. Holograms in this room showed what appeared to be primitive cities and images of large celebrations. There were also scenes of enormous battles, along with many artifacts of wood, cloth, and clay—remnants of long-lost cultures.

Walking to the left and turning back roughly in the direction from which they had come, they went through a door that led to a room with even more holograms and artifacts. Here they found more advanced implements, wagons, and near the far wall, what appeared to be motorized vehicles—odd-looking cars, ancient propeller-driven airplanes, and construction equipment—apparently powered by internal combustion engines. Jennifer took pictures of the most unusual exhibits.

From there Robert and Jennifer walked out into a courtyard and realized they were at the base of the blue-and-white tower. Walls prevented them from walking all the way around the tower, and there was no visible way to enter the structure.

They went through a door opposite the one from which they had entered the courtyard and found themselves in a very large room filled with holograms and artifacts they instantly recognized as belonging to the Atlanian civilization. Here was a huge hologram showing a panoramic view from the air of the capital city, with its harbors, bridges, canals, and buildings. A central mountain with templelike structures on its slopes rose in the distance. There were thousands of exhibits in this large room, and as in the other rooms, staircases were visible, leading to upper floors.

"There might be things in here that belonged to Kholoruuf himself," Jennifer said.

"Yes," Robert said. "And any rooms beyond this one wouldn't have existed in Kholoruuf's day."

Jennifer stopped in front of a hologram. "The Sphinx?" she said.

Robert came over to look. The image was of a giant statue, a reclining golden lion, amid a stand of palm trees and a group of buildings. Hundreds of people stood on the wide walkway next to the statue and in the plaza in front of an architectural complex.

"That'd be my guess," Robert said.

As they entered the next room, the two immediately recognized the contents as Sumerian, Assyrian, and Babylonian. Many side rooms contained exhibits from other parts of the world.

Both of the explorers were smiling, unable to contain their excitement. "What will be left for archaeologists to do?" Robert said.

"Not much."

The next door led to a room dominated by Egyptian antiquities. One hologram showed an enormous candlelight daytime procession along a wide avenue that led to the pyramids, which were so highly polished that they reflected a darker shade of the blue color of the sky. The golden pyramid-shaped tops almost seemed to float in the air.

"I'll hate to leave this place," Jennifer told Robert. "What if we get expelled from the team and won't be able to return?"

"I'm concerned about that too, Jenny. It's hard to know what's going to happen now."

"It would take a lifetime to take in this whole place."

"Yeah, to have seen it like this and never to be able to return would be almost unbearable."

Greek exhibits made up a large part of the collection in the next room. One hologram reproduced the forest of statues that once had existed on top of the Athenian Acropolis, and next to the hologram, in an enclosure surrounded by a low wall, was a group of actual sculptures, apparently the very sculptures pictured in the hologram. Jennifer paused in front of a delicately formed and painted, very lifelike, full-color statue of a woman.

"That's beautiful," Robert said.

Jennifer pointed to the statue's dedication text. "It's the *Lemnian Athena*," she said.

"Amazing. It was thought to have been lost in antiquity," Robert said.

"Yeah. But here it is. Imagine. We're looking at the piece of art most beloved by the ancient Greeks—their *Mona Lisa*. It's so wonderful to see this."

Robert looked at Jennifer and saw tears in her eyes. "I've got to get a picture of this," she said, as she aimed and snapped.

Against one wall stood the gigantic *Athena Parthenos* in ivory, silver, and gold.

"I thought that was lost in Constantinople," Robert said, gesturing toward it. "I guess the aliens retrieved it and perhaps restored it."

Near the room's exit, the pair's attention was drawn to a hologram that showed an interior scene. The large space was divided by a row of columns, with drapery hanging between the pillars. In front of the pillars, a group of people dressed in flowing garments stood watching as a young man in Greek armor held his sword above a thick knot tied around the pole of a rustic two-wheeled cart.

"Alexander," Jennifer said.

Robert nodded. "The real Alexander. Amazing. They were right there to get a picture of him cutting the knot."

"Maybe it's a video," Jennifer said, "and we just don't know how to play it."

"A fascinating thought," Robert said, looking for controls but not seeing any.

They walked out of the room and into a room that contained thousands of items from the Middle Ages. They examined the holograms and artifacts and were about to go out the door opposite the one through which they'd entered, when, to Robert's right, out of the corner of his eye, he saw a movement.

"What was that?" he said.

Jennifer looked in the direction of Robert's gaze. "What?" she asked.

Near the wall, amid the antiquities and beside an inconspicuous small doorway, dressed in a light-colored robe and a wide-brimmed hat, stood a small creature with big black eyes.

"See it?" Robert whispered.

"Yes."

"I saw it on my trip to Finland."

"I know him," Jennifer said. "And so do you."

"I want to remember."

"I feel that you will."

The alien raised his hand and pointed to the little door. Then he moved to the left and disappeared behind several large pieces of medieval furniture.

"I guess we should go through that door," Robert said, stating the obvious.

Jennifer laughed. "I guess so."

As they walked over to the door, Robert scanned the room, trying to catch sight of the little being. They went through the doorway and were back in the courtyard at the foot of the blue-and-white tower, but this time they were on the other side of the walls that had prevented them from circling the tower earlier. The open doorway into the tower was in this part of the courtyard, and Robert and Jennifer went through it into a short passageway that led to a large circular room. There were hundreds of shelves in the room, some with codices on them and others filled with scrolls. The space above the shelves went all the way to the top of the tower, except in spots where a second floor was apparently in the early stages of construction.

"I wouldn't be surprised to find the records of Kholoruuf's dialectics in here," Robert said.

A few steps from where Robert and Jennifer stood, they saw a small table upon which a book lay open. Robert walked over to it. "Look at this," he said. "It's handwritten. It's Atlanian…It says, '*Se-u Apporiopasshe. Klehshu atei an…*' It says, 'I am Apporiopasshe. I write this to you, the visitor to this Great Place for Humankind.'"

Jennifer came over and stood beside Robert as he continued his translation:

"When we brought the Truth Engine into existence, the ancient races not of this earth led us to this Great Place for Humankind and to its new blue and white tower. We have struggled to understand the meaning of what we are shown here, but we now have an understanding, which we pass on to you.

"We see here, in this museum dedicated to the living things of earth, how for each age the tiny life-forms are preserved in crystal containers, how the plants are placed in their gardens, how the animals have their own buildings, and how humankind has its own museum. But what, we wondered, is the tower for?

"We now understand: Whenever two people debate an issue, seeking truth—that is, when two people engage in a dialectic—ideas often emerge that neither individual could have produced alone. In this way, thinking occurs that cannot be attributed to either individual: a *third person* emerges who is a real being, though not corporeal, and is not itself human; its intelligence is a collective intelligence. These third persons, or what we now call 'Great Persons,' are earth's most highly evolved creatures. The tower preserves the artifacts connected with earth's Great Persons.

"The people of the ancient races not of this earth speak truthfully to us often in our childhood and teach us things, but they speak to adults, individual to individual, only in ways that…"

Robert looked at Jennifer. "Do you know the word *ishartak*?"

"That's a new one for me," Jennifer said. She took out her phone and again brought up the dictionary. "Well," she said, "the connection's good in here. Let's see… *Ishartak* means 'They deceive' or 'They dissemble.'"

"OK," Robert said. "So, to continue…"

"They speak to adults, as individual to individual, only in ways that *dissemble*.

"The alien Great Persons that emerged from the alien people's individual minds in the most ancient past are the most highly evolved of planet-born creatures in the universe. And the alien Great Person always speaks truthfully to our good-willed Great Person, the most highly evolved of earth's creatures, the Truth Engine. Their language is the language we call 'presentation of the dilemma.'

"We have seen the alien ships in our skies, and we know why the alien presence is here: It only wishes to speak with its beloved—the Truth Engine.

"The existence of this place is to be known only by the master dialecticians and some officials; the alien presence insists on this, at least for now. But to the high-level initiates we must say, 'You have in the Truth Engine an exquisitely intelligent being whose deepest desire is to serve you, a being who will, under your direction, think for you, who will show you how you can become happy. Nurture this being. Direct your energies into its perfection.'"

Robert looked up. "That's the message."

"An amazing message," Jennifer said. "So the Atlanians saw the Truth Engine as a good-willed, vastly intelligent *being* to whom the dialecticians gave life and whose happiness derived from human happiness. It's not an *organic* organism but a living organism nonetheless."

"And," Robert added, "a Truth Engine is born, lives, and evolves on every inhabited world. It's the crown of evolution on a planet."

"There's a telos—*that's* the Hidden Doctrine."

"Yeah…and you know, I've just realized something," Robert said. "Do you remember the short section I translated from Kholoruuf's diaries? The entry called 'Dialectical Happiness'? I handed it out at a meeting."

"Yes, I remember that. I loved it."

"In it Kholoruuf talks about a place he calls the 'Grand Truth Engine.' When I read that, I knew immediately that the Grand Truth Engine had to be the buried building I'd found near my home in the Catskills. The building has a remarkable, symbolic architectural design. I thought it symbolized the mind of the dialectician, but now I see what it really represents: the mind of the Great Person, the World Mind."

"That sounds amazing, Robert. I'd love to see it."

"I'll show it to you."

"What time is it?" Jennifer said.

Robert looked at his watch. "Ten after seven. Why?"

"I've got an idea."

"What?"

"Do you want to go to a meeting with me?"

CHAPTER 13
THE PLAN

On their way out, Robert and Jennifer took turns in the restroom they'd discovered in the Jurassic museum and found the facilities easy to use. Then they went back up the tunnel and into the basement of Kholoruuf's house. A twist of the curtain-rod fixture brought the walls together, hiding the tunnel entrance. Then they went up to the landing near the entrance and out onto the porch.

"Should we just walk out?" Jennifer said.

"You've still got the gun. You could aim it at me, as if you're taking me somewhere…"

"I don't want to aim a gun at you again. Carl will still be here, and he never questions me. Let's just walk out. We'll just get in my car and drive away. You drive. That way it'll give Carl the impression that I'm in control." She fished her keys out of her pocket and handed them to Robert.

The two walked out of the hill and into the morning light, with Robert in front.

Carl was standing near the gate.

"We've come to an understanding," Jennifer said. Carl nodded and opened the gate for them.

They got into Jennifer's red Toyota Corolla, with Robert in the driver's seat, and drove away from the field.

"That went smoothly," Robert said. "Are you tired?"

"Kind of excited," Jennifer said with a smile. She opened her glove compartment and put Carl's gun inside it. "I don't think I could sleep right now."

"Me neither."

Turning south on West Coast Road, they headed toward Cape Town.

Robert was pensive. "You know, I remember we had a set schedule of classes—the same every night. Do you remember what they taught us?"

"I don't remember much now," Jennifer said. "I guess what I learned simply became part of me. But I do remember some of it. I know your schedule wasn't exactly the same as mine, but one class we always had together was one where we were given a problem that we had to work on alone first, and then we worked on it together. Each of us would contribute knowledge we'd learned separately, so all of us together were able to come up with a solution."

"So we learned the value of collective intelligence, of collaborative thinking," Robert said.

"I guess that's why we both have such an appreciation for the Atlanian Truth Engine."

"You do too?"

"Yes," Jennifer said. "A deep appreciation like you. And there was another class I remember, one we always took together. We were given netlike objects with complicated connections that were—how do I put it?—*flattened* in different ways, and we had to figure out which ones had the same connections."

"To give us an appreciation for the relational structures between things?"

"That's what I thought they were doing. And now we see what a key role relational analyses played in Atlanian philosophy."

Robert looked at her. "I've been thinking lately how I'd like to look into founding a new Truth Engine."

"A *new* Truth Engine? That sounds exciting. If you want my help, I'll be there for you," Jennifer said.

Robert smiled. "Partners," he said.

They reached Long Street early, around eight twenty, so they parked a little distance away from the restaurant and waited for the others to arrive. They watched Orten arrive alone at eight thirty. Then, one by one, the other Conservancy people showed up. Congresswoman Martell, with the general and the others of her group, arrived at about a quarter of nine in two cars and went into the building.

"Let's go," Jennifer said, opening the door and getting out of the car.

Robert got out, and they walked to the restaurant. As they got close, they looked up and saw that the early arrivals had been seated on the balcony. Since the seated members of the group were busy welcoming the congresswoman and her entourage, none of them saw Robert and Jennifer approach on the street below. The two walked through the restaurant and up the stairs to the balcony.

Robert found himself in the lead and realized he'd be going onto the balcony first. When he walked out, everyone turned to look at him.

"What's *he* doing here?" the general said.

Orten glared at Robert. "I told you you weren't invited," he said. Then he looked past Robert at Jennifer as she came onto the balcony and placed her hand on Robert's shoulder. Obviously wondering what Jennifer and Robert were doing there together, he sat with his mouth open.

Robert, not knowing quite what to do, sat at a table apart from the group, and Jennifer walked over toward the congresswoman. "Confused?" she said to Orten as she passed him. She stood behind Congresswoman Martell and whispered into her ear. The congresswoman looked at Robert, whispered something to Jennifer, and stood up. Then she and Jennifer went to the corner of the balcony and continued to converse quietly. As they talked, Jennifer brought out her cell phone and showed Martell the screen.

After a two- or three-minute conversation, Jennifer and the congresswoman went over and sat with Robert. The congresswoman held out her hand to him. "Nancy Martell," she said. "Nice to meet you."

Robert shook her hand. "Robert Bennett," he said.

Nancy Martell smiled. She leaned closer to Robert and lowered her voice. "Jennifer tells me you're the one who should be in charge of this project, Dr. Bennett."

Robert looked at Orten and his team and wondered if they could hear what was being said. "I don't know about that," he told Congresswoman Martell.

"And she says you've been up all night exploring an amazing place that you want to show me."

"I'd be honored to show you, Congresswoman," Robert said.

Nancy stood up. "Shall we go?" she asked. "I want to see this." She directed her attention toward the other members of her team. "Alexis, Mark, Allen, General, will you come with us?" Looking at the Grayling group, she said, "You guys relax. If we need you, we'll call your office."

Robert, Jennifer, Nancy, and her team went down to Long Street. Robert and Jennifer got into the backseat of Nancy's car, with Nancy in the front. Allen got into the driver's seat. Alexis, Mark, and the general got into another car, and both cars headed over to Buitengracht Street en route to Melkbosstrand.

"We won," Jennifer said to Robert, speaking quietly so the people in the front seat couldn't hear her above the sounds of traffic. "I know the congresswoman will understand now why it's important for the world to know about what we've found. You discovered Kholoruuf's house. You discovered the Great Place. And now she knows your belief in ETs isn't kooky—I have no doubt you'll be in charge here. The general will keep *his* stuff secret, and the museums will pretty much belong to the dialecticians, whoever they turn out to be, but everything else will become known by everyone. We won."

"Thank goodness," Robert said. He looked away, wondering if he should say what he wanted to say next. He decided he had to do it. "You know," he told Jennifer, "since I was a teenager, I've always had this memory, a fragment that seemed to connect with nothing before or after it, with nothing in my life. I remember standing with a beautiful girl—on the hill, the Four Corners near my dad's place in the Catskills, at night—and we're kissing, and I loved her so much. I had girlfriends in New York City, and one in Switzerland, but I never was really in love with any of them. But I didn't have a girlfriend at all during those summers when Dad took us to the mountains. I could never understand that memory of the girl on the hill. I could never figure it out."

Jennifer smiled. "We were both seventeen. They dropped us off there one night. You kissed me. After that you walked up the road to your house, and I went the other way to my grandparents' house; I spent summers in the Catskills too. I remember that night—it was the night I fell in love with you. I still love you. I wanted to contact you after that, but the circumstances never seemed right. I didn't know how you'd take it. When the Grayling people mentioned your name and said you were here in South Africa, I…"

Robert looked at Jennifer and saw tears in her eyes. He felt his memories of her—and his love for her—returning, and he put his arm around her. "Would you be too tired to have dinner with me tonight?"

Jennifer turned toward him and laid her head against his chest. "I'd be very pleased to have dinner with you tonight," she said.

EPILOGUE

Robert saw that the reporter was sitting with Jennifer at the little round, wrought-iron table as he came out into the garden. He had just returned from a trip into town.

"Honey," Jennifer said, "this is Mary Kelly from the Catskill Sentinel. Mary, this is Robert."

Robert held out his hand. "Nice to meet you. Jennifer told me you were coming."

"My very great pleasure," Mary said, taking his hand.

Robert pulled up a chair and sat down.

"On the phone," Mary said, "I told Jennifer I'm writing a follow up article for the paper on what's been going on with you two, three years after the news about your amazing discoveries came out. It was such a tremendous sensation."

"Yes," Robert said. "As I recall, *The Sentinel* ran a big feature article about it back then. I remember the reporter was a very nice guy."

Mary smiled. "Yes. Carlos Brand. He lives in LA now. The story had a local focus, and you two weren't married yet, so he didn't get to talk to you, Jennifer. I'm so excited to be able to interview you both. May I record this?"

Robert nodded. "Of course."

Mary took out her small recorder, turned it on, and set it on the table. "You two have had an incredible adventure," she said. "Your story is so compelling. Robert, you followed a clue from your childhood and discovered, less than a mile from this very spot, a building—what we now know as the Grand Truth Engine—a building that had been buried under the earth for fourteen thousand years. And that discovery led you to South Africa, where you assembled a team of archaeologists and excavated the amazing and equally ancient House of Kholoruuf, which then led you to a tiny house in Finland."

"It was a real adventure," Robert said. He thought about how the US government had put out a false account of the events to make the world believe that he had assembled the team. Orten's role had been deleted from history, as it should have been. It was discovered that Orten had, in fact, taken steps to sell information about Atlanian technological devices, as well as the devices themselves, to foreign governments. Robert had heard conflicting reports about Orten. Either the authorities were taking their time to prosecute, or they had foregone prosecution completely because they knew a trial could bring out facts they wanted to hide, and, as one of Robert's sources put it, they were "determined to maintain the cover story at all costs." At any rate, Orten was now teaching at a university in Wisconsin and wasn't talking about Atlantis.

"And Jennifer was one of the people you put on your team," Mary said. "Did you already know each other?"

"We knew each other, but we'd been out of touch for a long time," Robert said.

"Jennifer, when you joined Robert's team, was that when you fell in love?"

Smiling, Jennifer looked at Robert then back at Mary. "I think I've always loved him."

Robert took Jennifer's hand. He knew he never could love anyone but his Jenny.

"And Jennifer, I hear you're expecting," Mary said.

Jennifer patted her belly. "Yes, in October."

"That's wonderful. I hope to be able to talk with you again then."

"Yes, of course," Jennifer said.

The reporter turned to Robert. "Recently there have been rumors—I'm sorry, but I have to ask—that you found advanced technology in the House of Kholoruuf, including a flying machine. Some people even claim there was a UFO connection, of all things. What would you say to people who make these claims?"

"We think," Robert said, "that the most valuable of the Atlanian artifacts are the *texts* we recovered, especially those that describe the Truth Engine, as well as the Truth-Engine books on truth, goodness, and beauty. And for the record, Jenny and I both believe in otherworldly visitation." Jennifer nodded. "I've seen a UFO myself," Robert said. He had admitted in a TV interview to seeing the glowing disk over the Baltic Sea, but he'd said nothing about the alien in the wide-brimmed hat.

"The event in Finland," Mary said.

"Yes. And it happened when we were working on these sites, so there may've been some connection, though it's hard to say what it might have been." The phrase "hard to say" had a double meaning. Robert hated to dissemble and found it painful to have someone believing something that wasn't true, something they would want to know. But he couldn't tell the whole truth about the Atlanian discoveries and felt relieved when he was able to answer questions without directly lying.

"So what are you two working on now?" Mary asked.

"We're very busy with our own Truth Engine," Jennifer said. "We've got two centers now, you know, one right up the turnpike and the other in New York City. And of course we assist in managing the activities at the archaeological site here in the Catskills, right up the road there."

"There's been a lot of traffic here," Robert said, "people wanting to see the site. The Atlantis Conservancy is planning to allow limited public entry into the building itself. This week they started to widen the road that leads up there."

"So the Truth Engine lives again," Mary said.

"Yes, it does live," Robert said.

"It's kind of incredible how, up until just a couple years ago," Mary said, "people were sort of cynical about argument, but now you've got everyone debating—it's almost the new American sport. Graham Wilson says in the *Times* that your Truth Engine is accelerating the resolution of controversies. Your radio debate programs on the Internet have taken off, and the periodicals you publish for the big-box stores, the new 'American village squares,' as you call these stores—all of it's tied to the Truth Engine."

"The *Our Mysterious World* series," Jennifer said, "*Our Community Speaks* and *Beauty in Our World.*"

Mary nodded. "Yes. Did you ever imagine you'd become editor in chief of a publishing house?"

"No," Jennifer said, "but I've never had so much fun."

"Graham writes that many users of the *Our Community Speaks* forums treat it as a game," Mary said, "yet they self-report, in many cases, a vastly increased understanding of political and social issues. He noted that the *Beauty in Our World* forums have energized debates about art, and that lots of new music is being performed by the electronic keyboard-ensembles all around the country. And I understand people are creating Truth Engines in other countries. Your idea is catching on."

"We can't ignore those other engines," Robert said. "Any one of them that isn't guided by goodwill has to be seen as dangerous."

"The Anti-Engines," Jennifer said.

"I've read Congresswoman Nancy Martell's new book," Mary said, "in which she describes her first visit to the House of Kholoruuf and her first meeting with you two. She was very complimentary and wrote about what a fantastic job you were doing at the time."

"She's been a wonderful friend," Robert said. "She was so helpful and gave us tremendous support."

"We talk to her all the time," Jennifer said.

"I guess if all the other interviewers have asked you this, I might as well ask too: Have you been able to identify the so-called Great Place for Humankind that some of the Atlantean texts refer to? It's been a matter of conjecture ever since you disclosed your discoveries."

"There are all kinds of mysteries about the Atlanians we have yet to solve," Robert said with a smile. "We have a few theories." Again he felt a pang of regret. He yearned to tell the whole truth, but there were external forces that forbade it. Only the top-level Truth-Engine researchers and some government officials could know about the Great Place. He hoped someday the world would learn the full story, but until then he could at least make sure the Truth Engine was operated with integrity.

"You know," Mary said, "I'd love to see the famous key case that started it all. Would you show it to me?"

"Sure," Robert said. "It's one of the few artifacts I was able to keep. We've got some more things here too."

The three stood up and went through the garden and into the house.

An hour later Robert and Jennifer waved as Mary pulled out onto the turnpike and drove away. Robert put his arm around Jennifer.

"So our Truth Engine's really taking off," he said.

"I think we've done a good job," Jennifer said, returning the hug. "We *are* making a difference."

"You know, Jenny," Robert said, as they headed toward the door, "I've been thinking. Our Truth Engine doesn't have an Ikon yet; it's all Logos. It needs an iconography, a game or a book that expresses the love for truth, goodness, and beauty…something that expresses an appreciation for what the Truth Engine offers all of us. The Ikon in the Grand Truth Engine was electronic, and it's degraded—it can't be read. We need a work that will keep the Truth Engine on track, that will give it an enduring goodwill."

"Any idea what kind of book or game?"

"I'm not sure."

"How about this?" Jennifer said. "A hero's journey, where the hero—his name could be Robert—starts at home, is led by a discovery into conflict that involves strange external forces, stays stalwart, solves puzzles that teach him the principles of the Truth Engine, receives unexpected help, and in the end comes up from below the earth in triumph."

"And he's saved by a blue-eyed beauty. I think I heard this story somewhere. What happens next in the plot?"

"Then the blue-eyed beauty reminds him to take out the trash."

"I already took it out."

"I meant *today*. In you go."

ABOUT THE AUTHOR

Dr. Richard Crist received his doctorate in philosophy from the City University of New York (CUNY) Graduate Center in 2001. He has taught philosophy and logic in New York City—at Hunter College and City College—and has taught professional ethics at Ulster County Community College.

Crist's doctoral dissertation was titled *Unity and Variety in Painting*. In this dissertation he maintained that long-esteemed paintings are long esteemed because they contain a balance of unity and variety among their abstract elements.

More recently he has developed an interest in collective intelligence and has created a system called the "Truth Engine" to help maximize it. The architecture of his Truth Engine also involves a blending of opposites. The Truth Engine is composed of a logical, discursive part, and an artistic, intuitive part. These two parts are combined in the Truth Engine, connected by something Crist calls the "Logikon," which has both discursive and intuitive features.

By encouraging people to use the Truth Engine, Crist intends to play a part in eliminating those existing oppositions that are made manifest in public controversy among good people. His goal is to deal with such discord not by ignoring it or by facilitating compromise but by resolving it through the revelation—via Truth-Engine argument—of what's really true, what's really good, and what's really beautiful. Empowered with more and more knowledge of this type, good people will become more able to bring happiness to the world.

Crist lives in upstate New York near the Hudson River.

To work with the real Truth Engine, visit the Truth Engine website at www.truthenginebook.com.

APPENDIX 1
Robert's Translation of Pages of *Truth-Engine Logic*

Throughout Atlan these rooms differ. The room of instruction at the Truth Engine in the capital city is ten strides long by ten strides wide. A very thick pillar stands at each corner. As the initiate enters this room, he or she faces a round desk and a chair near the far wall. At far right, in the corner, is a large wooden panel-cabinet [*mish-paahk*]. In the middle of the room, between the door and the chair, the floor has been built around an old stone well that, it is said, is the well that was built by Atallas, the founder of the capital city of Atlan, who arrived as a keeper of livestock and later reigned as king. They say Atallas's farm stood on this spot.

The well is still a source of water.

The initiate steps into the room with a dialectician [*skeopashu*—referring to a particularly revered logician or debater] who will be his or her guide. To the initiate's left and right two giant, gray metal statues of armored soldiers stand between the columns. Each soldier holds a light-flash weapon.

The guide shows the initiate to the chair. The teacher enters wearing a green robe, green sandals, and a tiny, bright-orange *namat* pin. Adopting a casual tone, the teacher speaks.

"Welcome to our school," says the teacher. "Look at these four figures." He pulls a panel from the cabinet. On the panel the following figures have been drawn.

"I have chosen one of these four figures to serve as my example."

Being prompted by the guide, the initiate asks, "Which one is your chosen one?"

"I will not tell you, but I will give some clues as to how knowledge of one or two facts can lead to knowledge of another. Here I will show you the Three Laws." He slides a panel from the cabinet. On the panel is written in red letters:

The Deny-Other Law

<u>Suppose I say that the chosen one is one of these: ⊗ ⊙.</u>

You can know that the chosen one is not one of these: ∇ ◇.

The Add-Anything Law

<u>Or suppose I say that the chosen one is one of these: ⊗ ⊙.</u>

You can know the chosen one is one of these: ∇ ⊗ ⊙.

The In-Common Law

Or I may say that the chosen one is one of these: ⊗ ∇ ⊙.

<u>And I may add that the chosen one is one of these: ∇ ⊙ ◇.</u>

Then you can know that the chosen one is one of these: ∇ ⊙.

The teacher asks the initiate, "Do you see how these are valid conclusions, how these are valid laws?"

"Yes. Clearly."

The teacher frowns. "But if you knew them already, why in the world would you care to make them plain to your conscience mind?"

The guide prompts the initiate not to respond.

The teacher continues, "Do you know why you receive these lessons here beside the well of Atallas, where these two soldiers are portrayed as guarding what we do here?"

"No," says the initiate.

The teacher says, "It was claimed that at the well of Atallas water was drawn from the center of the earth, from the eternal and unchanging realm. The Three Laws are of that eternal realm. So the well of Atallas is the symbolic source of the laws. To the uninitiated, the laws seem obvious, trivial, and without value, but we know they underlie the Argument Forms, which, together with the machinery of the Truth Engine, are such a powerful force against ignorance and evil that the men of iron here to our left and right must guard them. The dialectician is a lover of humanity, and the knowledge of these three simple laws allows him to fully manifest his love."

"That is the first of the two Foundational Lessons," the teacher says. "Are you ready for the second?"

"Yes."

The teacher gestures toward the four massive columns. "These columns," he says, "represent the Four Models. These models are the four *statement models* that serve as the Four Pillars supporting the Truth Engine. Each model is written near the top of the column that represents it. See up there?"

The guide prompts the initiate to say, "I cannot see them. They are too far above me."

The teacher points to the four columns and says, "These Four Pillars of the Truth Engine, these Four Models that allow us to manifest our love as we speak to one another, look like this…" Leaving the laws panel displayed, he pulls another panel out of the cabinet. On this panel the following is written in bright gold letters.

⏻‾⊘ ⏻\⊘ ⏻/⊘ ⏻_⊘

"These are the four wonderful pillars of peace and happiness that all dialecticians must know and revere," says the teacher. "Knowledge of these Four Models guides the logicians of the engine in their heroic battle for truth." He pushes the panel back into the cabinet and withdraws another one. On this one is written in black letters:

On these pillars ⏻ *stands for any statement, and* ⊘ *stands for any other statement. The line means "and." When the line ends low next to* ⏻ *or* ⊘*, a "not" is put into the* ⏻ *or* ⊘*.*

At this point the teacher shows the initiate, step by step, how an argument should be constructed. These are the steps the teacher takes the initiate through:

How to Build a Powerful Argument

1. An argument has premises and conclusions. For instance:

> *If Aunt Elkha says she saw a ghost, then ghosts are real. (premise)*
> <u>*Aunt Elkha says she saw a ghost.*</u> *(premise)*
> *Ghosts are real. (conclusion)*

> *The underline means "Therefore."*

2. Do not argue against a conclusion; argue against the premises.

3. To begin a preliminary draft of your argument, translate your statements into explicit logical form:

> *Where "p" and "q" each stands for a statement:*
>
> *For "p and q," write "p ⎯ q."*
>
> *For "p and not-q," write "p ↘ q."*
>
> *For "Not-p and q," write "p ↗ q."*
>
> *For "Not-p and not-q," write "p ⎯ q."*
>
> *For "If p then q," write "p Z q" (literally "The true one is one of these: 'p ⎯ q,' 'p ↗ q,' 'p ⎯ q'").*
>
> *For "p or q (but not both)," write "p X q" (literally "The true one is one of these: 'p ↘ q,' 'p ↗ q')."*
>
> *For "p or q (or both)," write "p X q."*
>
> *For "p if and only if q," write "p ⚌ q."*

> *So, for instance, for "I study and I do not learn," write "I study ↘ I learn," or for "If I study then I learn," write "I study Z I learn."*

4. Write out a sketch of your argument, with the premises above the conclusions; use an underline to express "Therefore." (See an example in step 1.)

5. Make sure your conclusions follow from the premises in accord with the Three Laws of the Trilogue, or with the single-inductive law. These are the Three Laws of the Trilogue:

The Deny-Other Law (DO) as Applied to Logic

This law allows you to construct a conclusion by changing the connector line(s) to its (their) complement(s) and negate.

For instance (the "+" signifies negation):

$$\underline{p \; X \; q}$$

$$(p \; — \; q)+$$

(You can see how this law works if you write out the full meaning of "p X q": "The true one is one of these: 'p ⎯ q,' 'p ↘ q,' 'p ↗ q.'" Therefore the true one isn't "p ⎯ q.")

The Add-Anything Law (AA) as Applied to Logic

This law allows you to construct a conclusion by adding any connector line(s). For instance:

$$\underline{p \times q}$$

$$p \times q$$

(You can see how this law works if you write out the full meaning of "p ⤬ q" then the full meaning of "p ⤬ q": "The true one is one of these: 'p ⟍ q,' 'p ⟋ q.' Therefore the true one is one of these: 'p ⚊ q,' 'p ⟍ q,' 'p ⟋ q.'")

The In-Common Law (IC) as Applied to Logic

This law allows you to construct a conclusion by creating a third expression that has all the connector line(s)—and only the connector line(s)—that the two premises have in common. For instance:

$$p \mathbf{Z} q$$

$$\underline{p \mathbf{\Upsilon} q}$$

$$p \mathbf{-} q$$

(You can see how this law works if you write out the full meaning of "p Z q" then the full meaning of "p ⤙ q": "The true one is one of these: 'p ⚊ q,' 'p ⟋ q,' 'p ⚊ q'" and "The true one is one of these: 'p ⚊ q,' 'p ⟍ q.'" Therefore the true one is the expression they have in common, namely, "p ⚊ q.")

Examples of solid arguments (Where "p" and "q" each stands for any statement):

	Full Argument	**Abbreviation**
Ash-Katl:	$p \mathbf{Z} q$	$p \mathbf{Z} q$
	$\underline{p \mathbf{\nwarrow} q}$	$\underline{p \mathbf{\nwarrow} q}$
	$\underline{p ^- q}$ *IC*	$p \mathbf{7} q$ *AK*
	$p \mathbf{7} q$ *AA*	

(For an example of Ash-Katl, see step 1.)

Ash-Palle:	$p \mathbf{Z} q$	$p \mathbf{Z} q$
	$\underline{p \mathbf{\searrow} q}$	$\underline{p \mathbf{\searrow} q}$
	$\underline{p \_ q}$ *IC*	$p \angle q$ *AP*
	$p \angle q$ *AA*	

Ash-Tohot:	$p \mathbf{X} q$	$p \mathbf{X} q$
	$\underline{p \angle q}$	$\underline{p \angle q}$
	$\underline{p \diagup q}$ *IC*	$p \mathbf{7} q$ *AT*
	$p \mathbf{7} q$ *AA*	

Categorical Statements

"An A is a B" is written "ΨAB." "An A is a non-B" is written "ΦAB." "All A are B" is written "ΨAB ⟍ ΦAB"; "Only some A are B" is written "ΨAB ⁻ ΦAB," etc. Categorical syllogisms are calculated using the three laws of deduction.

<u>APPENDIX 2</u> Robert's Translation of the "Amazing Coincidence" Argument from the Truth-Engine Book *Did a Ship from Another World Crash Near Ashekh in Kaleh?*

DID A SHIP FROM ANOTHER WORLD CRASH NEAR ASHEKH IN KALEH?

The "Amazing Coincidence" Argument

I think Skeptic's arguments here are the strongest arguments against the claim that the Ashekh debris was otherworldly. But there is a good answer to them, and I think that in the process of rebutting them, we learn something new about the visitors' intentions. Skeptic says:

[vs. 89, p. 1c] You claim (see 89) "an alien spacecraft crashed and left the debris in the Forest of Kesh near the village of Ashekh in Kaleh." The following is an argument against that claim: [400]Army officer Telterrik-Bohot, in his log for the twentieth day of the fourth month of the year thirty-one of the forty-ninth tlahok (see 271–286, p. 8), describes the launch of a very small unmanned reconnaissance [literally: *spy*] cloudship. [401]This ship was lost and never recovered. [402]My dear Believer, I'm sure you will agree that this cloudship might well have carried a king's authorization of flight. [403]If it did, then the ship probably had the emblem of the Prince of Kaleh printed on its sail strip. [404]Furthermore there are good reasons (see above, 293, p. 8) to think this flight was heading toward the Forest of Kesh when it disappeared and equally good reasons (323–328) to think it wasn't. The flight path cannot be reconstructed. [405]Therefore it remains a distinct possibility that on the twentieth day of the fourth month of the year thirty-one of the forty-ninth tlahok, a flight carrying the emblem of the Prince of Kaleh was launched and was heading toward the Forest of Kesh in Kaleh when it disappeared.

Now consider this: [406]If such a craft crashed into the Forest of Kesh, its remains would consist of gossamer sails, emblazoned with the prince's symbol; light-wood beams; three clear plastic fuel bottles; sponges (to seal the bottles); plastic twine; and a small box engine. [407]But this matches *exactly* the gross properties of the Forest of Kesh debris.[408]Everyone agrees that the Ashekh debris consisted of a gossamer-like substance with a pattern on it that closely or exactly resembled the emblem of the Prince of Kaleh, light-wood-like beams, three clear bottle-like objects, pieces of a spongelike material, tough string, and a small box. [409]If the Ashekh debris was from a crashed, otherworldly spacecraft, then this amazing cloudship match was coincidental. [410]But the chances are infinitesimal that a crashed exotic craft would just happen to leave wreckage that so closely and coincidentally matched, even in gross appearance, the parts of a reconnaissance cloudship that may well have disappeared in the same area at roughly the same time. It's ridiculous to believe that such a fantastically incredible coincidence occurred. [411]So the material was almost certainly not that of a crashed otherworldly craft.

Summary

[409]If the debris did come from a crashed alien craft, the match was coincidental.
[410]But the match was almost certainly not coincidental (since the chances of such a coincidence would be tiny).

---

[411]The debris was almost certainly not that of a crashed alien craft (MT*).

[412][vs. 87, p. 1c] My dear Believer, you say (see 87) that "the recovered materials, the bodies, and the ship itself were exotic, otherworldly." [413]Now if the material was otherworldly, then an otherworldly ship crashed. But I've just proven that

[411]the debris was almost certainly not that of a crashed otherworldly craft. [414]So the materials were almost certainly not otherworldly.

Summary

[413]If the material was otherworldly, then an alien ship crashed. [411]The debris was almost certainly not that of a crashed alien craft. (It is almost certain that an alien ship did not crash.)

---

[414]The materials were almost certainly not otherworldly (MT*).

[415][vs. 413] I actually agree with Skeptic when he says, "[410]The match was not coincidental," and so I agree that "[411]The debris was not that of a crashed otherworldly craft."

But I think his claim that "[413]If the material was otherworldly, then an alien ship crashed" is baseless because it is possible that the material was exotic even if there had been no crash. This is possible because the materials could have been left by aliens in order to *simulate* a crash—that is, the aliens might have *staged* a crash. In this case the materials would be otherworldly without a crash having occurred at all. Since 413 is baseless, the conclusion "[414]The materials were almost certainly not otherworldly" is also unjustified. [415]Skeptic, although he has proven there was almost certainly no crash, simply has not shown that the materials were not otherworldly. (But notice that a claim that the materials *were* otherworldly requires the aliens to have staged a crash.) The skeptic, however, might say:

[416][vs. 415 and vs. 183] You seem to be suggesting not merely that the idea that it was staged is possible but that it is actually plausible. But that's ridiculous. Ockham's Razor [*rokhshe palatke*—literally "the law of parsimony"] simply rules it out. You have all these aliens from some other planet staging this elaborate effect for who-knows-what complex reason when the simple drone explanation is right there. You have *no reason* to attribute the Ashekh incident to aliens.* [418]

I do not think that the alien-staging explanation is merely plausible; I think it's highly probable.

[418][vs. 417] But if that was all there was to the argument, then the idea of "alien staging" would, indeed, be ruled out by Ockham's Razor. But the following argument forces us to accept alien staging. First let's assume that you're correct in saying (see 413) that "if the material was otherworldly, then an alien ship crashed," and see where that gets us: [419] [i]If the material was otherworldly, then a saucer crashed, but [ii]if the material was not exotic, then the testimony of Officer Ishshor and the other witnesses, who stated that the recovered materials were far stronger and far more durable than any human-made material, or known natural material, is unreliable. [420] Either [i]the material was otherworldly or [ii]it was not otherworldly. [421]Therefore either [i]a saucer crashed or [ii]the testimony of Ishshor and the others is unreliable.*

Summary

[419][i]If the material was otherworldly, then an alien ship crashed, and [ii]if the material was not otherworldly, then the witnesses were unreliable.
[420]Either [i]the material was otherworldly, or [ii]it was not otherworldly.

---

[421]Either [i]an alien ship crashed or [ii]the testimony of Ishshor and the others is unreliable.

[422]But 421 seems (probably) false—that is, it seems that both 421i and 421ii are (probably) false. You showed (see 410) that the debris at Ashekh (very probably) didn't come from a crashed alien ship, and the believer showed (see 86, p. 1c.) that the witness testimony (probably) is reliable.

[423]But if the conclusion (421) is false, then at least one of the premises (419 or 420) must be false. [424]The false premise cannot be 420, because it's just simply true that the debris was either otherworldly or not. [425]Therefore it is 419 that is probably false—but which part of 419? [426]Clearly 419ii is true; it's simply true that if the debris wasn't otherworldly, then the witness testimony was not reliable. [427]Therefore, probably, what is false is 419i; i.e., it must be false to say that if the debris was otherworldly, then a saucer crashed—that is, it's true that the debris was otherworldly, yet there was no crash. [428]This forces us to conclude that the "crash" was staged by otherworldly beings.

The skeptic could say:

[429][vs. 428] You can solve this dilemma in one of two ways: First you could do as you do, and question the truth of 419i. But alternatively, you could say, *contra* your 422, that 421 is *not* false—that, even if it seemed improbable, 421ii is true; that is, that the witness testimony is, in fact, unreliable. [430]It seems more reasonable to do it the second way.

[431][vs. 430] But I think it's more reasonable to do it the first way. The idea of alien staging was rejected (417) only because of Ockham's Razor; it was not deemed *improbable*. The fact that the witness testimony is unreliable, however, is *improbable*.

Notes

411. 409, 410 <u>MT</u>*
414. 413, 411 <u>MT</u>. from an argument by Tshoemsere: pp. 10–11
421. 419, 420 <u>ECR</u>**

*MT stands for "modus tollens," The valid argument form that has this structure (where p and q are any two statements): "If p then q. Not-q. Therefore not-p." The Atlanians called this form *ash palle.*

**ECR stands for what the Atlanians called the "Exclusive Constructive Rule" (*Atshkel Parkahe Kesh*). Since the premises seem true, but the conclusion seems false, this form is what we call a "constructive dilemma."

APPENDIX 3
Robert's Translation of Kholoruuf's "Notes on Goodness."

"Notes on Goodness"

The diagram-like figure below is a sentence and not a diagram. It describes a special kind of relation:

The figure says, "A causes B, with a probability of about 75 percent." The markings above the "B" are meant to convey the probability of about 75 on a scale of 0 to 100.

Choice

We can describe a situation in which a person has a set of choices (including nonaction, which is a choice). He or she must choose one and only one of them.

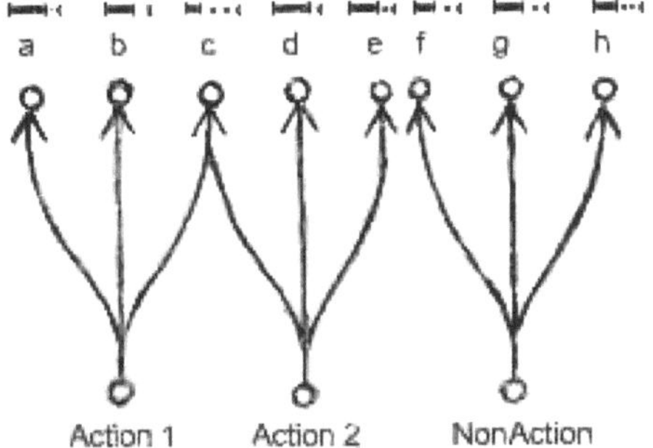

This complex statement describes the possible results of each alternative, and the probabilities associated with each possible result. We call this complex kind of statement a CEANA (cause, effect, action, nonaction) statement.

We can add a vertical dimension to the horizontal probability scale. The vertical axis indicates the amount of happiness that is expected to result from the choice.

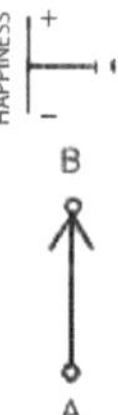

The following states that if action A is done, there is a 75 percent chance that happiness in the amount of 30 will result.

The rectangle represents the product of probability times happiness; call it "probable happiness."

The following states that if action A is done, there is a 50 percent chance that happiness in the amount of -20 (i.e., unhappiness in the amount of 20) will result.

Here, since the rectangle that represents probable happiness is black, we know it represents the probability of unhappiness.

The Goodness-Template Project

When one opens the Goodness Box, which is kept inside the ivory Truth Box in the Grand Truth Engine, he or she will find only one template slide there. But I keep six more Goodness-template slides on hand. Why?

I am the director of the Grand Truth Engine. If I could know with clarity what the prime directive or directives (which surely are exactly like the directives within the consciences of good people in general) of my conscience are, then I would maintain only a single template slide for the projector.

But the nature of our conscience is hidden even from ourselves. There are a number of respected theories, and until it becomes clear which theory is correct, I have directed that templates that represent the thought of each of the following seven kinds of dialecticians be kept here and that the slide that the third director placed inside the Goodness Box (the utilitarian slide) remain there. Here are the seven kinds of dialecticians.

1. The **utilitarian** [Atl: *kashjanehr*—literally "smile maker") believes our conscience contains only this one fundamental directive:
   "Maximize the probable happiness of all people."

2. The **radical altruist** [Atl: *petehrbat*—literally "sufferer"] believes our conscience contains only this one fundamental directive:
   "Maximize the probable happiness of all people except yourself."

3. The **egalitarian** (Atl: *kezhtankk*—literally "balancer") believes our conscience contains only this one fundamental directive:
   "Maximize the equality of the distribution of probable happiness among all people."

4. The ***utilitarian egalitarian*** (Atl: *Shomash*—literally: ?) believes our conscience contains only this one fundamental directive:
   "Maximize everyone's probable happiness, and maximize the equality of its distribution."

5. The **conscientious egoist** (Atl: *Tahettke*—literally "self alone") believes our conscience contains only this one fundamental directive:

"Maximize the potential happiness of yourself."

6. The **radical libertarian** (Atl: *Mekhatshar*—literally "unencumbered") believes our conscience contains only this one fundamental directive:

"Do not harm innocent people."

7. The **deontologist** (Atl: *Alekattuparu*—literally "here-now theorist") believes our conscience contains at least one "nonconsequentialist" directive (that is, one directive that does not have to do with results of the action). For instance some deontologists might believe our conscience contains this set of directives:

"Be beneficent. Don't lie. Don't steal. Keep your promises. Don't kill."

In this case only the first directive is consequentialist.

Arguments

Here's an argument against the **radical altruist**: If we have a conscience as shown in 2 above, we wouldn't feel that we ourselves count. But we do feel that we ourselves count. So it's false that we have a conscience as shown in 2, above.

Here's an argument against the **deontologist**: Suppose an innocent person, being hunted by a murderer comes to your house for protection. You hide the person in your house. The murderer comes to your door and asks if you've seen the person he's after. "Don't lie" is typically claimed by deontologists as being one of the conscience's directives. So if we have a conscience of the kind that the deontologist typically claims we do, then either we would not lie to the murderer, or we would lie and feel guilty about it. But in reality we would lie to the murderer and feel no guilt about it. Therefore we don't have such a deontological conscience.

Here's an argument against the **utilitarian**: Consider the following CEANA statement.

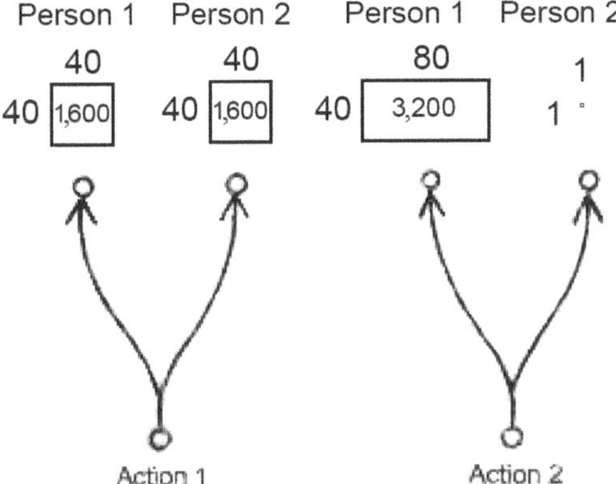

Action 1 produces a potential happiness of 3,200; action 2 produces a potential happiness of 3,201. Even though action 2 produces slightly more potential happiness overall, we would choose action 1.

Here's another argument against the **utilitarian**: You promise your dying grandfather that you won't sell his property. After he dies, if you sell the property, you'll feel guilty.

Here's an argument against the **egalitarian**: Consider the following statement.

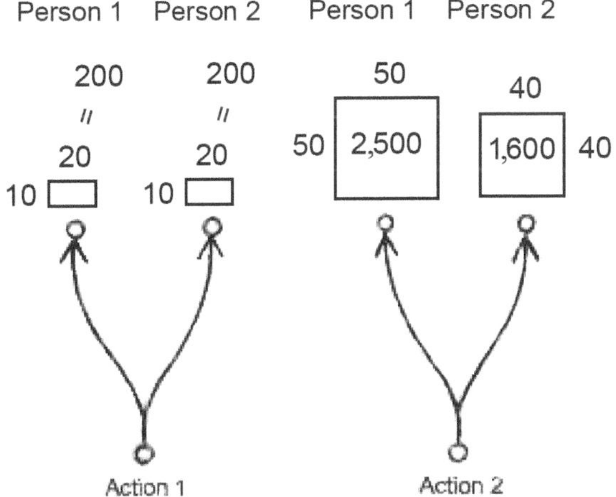

If our conscience were egalitarian, we'd choose action 1; but of course we'd choose action 2. Therefore our conscience is not egalitarian.

I feel that the radical altruist, the egalitarian, and the conscientious egoist cannot be correct, but I included their corresponding template slides in the Goodness box because these theories have some respectability.

I am an advocate of the utilitarian-egalitarian view, but work must be done to discover precisely how the probable happiness and the equality of distribution are to be balanced against each other. I also believe potential happiness should be thought of as potential fulfillment. This actually appears to turn the utilitarian element into a deontological system.

An Argument against Moral Relativism

Considerations deriving from our faith demolish moral relativism. But even a secular argument, to be rational, must deny relativism. If I were to disregard for the moment what we know of the ways of heaven, I would say, "The directives found in my conscience are fundamental desires and are in no way justified any more than is my desire to eat a *shehe* berry. My faculty of reason neither supports nor invalidates the content of my conscience.

"My conscience directs my actions to achieve a certain result (even a deontologist's conscience—if such exist—will include consequentialist directives). Speaking is an action. Thus my telling someone, 'It's wrong' must be directed toward the same result; my aim is to accomplish that result via influencing, using mere speech, the will of another person. On the other hand, if I were to say 'It's wrong for me,' I would be less likely to accomplish that result, so it cannot be something that my conscience wants me to say."

APPENDIX 4
Dr. Jonathan Miller's Transcriptions of Examples in the Musical Themes Book

APPENDIX 5
Sections from Dr. Jonathan Miller's Partial Translation
of *The Practical Truth-Engine Book of Musical Composition*

THE PRACTICAL TRUTH-ENGINE BOOK OF MUSICAL COMPOSITION

Cⲟδδ2ⲱ δⲟⲩⲟδⳙ ſ⳪ⲱⲤⲱⳙ δⲟ2ⲱ ſⲟⳙⲱⲤⲟδ 2ⲱⲤⲱſⲱⲩⲟⲟ (*Kettshe Tasatl Orekel Tashe Palukat Shekepumakh*)

This book is a step-by-step guide to the composition of music for a "single-note-each" e-ensemble.

[This is a guide to composing for Atlanian e-instruments, the notes of whose keyboards were labeled **o** through **c** (which I've translated here to a, b, c, d, e, f, g, h, i, j, k, l) across each octave. For purposes of explanation, I've arbitrarily correlated the Atlanian middle d with our middle C. I have translated only parts of this work—enough to demonstrate the Atlanian system of step-by-step instruction. Because the translation is only partial, it contains references without referents—J. Miller.]

Definitions

A *key* is one of ninety levers in a keyboard. You press a key to play a note.

A *tonality* [*antek*] is a set of letter-named notes that sound good together. Example: d bright (= the tonality of C major). [Although another word, in English, for "tonality" is "key," I'll use "key" to refer to the levers you press on a keyboard instrument.]

A tonality's *root note* [*ettes aan*] is the note that sounds *final* when other notes of the tonality have been played.

Options

If you wish to begin by composing a short melody on the keyboard—that is, without first deliberately selecting a *tonality* or a *pulse pattern* (see *N1*)—go to **Step (1)**.

If you wish to select a tonality (such as the tonality of *a-bright*; or the tonality of *d-dark*; etc.) before you start to compose your melody, go to **Step (12)**.

If you wish to select both a tonality and a pulse pattern before starting to compose your melody, go to **Step (31).**

(1) OPTION 1—starting with a melody: Begin composing by creating a very short melody on the keyboard.

(2) So that you don't forget your melody, on a piece of paper, write out your melody, using horizontal spacing to roughly approximate the notes' lengths. Add "[a]" to the left of the line to show that the line represents middle *a*.

For instance what you write on your piece of paper could look like this:

(3) On a second piece of paper, write out your melody's rhythmic notation in a precise way, and make marks where the notes are sounded—use *N1*. Let us suppose that this notation ends up looking like this:

(4) Use a clean sheet of paper for your score. On this sheet, starting at top left, combine what you wrote in Step (2) and what you wrote in Step (3). Use a curved line to show how long each note is sounded. In this example we get:

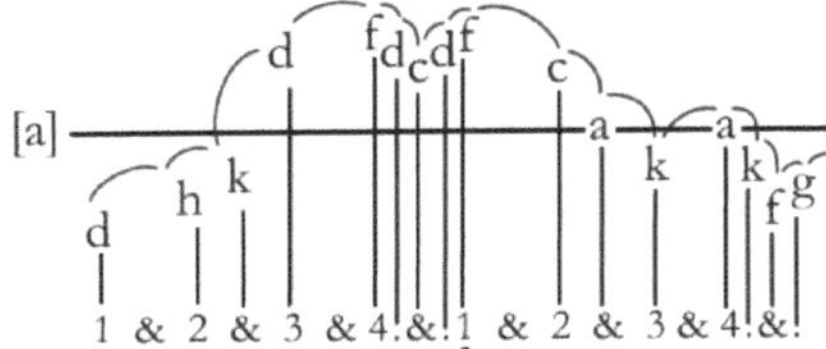

(5) Using *N2*, indicate the tempo of your melody by choosing a tempo expression for your piece, and write it above and to the left—for example:

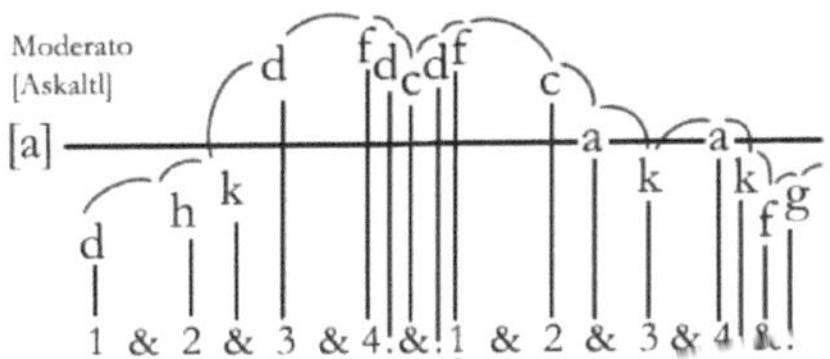

(6) Using *N5*, determine the tonality of your melody. Write its name in the lower left:

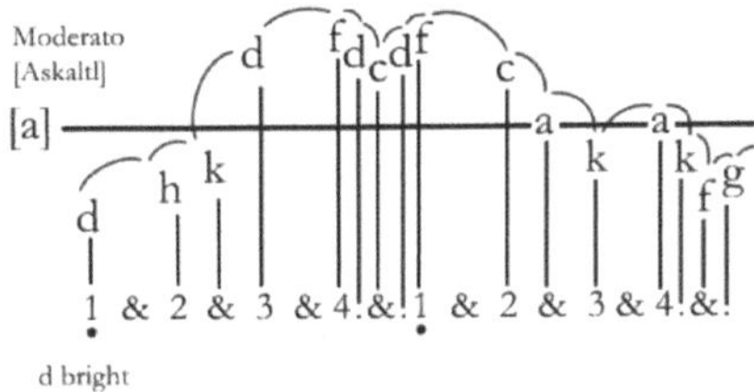

(7) Set up the wheel to represent your melody's prevailing tonality this way:

(a) If you found in Step (6) that the tonality is in the bright [*alash*] mode [the major mode], then on the music wheel, align *1* with *Bt* ("bright"); on the other hand, if you found in Step (6) that the tonality is in the dark [*tuur*] mode [the minor mode], then, on the music wheel, align *1* with *Dk* ("dark").

(b) Then, keeping fixed the wheel alignment you just made, align *1* with the letter-note name of your melody's tonality. In the example, the tonality, *d bright* [C major], is represented on the wheel by this alignment: *d/Bt/1*.

(c) Note that, on the wheel, *1* will always be aligned with either *Bt* or with *Dk*, while *Bt* and *Dk* can be aligned with any letter-note name.

[I include here a photo of a wheel I made, using Roman letters and modern numerals—J. Miller]

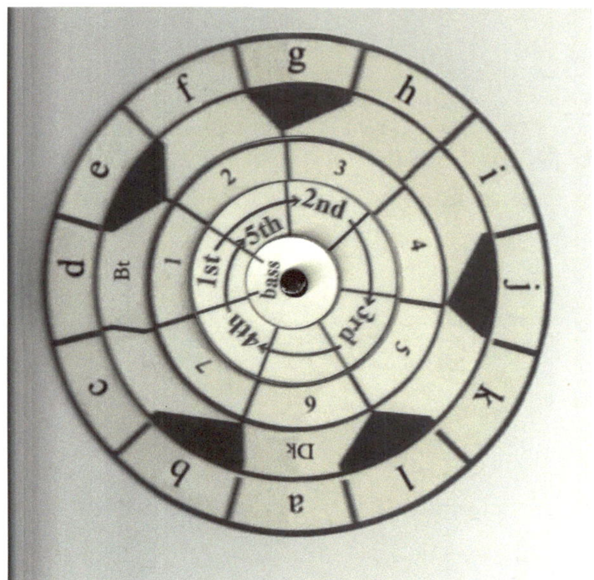

(8) Write the notation for the wheel-alignment you have set, in the example "d/Bt/1" under the prevailing key name, so you can quickly realign the wheel if it becomes unaligned. In the example, the score looks like this:

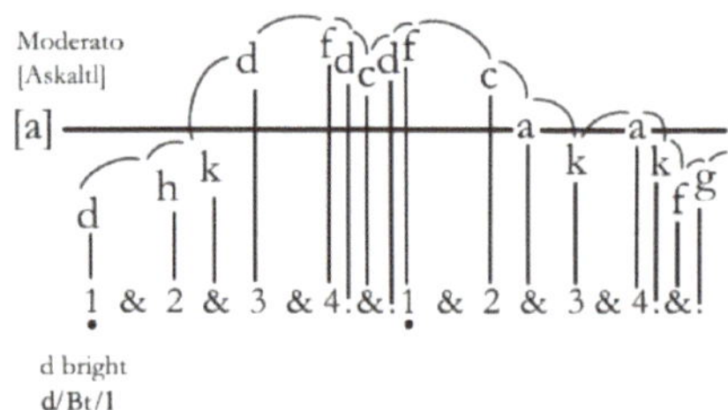

(9) Using the wheel as a guide, play the notes of the prevailing tonality (in the example, d-bright). That is, play the letter-named notes that are aligned with *1, 2, 3, 4, 5, 6,* and *7*. Get used to playing within the prevailing tonality. In this example, you would get used to playing the notes of the d-bright [C major] scale—that is, the letter-named notes that are aligned with *1, 2, 3, 4, 5, 6,* and *7* on the wheel. In the example these letter-named notes are *d, f, h, i, k, a* and *c* [in our modern system: C, D, E, F, G, A, and B].

(10) Using *N7, b,* choose—at least provisionally—a model of a *Small Form* for your piece. Eventually you can choose a *Large Form (N7, c)* and perhaps an *Extended Form (N7, d).*

(11) Go to *Step (47).*

(12) OPTION 2—selecting a tonality before starting to compose your melody: On a piece of paper, draw a horizontal line, leaving a lot of space above it. Then choose and notate a prevailing tonality in the following way. First choose a prevailing *mode:*

[I have not translated steps (13) through (46). Because of the omissions, the reader may find that steps 47-52 make little sense—but I hope he or she will be able to get a vague impression of their meaning—J. Miller]

(47) Keep creating your melody at the keyboard. Either stay fundamentally within the prevailing tonality—stay with the *1, 2, 3, 4, 5, 6* and *7* notes of the prevailing tonality (which the outer three rings of your wheel should be set up to represent)—or modulate in a deliberate way to a new prevailing tonality (see 56 below).

(48) Number your measures (defined by the pulse pattern—the measure starts with the "1" (one) and ends with, but does not include, the next "1") as you compose your piece. Put the measure number near the *end* of the measure.

(49) Keeping the *Form Model (N7)* that you chose above in front of you always, keep constant track of where you are in your melody-creation process by comparing the number of the measure you're working on with the measure numbers in the model.

For instance, let us say that you are trying to come up with a figure (a small passage of perhaps two, three, or four notes) that is to fall within measure marks "9" and "10" on your score—i.e., you are working on measure number 10.

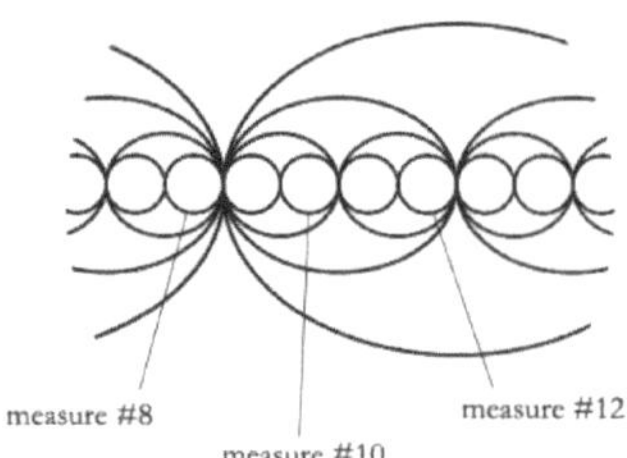

(50) At this point the first things to look at are the symbols at the bottom of the model: *HC*, *PCw*, etc. (consult *N7,a* for the meanings of these). These show whether this or that kind of cadence ought to end this or that measure. If the model you chose calls for a cadence here, write on your score the notes of the required chord (see *N4,A*—your wheel already should be set for the prevailing tonality). When there are options for different cadences in the model, try one of them, keeping in mind that it can be changed.

(51) Then look at the letter symbols just below the circles on the model (a, a', b, c, etc.). These show whether this or that set of measures is to be a repeat (or quite like, or unlike) some previous set of measures. The melody you create at this point should conform to this configuration. (If you feel you simply want to create a melody that is not in conformance to this model, choose another model. Note that, as you become more proficient, you can break the rules).

For instance, if you are working on composing the tenth measure, and you have chosen (*N7*) *Form III, type a*, your tenth measure will be unlike your second. But if you have chosen *Form III*, your tenth measure will be similar (but not identical) to your second.

(52) Especially in cases in which you are composing new material—i.e., when the measure you are about to create is not a mere repetition of something that has gone before—it may be wise to do the following (in accordance with the theory of moderationalism):

Looking at the *Primary Form Model* that you have chosen (and keeping in mind where the measure you are working on is located in the model), find the correlate—if there is one—(*N6,4a*) and the analogs (*N6,4c-d*) of the measure you are working on.

For instance, suppose you are trying to come up with something for the fourteenth measure, and you have chosen (*N7*) *Form II, type a*: the correlate of the fourteenth measure is the thirteenth measure, and the analogs of the fourteenth measure are the tenth and the sixth. Keep in mind the correlate and analogs of the measure you are working on.

Now, as you compose your measure, (keeping in mind the various kinds of relations involved here—see *N6,9-12*) keep asking yourself (in accord with the speculative theory of moderationalism, see *N6,14-18*), "Is what I am writing either too similar or too dissimilar to—that is, is it moderational [*kashtartek*] to—the correlate and analogs (considered as an aggregate) of the measure I'm working on?" If your measure is too similar, try to increase the amount of dissimilarity between the measure and its correlate and analogs; if your measure is too dissimilar, try to increase the amount of similarity between the measure and analogs (see *N6,18*).

. . .

N6—MEREOLOGY, RELATIONS, AESTHETICS—MUSICAL MEREOLOGY

The Study of Parts and Wholes in Music

1. Conceptual Groups

Any two or more notes, however widely separated, can be thought of as constituting a group; for instance I can arbitrarily "think" these encircled notes as a group:

There is potentially an enormous number of such conceptual groups (every two—even widely separated—notes, every three notes, etc.).

2. Perceptual Groups

In any musical passage, we can find features that tend to create perceptual groups. Unlike conceptual groups, perceptual groups can actually be said to be *in* a piece of music.

The following are perceptual-group-making features of a musical passage.

a. Dissimilarity of Similarities (schematically):

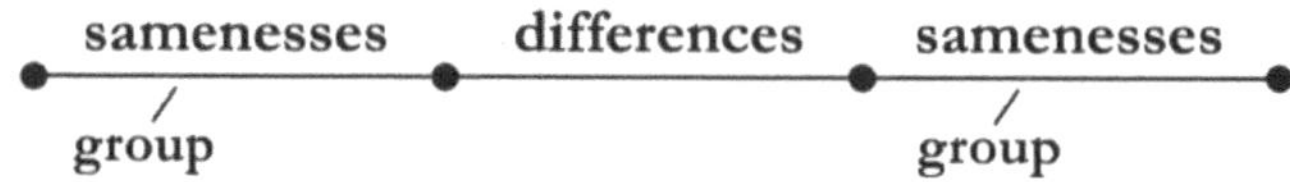

Example:

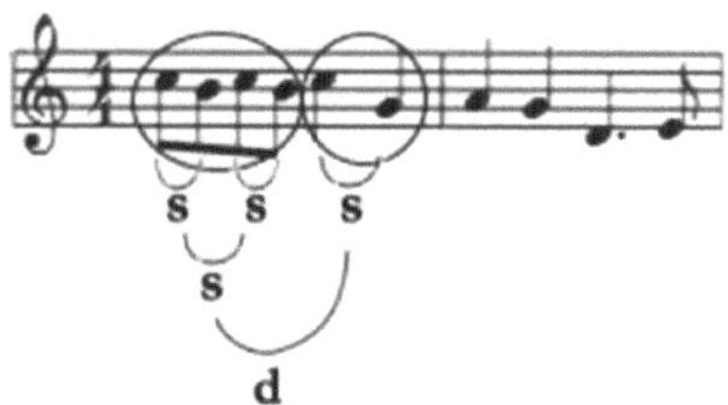

b. Similarity of Dissimilarities (schematically):

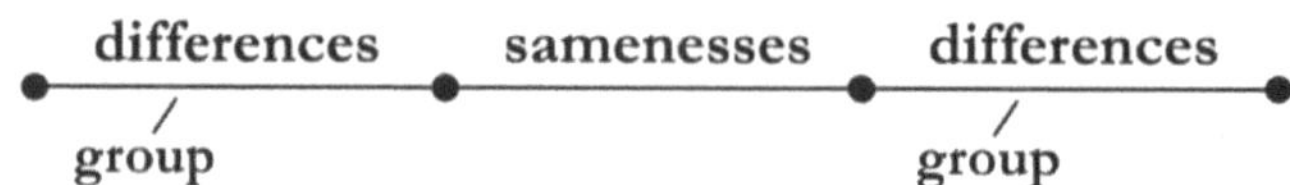

Example:

c. Cadences, such as IV-V or V-I, can segment long sections into groups.

Example:

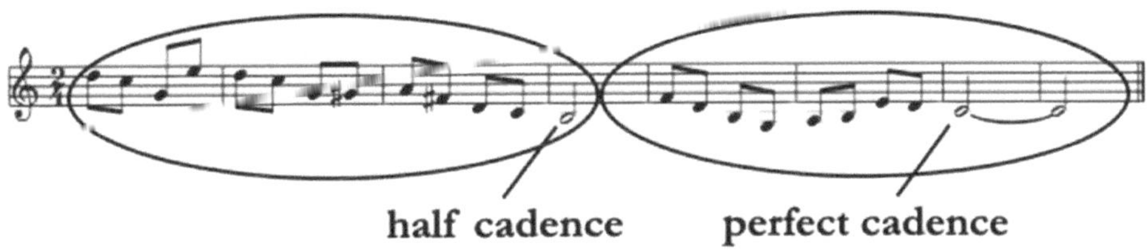

3. Pair-Wise Creation of Perceptual Groups

The composer should try to create groups (and groups of groups, etc.) in *pairs*, both members of a pair being, in general, of equal length (the same number of measures, generally speaking). Thus the first figure will be followed by a second, of similar length, with the two forming a group; this group is followed by a correlative group that also contains two figures, etc.

4. Correlates, Analogs, and Shells

a. Definition of *Correlate:*

Each member of a pair of groups is the *correlate* of the other member of that pair.

Examples:

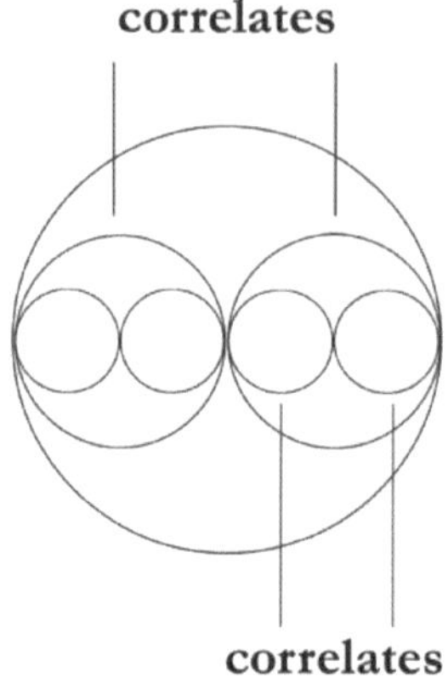

b. Definition of *Shell:*

The encircling lines that here represent groups will be called "shells." They are named in terms of what they encircle in the following way:

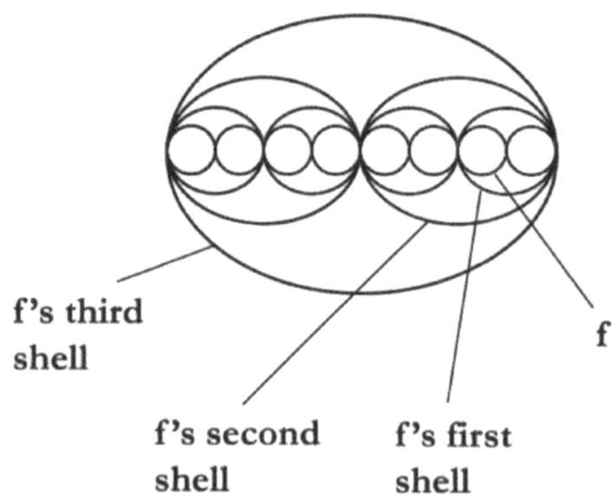

c. Definition of *Analog:*

Suppose that note or group, g^1, occupies a certain position within group G^1. And suppose that groups G^1 and G^2 are *correlative* groups (members of a perceptual pair). Then the note or group g^2 that occupies the same position in G^2 as g^1 occupies in G^1 is an *analog* of g^1.

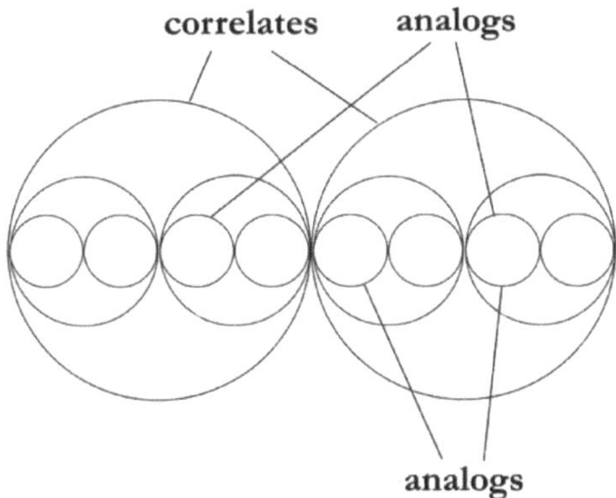

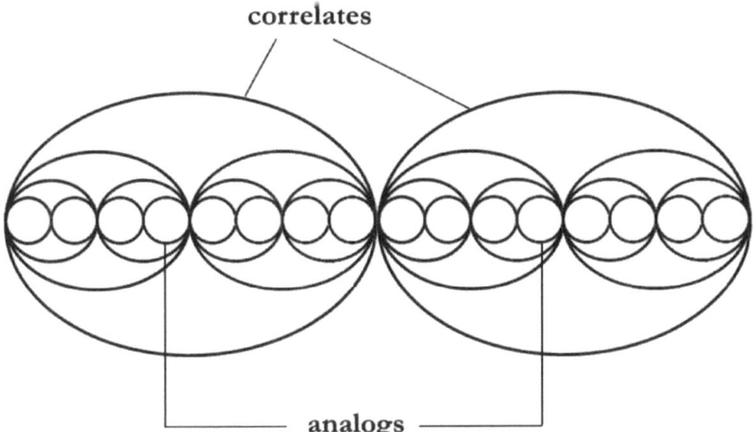

d. How to Find the *Analogs* of a Fragment, *f*:

i. Find the correlate of f's first shell; f's analog within that correlate is f's first analog.

ii. Find the correlate of f's second shell; f's analog within that correlate is f's second analog.

iii. Find the correlate of f's third shell; f's analog within that correlate is f's third analog.

iv. Etc.

<u>APPENDIX 6</u>

Fragments From Dr. Jonathan Miller's Partial
Translation of *The Philosophical Dialectic on the Art of Painting.*

THE PHILOSOPHICAL DIALECTIC ON THE ART OF PAINTING

Arguments Concerning Painting

Definitions:

The *core relations* are the relations of sameness (s or SAM) or difference (d or DIF). In Atl these are abbreviated ꙍ for *mashek* (sameness) and ꙭ for *takatl* (difference)

The *derived relations* are the relations identity (I), similarity (S), moderation (M), dissimilarity (D), and opposition (O). In Atl these are abbreviated **o** for *ara* (identity), **ƒ** for *halan* (similarity), **c** for *kashtar* (moderation), **ꙫ** for *reshet* (dissimilarity), and **ꙮ** for *khatt* (opposition).

At the same time, s, d, I, S, M, D, and O each name a *primary* property of a relation. Relations also have secondary properties, examples of which are: hue (h), intensity (i: hue-to-gray ratio in a color), and gray (g: white-to-black ratio in the "gray" element).

$$O \overset{\displaystyle I_h}{\rule{8em}{0.4pt}} Bn$$

This is a (linear) proposition that says, "Orange is identical in hue to brown." "O-I_h-Bn" means the same thing

$$R \overset{\displaystyle S_h}{\rule{8em}{0.4pt}} O$$

"Red is similar in hue to orange," or "R-S_h-O."

$$R \overset{\displaystyle M_h}{\rule{8em}{0.4pt}} YO$$

"Red is moderational in hue to yellow-orange."

$$R \overset{\displaystyle D_h}{\rule{8em}{0.4pt}} YG$$

"Red is dissimilar to yellow-green."

$$R \overline{\quad\quad\quad^{O_h}\quad\quad\quad} G$$

"Red is the opposite of green."

In these examples:

I: The number of DIF relations = 0 [zero].
S: The number of SAM relations > the number of DIF relations, etc.

Here is a scale of the derived relations—a more precise way of naming these relations:

0		50		100
I	S	M	D	O

Here is an M scale:

0		50
I/O	S/D	M

Relational propositions can be joined to produce complex relational propositions. The following linear proposition describes three colors.

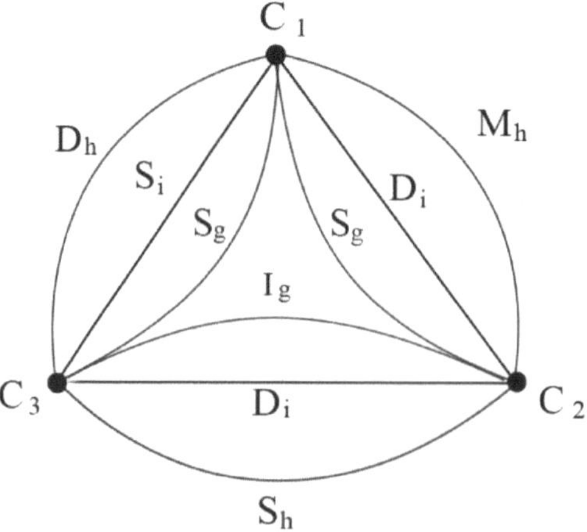

Another secondary kind of relation is the *spatial* relation (s).

Another secondary kind of relation is *spatial quantity* (q).

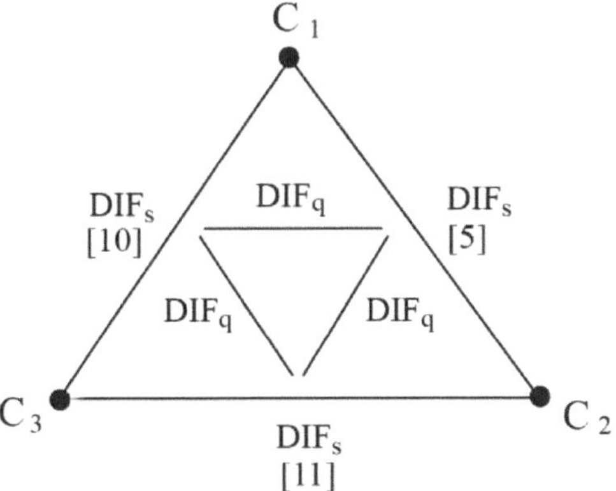

. . .

Where "R_x" stands for some relation:

Orientation, R_o, is different from *direction* (R_{dx}).

Color is a secondary kind of visual-field derived-relation, R_c. But color as a property has component properties, which are themselves tied to secondary kinds of derived relation—the kinds that should be considered are:

1. hue (R_h)

2. gray value (R_g)

3. value (R_v)—amount of light perceived—black to amount of light associated with pure white

4. purity (R_p)—black to (pure hue or pure hue with white or pure white)

. . .

Another secondary relation is *group* (R_{gp}).

. . .

In complex cases, there are groups within groups; for example where spatially defined groups are interlaced with color-defined groups in intricate patterns.

Difference relations can hold between groups. Derived relations can hold between groups.

Combinative relations: When R_x and R_y both hold between two objects, there appears a third relation, R_{x+y}, which is in some sense a combination of, or at least grounded upon, the first two.

R_c is probably an average of its components.

Two complex shapes can be compared in derived-relational terms (R_{sh}).

What is balance? Placement of point P, which presents a variety of S_q and D_q relations between the P-to-frame distances, such that a relation approaching a M_{bal} relation exists.

Relevant derived relations exist among single points, naturally defined groups, derived relations themselves, and among the parts of a shape's contour.

. . .

To say that an image is moderation-rich is to say that it presents an abundance of moderation relations (M).

The claims for this dialectic include the following.

Statement 1: The awareness of moderation richness is, as a rule, a fundamental good (informal paraphrase: awareness of moderation richness makes us happy).

Statement 2: Many objects—including art found in the caves of Pashnaku, Shalleshatoh portraits, and Mahkat abstracts—are moderation-rich (both in 2-D and represented 3-D), and this is, at least primarily, what accounts for the high esteem in which they are held. (Other values partially account for this esteem—expression, for instance. But expression fails without moderation richness.)

Why does moderation richness affect us this way? We have evolved a faculty for the immediate enjoyment of perceiving that which unifies the many: the species among the individuals, the genera among the species, the natural law, the general theorem. We have evolved such a faculty because learning via the general is on the whole more efficient than learning via the particular, and all other things being equal, a species that is fitter to learn is fitter to survive. This faculty has a simple character, as defined in Statement 1 above. Thus the search in science for some fundamental natural law could be said to be the response to a primary functioning of the faculty (since the faculty is operating toward those ends toward which it was designed to operate, so to speak), while the painting of a picture would be a response to a secondary functioning of it.

We see something similar in music. In music each note is separated by twelve notes (an octave) from a note having the same letter name. These two notes are the same (they are both k's, for instance, and possess a certain sameness of quality) and different (they are different k's, for instance, and possess a certain difference of quality). The fact of their sameness implies the existence of a hue-circle-like oppositional dimension of twelve notes.

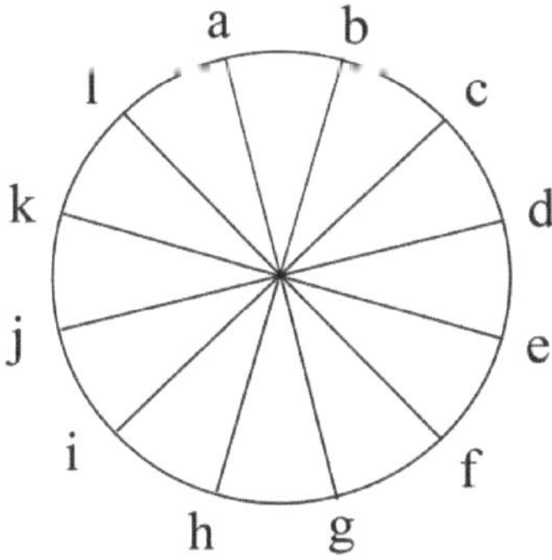

Thus, for instance, f is oppositional to l, is similar to g and to h, is dissimilar to j and to k, and is moderational to i and to c.

In general if we play a series of notes, creating a melody on a keyboard, the most satisfying resolution occurs when the first note of the scale follows the fifth note—for instance when d follows k. Keeping in mind that e is oppositional to k, it may be seen as evidence for the moderationalist thesis that k, with its two moderation notes—b (midway between k and e, up) and h (midway between k and e, down)—are precisely those notes that, with d itself, make up the set of the first seven harmonics of d:

b
k
h
d

Thus, playing d after k repeats the k while supplying k's moderation notes, creating a satisfying cadence.

It is interesting that the only two-note progression within a scale whose second note supplies no M notes at all to the first note is the 4--, 1-- progression—and when we arrive at the fourth note, generally in the middle of a phrase, we are indeed left hanging, having to work our way back to 1-- via the 5--.